"It's late. Past midnight. Why don't you come to bed?" Taryn said. *Let me take care of you.*

Chance didn't say anything, but kept staring out the window at the river. Red Thunder looked innocent enough tonight. Romantic even, with the moonlight dancing on its surface.

"The river has stolen a lot from you, hasn't it? Twice now, it's taken your memory."

He started to turn from her, but she hung on to him. "I won't let it take anything more from you."

Tentatively she pressed a kiss against his neck, felt the answering leap of his pulse against her lips.

Chance growled, "No." But there was no strength to his denial.

She could reach him on this primal level. She knew she could. "Let me love you, Chance."

"No," he said, then leaned forward and kissed her....

Dear Harlequin Intrigue Reader,

Harlequin Intrigue has four new stories to blast you out of the winter doldrums. Look what we've got heating up for you this month.

Sylvie Kurtz brings you the first in her two-book miniseries FLESH AND BLOOD. Fifteen years ago, a burst of anger by the banks of the raging Red Thunder River changed the lives of two brothers forever. In *Remembering Red Thunder*, Sheriff Chance Conover struggles to regain the memory of his life, his wife and their unborn baby before a man out for revenge silences him permanently.

You can also look for the second book in the four-book continuity series MORIAH'S LANDING— *Howling in the Darkness* by B.J. Daniels. Jonah Ries has always sensed something was wrong in Moriah's Landing, but when he accidentally crashes Kat Ridgemont's online blind date, he realizes the tough yet fragile beauty has more to fear than even the town's superstitions.

In *Operation: Reunited* by Linda O. Johnston, Alexa Kenner is on the verge of marriage when she meets John O'Rourke, a man who eerily resembles her dead lover, Cole Rappaport, who died in a terrible explosion. Could they be one and the same?

And finally this month, one by one government witnesses who put away a mob associate have been killed, with only Tara Ford remaining. U.S. Deputy Marshal Brad Harrison vows to protect Tara by placing her *In His Safekeeping*— by Shawna Delacorte.

We hope you enjoy these books, and remember to come back next month for more selections from MORIAH'S LANDING and FLESH AND BLOOD!

Sincerely,

Denise O'Sullivan
Associate Senior Editor
Harlequin Intrigue

REMEMBERING RED THUNDER

SYLVIE KURTZ

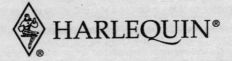

HARLEQUIN®

TORONTO • NEW YORK • LONDON
AMSTERDAM • PARIS • SYDNEY • HAMBURG
STOCKHOLM • ATHENS • TOKYO • MILAN • MADRID
PRAGUE • WARSAW • BUDAPEST • AUCKLAND

For Chuck—For your enduring love

A Special Thanks to:
Sandy Emerson for answering my bail questions.
Jerry Fletcher—Chris's Class A mechanic dad—
for scenario #2. It fit the bill perfectly!
Any errors in procedure are the author's.

ISBN 0-373-22653-5

REMEMBERING RED THUNDER

Copyright © 2002 by Sylvie L. Kurtz

ABOUT THE AUTHOR

Flying an eight-hour solo cross-country in a Piper Arrow with only the airplane's crackling radio and a large bag of M&M's for company, Sylvie Kurtz realized a pilot's life wasn't for her. The stories zooming in and out of her mind proved more entertaining than the flight itself. Not a quitter, she finished her pilot's course and earned her commercial license and instrument rating.

Since then, she has traded in her wings for a computer keyboard, where she lets her imagination soar to create fictional adventures that explore the power of love and the thrill of suspense. When not writing, she enjoys the outdoors with her husband and two children, in addition to quilt making, photography and reading whatever catches her interest.

You can write to Sylvie at P.O. Box 702, Milford, NH 03055. And visit her Web site at www.sylviekurtz.com.

Books by Sylvie Kurtz

HARLEQUIN INTRIGUE
527—ONE TEXAS NIGHT
575—BLACKMAILED BRIDE
600—ALYSSA AGAIN
653—REMEMBERING RED THUNDER*

*Flesh and Blood

All underlined places are fictitious.

CAST OF CHARACTERS

Chance Conover—His memory is wiped clean of everything except a nightmare.

Taryn Conover—Her husband is turning into a stranger before her eyes.

Angus Conover—Does Chance's adoptive father know more than he's willing to say?

Nola Barnes—Taryn's grandmother is dead set against her granddaughter chasing after any man, even her husband.

Tad Pruitt—The deputy wants to discover if Chance is fit to serve.

Dr. Benton—Does the staff psychiatrist have reasons of his own to want Chance to stay put?

Carter Paxton—He's the law in Ashbrook. Revenge has been eating at him for fifteen years.

Ellen Paxton—Is the shell of a woman in the nursing home the girl in Chance's nightmare?

Garth Ramsey—The boy from the wrong side of the tracks has done well for himself. How far will he go to protect his own interests?

Joely Brahms—The town librarian has answers, but fear keeps her quiet.

Doug Talberg—The retired high school principal would just as soon not remember the past.

TARYN'S BUTTERMILK ANGEL BISCUITS

2 cups unbleached white flour
1 tbsp sugar
1 tbsp baking powder
1/2 tsp salt
1/2 tsp baking soda
1/4 cup vegetable shortening
1 package quick-rising yeast
1 1/4 cups 2% buttermilk, warmed
melted butter (optional)

In a large bowl sift together the flour, sugar, baking powder, salt and baking soda. Cut in the shortening until the mixture resembles coarse meal. Add yeast. Set aside.

Add the warm milk to the dry ingredients and stir with a fork until moistened. The dough will be sticky.

Turn out the dough onto a heavily floured breadboard and knead gently until smooth, about 30 seconds.

Gently roll out the dough to a half-inch thickness. Cut with a floured round or fluted cutter. Arrange the biscuits 2 inches apart on an ungreased baking sheet.

Preheat the oven to 400°F while the biscuits rise on the baking sheet, about 15 minutes. Place the biscuits in the oven and bake for 12-15 minutes. If desired, brush the tops of the hot biscuits with melted butter. Makes 12 biscuits.

Prologue

Ashbrook, Texas. Fifteen years ago.

She was late.

He'd known she'd be too chicken to show. Playing games wasn't Ellen Paxton's style. Still, he'd hoped she'd help spice up what was shaping up to be an otherwise dull evening.

Trespassing was the only thing that made this outing any fun. But even that bit of adventure was growing old in the buggy humidity of these backwoods.

All these trees made him claustrophobic. Heat suffused his every pore, glistened his skin with sweat and rendered his mind slug slow. Any second now, all this nature was going to drive him plumb crazy.

What they needed was a bit of excitement. And on this hot and sticky late-May evening, excitement wasn't likely to find them unless they met it halfway.

Garth Ramsey glanced at his companions. The Makepeace twins looked as contented as dogs who'd found a cool spot under a porch. Kent, he knew, could stay here all night and be happy. Kyle would be easier to prod along.

"Turkey tracks," Kent said, pointing at the three-fingered prints where the wild birds had followed the sandy riverbank then veered into the brush.

Who cares? Garth thought and swiped Kyle's Coke from the cardboard tray between them on the ground.

"And here we are nowhere near Thanksgiving," Kyle mocked.

Kent shot Kyle a narrowed gaze, then turned his attention to his burger. The jitter of his knee said he wanted to add something, but realized it wasn't wise when Kyle was in one of his moods.

And Kyle was in the mother of all moods. He'd had some burr under his saddle for the past three days. For once he hadn't bothered Garth with all the details—which only made him more curious and more determined to view the outcome. Too bad Ellen hadn't shown. Garth slurped the last of the Coke and batted away at the mosquitoes determined to eat him alive.

In a week, high school would be over and reality would kick in, but for now, he, Kent and Kyle were still free. Garth wanted to make the most of his time and not waste a precious evening vegetating along the river.

"I hear there's goin' to be a drag race out by the reservoir tonight," Garth said, feeling out his chances of seeing action any time soon. He hated depending on Kent for transportation.

"Who's gonna be there?" Kyle asked as he squeezed a second packet of ketchup onto his burger.

"Mac Renfro and his souped up Chevy for one."

Kyle snorted. With an overhand hook, he tossed the empty ketchup packet toward the fast-food bag and missed. "If he drives that thing like he rides, I'll put my money on whoever he's racing."

Undeterred, Garth tried another tack. "Shannon Blake's

havin' a party. Her parents are out of town for the weekend and I hear she's goin' to have a keg.''

''Yeah?'' Kyle flattened the top bun over the other half of his burger. Ketchup oozed out one side and plopped onto the ground. ''Might be worth checking out.''

''Sounds like trouble,'' Kent said. He tipped his cap to shade his eyes, crossed his arms over his chest and leaned deeper into the oak behind him.

Garth silently groaned. He wanted to cruise around town and find some sort of life. The curse of having two of his four older sisters still living at home was that one of them always had dibs on the family car before he did. Even his mother sided with them. Work came before pleasure. Like slaving at the local supermarket was worth the hassle.

''You don't have to stay.'' Garth poked the straw of his drink through the lid. ''You can just drop Kyle and me off. We can get a ride back.''

''Kyle can't go. He can't afford another run-in with Sheriff Paxton.''

''I can decide for myself.''

''It's a party—'' Garth started.

''A party that sounds like it'll get out of hand.''

Garth shrugged. ''So we leave when it does.''

''John Henry—''

''Won't care,'' Garth said.

When it came down to the doing, John Henry Makepeace couldn't always be counted on. Garth figured that was why Kent was such a pain in the butt at times. Someone had to be responsible. Since his grandfather and his brother weren't, Kent had appointed himself conscience to both.

''He'll care if he's called down to the sheriff's office one more time to explain why he can't keep Kyle in line,'' Kent said.

''And he'll get over it just as quick.''

Bull's-eye, Garth thought when Kent's eyes opened and his glare was cold enough to cool the stuffy air around them.

"We'll all go, then," Kent said after a while. "First hint of trouble and we leave."

Garth and Kyle shared a conspiratorial look over Kent's head.

"Fine."

"Sure." Garth picked up his carton of fries and started munching on them. Promises were made to be revised. He glanced at his watch. Half an hour to kill before he had to prod old Kent along.

The only thing around with any energy was Red Thunder. As its name implied, the river was never quiet. Unlike its meandering sisters, the Neches to the west and the Sabine to the east, Red Thunder ran straight and fast. And today, swollen by a week of rain, it seemed in a mighty hurry. Like him, Garth thought. He was in a hurry to get out of this one-stoplight town.

He had plans, big plans, and he'd set goals to reach them. Like a road on a map, he knew exactly where he was going and couldn't wait to get started on his trip to the top. And his drive was as powerful as the river's. Nothing was going to stop him.

Footsteps muffled by the thick padding of leaf litter drew nearer. A branch cracked. A pine bough swished. None of them stirred. The arrival was much too hesitant to belong to the forest ranger assigned to patrol the Woodhaven Preserve.

When the footsteps reached the clearing, Garth smiled. *Well, well, look who's here.* He might have drawn a pat hand from a stacked deck after all. He plucked another fry from the carton he was holding and glanced over at Kyle, wondering how his friend would react.

Kyle tossed his burger to one side and shot up, then busied himself with picking up rocks along the riverbank.

Pine bough in hand, Ellen Paxton hesitated before walking into the clearing. Her blond hair hung in a long braid down her back. Garth had told her to let it hang loose. He liked the way the gold glinted in the light, and often fantasized about running his hands through the silken strands.

She hadn't listened to his other advice, either. Her denim cutoffs were too short and her red T-shirt too tight. Not that the outfit looked bad on her. Watching her move, he was getting hotter by the second. She didn't have much to fill the top, but those firm, long legs of hers could give any man a hard-on. Thing was that neither the short shorts nor the tight shirt were her nature, and she didn't look comfortable playing the role of temptress she was striving for. Fresh innocence and loose, gauzy fabrics suited her more. He'd told her so.

Her gaze, with its anxious gray-green eyes, sought out Kyle, then swept quickly away to fixate on Kent. So that's how she was going to play it. He'd told her to use *him* to win Kyle over again. She was doing this all wrong.

The empty fry container collapsed in his fist. One day, he'd get to her, if only to prove to himself he could.

She sank next to Kent, swiveled the straw from his drink in her direction and sipped. A kiss of red lipstick branded the white straw. She looked better in pink. He'd told her so.

Kyle's jaw worked overtime as he pretended not to care.

"I saw your truck by the road and thought I'd stop and say hi."

Garth smiled and leaned back against the hickory tree. *Saw, my foot.* He'd called her from the burger joint, and knowing there'd be fireworks, he'd told her their plans. He'd laid out a perfect step-by-step course of action for her. But had she listened? No. She was playing a game she couldn't handle.

She should have listened to him.

But what the heck, this could still prove more entertaining than an evening drinking beer at Shannon Blake's party. And he might still get what he wanted in the end.

"So what are y'all's plans for the summer?" Ellen asked with a brightness that sounded exaggerated and an ease her tight muscles against Kent's side denied.

Ellen was crazy in love with Kyle. That was plain to see on her face even though she was trying hard to ignore him. Kyle was gaga over Ellen, too, even though he was pretending she was nothing more than a weed at the moment. Garth had had to suffer through enough of Kyle's fawning to know.

Kent started to get up, but she hung on to his arm. The straitlaced Makepeace didn't want to let Ellen use him to get to Kyle, but he was also too accommodating to hurt a lady's feelings, whether she deserved it or not.

"Kent'll be a gatekeeper at the state park," Kyle sneered. He hurled a pebble into the river. It splashed and was swallowed without even a ripple. "Safe. Solid. Dependable. Sound familiar?"

Yeah, that sounded like Kent all right. How he could find such dull work interesting was beyond Garth's comprehension. "Better you than me. Sounds boring."

"You got it wrong, Garth. He'll be right in his element. Smokey the Bear will get to lecture everyone who makes the mistake of wanting a camping vacation." Kyle tipped back his head and howled at his own joke.

"What's wrong with wanting people to be safe?" Ellen asked with much more intensity than the comment deserved.

"They don't want to be safe. They want to have fun."

Ellen's hold on Kent's arm tightened. Her face was an indignant scrunch.

"Let it go," Kent said between gritted teeth.

"I can't."

"That's right, Kent. She can't let go. She'll cage even someone as stodgy as you in the end." Without looking at Ellen, Kyle launched another missile into Red Thunder. The body English behind the motion told a story a mile long.

Garth licked the fry salt from his fingers. A mule facing a wall. He'd been right. Kyle wasn't ready to kiss and make up yet.

"It's not the job, Kyle," she said.

"Then what is it?"

She blushed a deep shade of red. Her gaze darted from Kent to him. "Can't we talk in private?"

"Hey, you're the one who came barging in uninvited."

Ah, there it was. Body language never lied. Why hadn't he seen it sooner? So they'd done it and innocent little Ellen was a virgin no longer. Funny how Kyle hadn't mentioned that bit of news. He was usually more than eager to brag about his conquests. What would the sheriff say if he knew his precious daughter was no longer pure? Garth filed away the tidbit.

So Ellen had finally given herself to Kyle and was having a hard time accepting her lover's imminent departure to a ranch out in West Texas. Not that he blamed her. Kyle had a way of attracting trouble. If she weren't around, she probably figured some of that trouble would be of the female persuasion. She'd more than likely be right. Kyle lived the cowboy image to the hilt—from hat to boots to horse—and the girls did swoon over his dark good looks when he was all dudded up and riding his flashy black horse. Those high cheekbones, those blacker than black eyes, that singular stamp of pride made a Makepeace stand out from a crowd and attracted women like flies to honey.

But if that's all Ellen saw, she was missing the most important element. Once Kyle made something his, there was no taking it back—which was the only reason Garth hadn't made a move on her himself. As pretty as she was, she wasn't worth getting his eye blackened or his lip fattened because Kyle had trouble controlling his temper. Too bad Ellen didn't understand that. Or maybe it was good. Maybe while Kyle was gone, he'd finally get a shot at her.

The going would be good for Kyle. He was too much of a dreamer and needed a little dose of reality. A summer sweating on the range would see to that. Then maybe Garth could talk some sense into him. Owning the ranch would be much more satisfying than working it. Once Kyle had a taste of hard labor, maybe he wouldn't be so hesitant to spend the trust fund that would be his when he reached twenty on one of Garth's plans. Oil, lumber, cattle, horses, real estate. He'd get back the fortune his father had squandered.

Let him go, he wanted to say to Ellen. *He'll come back.* Garth quirked a smile. *I'll help you get over the heartache, darlin'.* That had been the whole idea behind inviting Ellen to join them tonight.

Kent was looking ill at ease as he gently tried to extricate himself from Ellen's hold. But she just hung on to him as if he were a lifeline and she was drowning. She should have played it the way he'd told her.

Without letting go of Kent's arm, she snapped her head and an overbright smile toward him. "What about you, Garth? What are your plans for the summer?"

He was glad to oblige. This situation was proving more entertaining than any drag race by the reservoir. "My uncle wants me to help him out with his real estate business. Says

I've got charisma and charisma is important for attracting business." He flashed her a grin to prove his point, saw Kent roll his eyes.

"Your uncle'll probably have you doing all the grunt work," Kyle said, peppering the river with a handful of stones.

Ellen ignored Kyle. "Why, that's wonderful, Garth! Since you're aiming to get yourself a degree in business administration, it's right up your alley."

An in with the scholarship committee guaranteed him a free education. And Garth didn't plan on doing grunt work for long. Unlike his father who'd struck out in too many directions without thought, Garth knew exactly what he was after. His planning and dedication had already shown him many shortcuts on the path to success. Give him a few years, and he was going to explode to the top. And like the river, nothing could stop him.

Soon the Ramsey name would no longer stand for his father's failures, but for Garth's own success. People wouldn't snigger behind his back anymore; they'd respect him and look up to him.

"You done?" Kent asked Garth as he gathered the remnants of their fast-food dinner.

"What's your hurry?" The tension between Kyle and Ellen was just getting interesting. He did like watching a good fight. And if it was good enough, he'd have a sobbing Ellen to console on the way home.

"I forgot I promised John Henry I'd stop by the Feed and Seed and pick up the oats he ordered. Come on. I'll need your help loading."

Yeah, right, and if I believe that, you've got a jackalope ranch to sell me. John Henry had no more ordered oats than he'd held down a steady job since his accident at the sawmill ten years ago.

Ellen latched onto the hem of Kent's T-shirt. "Kent..."

"Talk to him," he whispered.

"He's past listening to me," she murmured back, placing both her hands on Kent's chest. "You talk to him, please, Kent. He listens to you."

From Garth's vantage point, the touch looked mighty intimate—almost like a lover's caress. Kyle didn't miss it either or the way his brother and his girl stood, hip bumping into hip. Kyle could easily mistake her arms wound around Kent's neck and the pleading look in her eyes as a come-on, especially in his foul mood.

"This is between you and him."

"What are you two hatching?" Kyle asked. His fingers were flexing. His gaze narrowed. He was spoiling for a fight. Garth leaned back, ready to watch the spectacle.

"Nothing." As Kent picked up a wad of discarded napkins, Kyle grabbed his arm. "Let go, Kyle. This is between you and Ellen. I'm leaving, okay."

"Can you stop the river?" Fire burned in Kyle's dark eyes, bringing forward the exotic good looks of his Caddo ancestors. The heat of anger had his face tight and his breath short and shallow. His grip on Kent's elbow looked iron hard.

"Kyle—"

"I asked you a question. Can you stop the river?"

Garth had no idea where Kyle was going with his hot-blooded question, but the wrong answer could break the dam of what little restraint Kyle still had. Kyle was feeling bullied and he'd never backed down from a threat.

Kent glanced over his shoulder at Red Thunder rumbling behind him. Sweat glistened along his hairline. The convulsive swallowing had Garth believing Kent was having to choke down his own temper to keep the situation under control.

"It takes a lot to stop a river," Kent said calmly.

"Exactly." Kyle let go of Kent's elbow and gestured grandly. "The river has to flow. If something tries to stop it, it might slow for a while, but eventually it goes around or through or over. It still flows."

Lord help us, Kyle was getting metaphoric. Garth never understood Kyle when he started talking in pictures. Facts and figures Garth understood; pretty words were too fanciful for him. Still, Garth thought as he looked at the river, there was a power there that couldn't be denied. Its energy sang in his blood.

"You're talking to the wrong person," Kent said.

Kyle glowered at Kent. "You're afraid to swim. That's your problem."

"Kyle—"

Kyle didn't back off. He stepped forward and got in Kent's face. "You're afraid to even dip your toe in water just because you got stuck in a drainage ditch when you were five." With the heel of both hands, he gave Kent a shove.

"Your beef's not with me."

"What you're missing is life." Kyle pressed closer. Kent took a step back. "It's gonna pass you by. You're going to end up all brackish and stale and she doesn't see that. She doesn't see she'll hate you that way. She'll hate her life, herself in the long run."

"Kyle, that's enough!" Both hands around Kent's biceps, Ellen tried to tug him out of the line of fire.

Kyle's nostrils flared.

Kent gently set Ellen out of harm's way.

"Talk to Ellen."

"I don't give a damn about Ellen."

"Yeah, right. Don't know why she cares for a hothead like you, anyhow."

Kent made the critical mistake of starting to turn away.

With an explosive grunt, Kyle rammed Kent with all his might. The force of the blow made Kent backpedal. He caught himself, then took another step to steady himself. The sandy bank crumbled beneath the weight of his hiking boot.

Kent fell backward, seemed to hang in midair for an eternity. Horror etched itself into his face.

Garth shot to his feet, then stopped himself short.

Ellen screamed.

Kyle swore and reached forward, grabbing for his brother.

Kent hit the water hard.

Kyle thrust out his hand farther. "Grab it!"

He skimmed the tips of Kent's fingers. The water carried Kent away. Kent latched on to a root on the riverbank. Kyle threw himself against the bank for a third attempt to save his brother. The sandy bank crumbled beneath him. Gravity pulled him forward and he smacked headfirst into the turbulent water, casting both of them into the current.

Ellen shrieked. "Do something!"

The swift river tugged furiously at both brothers like a predator tearing at prey.

"Kyle, Kyle!" Ellen chased the water along the bank. "Do something, Garth! Help them!"

Garth knew his strengths and weaknesses. He took one look at the water, at his friends being whirled and spun downriver, and knew there was nothing he could do. He wasn't going to mess with power like that.

"Don't just stand there." Ellen grabbed the front of his shirt and pulled him toward the shore. "Do something. They're drowning!"

"I'll get help." He turned and headed for the truck.

Ellen pummeled his back. "Help them! You've got to help them before it's too late!"

A look over his shoulder showed him the river, bleeding red under the setting sun, had swallowed them both. Besides, he couldn't swim. "It's already too late."

That stopped the pounding, but did nothing to erase the fury narrowing her eyes and curling her lips. For the first time, he saw an underlying strength in Ellen he hadn't known existed. "Help them, you gutless wonder, or I'll tell your secret."

He sneered. "I don't have a secret."

"Alice Addison."

She knew. He didn't know how, but she knew.

He had plans, big plans.

He was getting out of this one-stoplight town. He was getting that business degree that would tell the world he was somebody. He was going to the top. Nothing was going to stop him.

Nothing.

He grabbed for Ellen....

Chapter One

Gabenburg, Texas. Present.

The house was cool, cozy and inviting, and a deep sense of contentment filled him as he silently slid the glass door closed.

He was home where he belonged.

The rich aroma of simmering chili tantalized. The anticipated sweet tartness of the cherry pie sitting on the counter made his mouth water. The woman at the stove, adding a dash of cumin to what he already knew was perfection, was more enticing still.

She hummed a tuneless song as she stirred. His mouth quirked in wry amusement. Taryn couldn't carry a tune to save her life, but if she was humming while she cooked, he knew everything was right. She couldn't have been home long since she still wore the white T-shirt and white cotton pants that were her uniform at the bakery she owned.

Without taking his gaze off his wife's back or the pleasing curves that had been on his mind all day, he quietly made his way across the kitchen. With a groan that was part surrender and part captivation, he wrapped his arms around her waist and dropped a greedy kiss on the side of her neck. She smelled like sugar and flour and roses heavy with dew. The combination never failed to make him hungry.

As expected, she jumped and whirled in his arms. "What are you doing here? I wasn't expecting you for another half hour."

The open welcome in her eyes, in her smile, deepened his sense of contentment, allowing him to shed the last of the weariness that had dogged him for the last hour of his twelve-hour shift at the sheriff's office.

Chance Conover grinned and pretended to look around the kitchen as if he'd walked into the wrong house. In truth, he'd tuned everything out but the woman in his arms. "Don't I live here?"

"I'm not ready for you."

Taryn plopped the spoon she was holding back into the pot and frowned her displeasure. But the effect was negated by the fact she stood on her tiptoes to kiss him back. Caught in a ponytail, the ends of her long brown hair tickled his arms. He loved the silky feel of her hair on his skin, of her body against his. After a long day at work, he wanted nothing more than to lose himself in her.

"Well, sweetheart, I'm ready for you." He kissed her again, long and slow, savoring the heady taste of her, reveling in her ardent response.

Made a man grateful to have a woman like Taryn waiting for him at the end of a long day. She made him feel like a somebody, not the nobody who'd washed up bruised and battered on the shore of the Red Thunder River fifteen years ago. She made him feel real and solid. She made him feel needed.

A man couldn't ask for more.

"You weren't supposed to see until I was ready."

He held her at arm's length and caged her gaze with his. He loved her eyes, the way they sparkled with life, the way they shone with love for him. "Well, now, I like what I see."

She blushed and batted her fingers against his shoulder. "You're impossible!"

Turning her head, she looked at the small round table in the middle of the kitchen floor. "It was supposed to be a surprise."

For the first time since he'd walked into the kitchen, he noticed the scene set for seduction. On crisp white linen, silverware gleamed in the late-afternoon light. The fancy cream and gold china that had once belonged to Taryn's mother scintillated. Red candles in their crystal holders were ready to be lit. The fragrance of pink roses from the garden competed with the chili's spice.

"What's the occasion?"

Coyly, she fingered the gold sheriff's star on his uniform shirt. "It's Friday night. Do we need an occasion?"

Her soft smile and the deepening blue of her eyes were having their usual combustible effect on him. A wave of craving clawed at his insides. Even though Taryn's chili was his favorite meal and her cherry pie was to die for, right now he'd skip the food for nourishment of the sensual kind. "You want me to leave and come back later?"

She hesitated, then shook her head. "We can eat later."

With swift ease, he scooped her into his arms and started toward the bedroom down the hall. "I promise I'll be hungry."

"I had everything planned." A hint of disappointment colored her voice. She shrugged it away and a Mona Lisa smile soon graced her lips. "I may have a bit of news."

"What kind of news?" Her full, pouty lips distracted him, so he kissed them and set a sweeping tide of desire surging through him. That he still wanted her this fiercely after seven years of marriage amazed him.

"It's a surprise. You'll have to wait."

But her voice had gone soft and her body molded itself to his with a liquid heat. Her arms twined at his neck and her fingers curled into his hair. And she kissed him back with such passion that his muscles quivered and weakened.

He placed her on the blue-and-white quilt in their bedroom and sat on the edge of the bed, admiring her. Her skin bloomed with need for him. Her sexy blue eyes had gone dark and dreamy. She reached for the hem of her T-shirt and pulled it over her head. That she still seemed unable to resist his advances after all this time struck him with wonder.

With a finger he traced the lace edge of her bra. The silk softness of her skin was a delight. The speeding of her breath caused an answering gallop of his pulse. He couldn't resist the invitation of the pebbling of her nipples beneath the satiny fabric. Her soft sigh, the curling upward of her body to meet his touch as he thumbed one hard peak then the other made him acutely aware of the pulsating hardness of his body.

"Dinner can wait?" He hated to ruin her surprise when she'd worked so hard to set the scene.

She smiled at him in a way that told him she was fully aware of his desire for her and reached for him, bringing his face close to hers. In a voice raw and seductive, she said, "Dinner can wait."

They came together in a kiss that could have melted the polar ice caps. Taryn was fumbling with the buttons of his shirt when the phone rang.

Both stopped mid-caress. Forehead rested against forehead. Breaths came in short, heated bursts.

"Don't answer," she said, clutching his shirt collar with a frantic hold.

"I have to."

The shrill sound was a counterpoint to their racing pulses. Then suddenly her eyes showed both disappointment and acceptance. "Tad's on duty."

"I'm on call."

He nibbled the lobe of one ear, but the ring of the phone was fast cooling his ardor. "I'll make it up to you."

Taryn bussed his cheek with a stiff peck. "I'll go check on dinner."

Heart heavy with regret, he picked up the receiver on the small night table beside the bed.

Before he could say anything, RoAnn McGarrity's cutting voice chimed in. "Chance? Are you there?"

"I'm here, RoAnn." Taryn reached for her T-shirt and pulled it back on. Quietly, she left the room and a sinking feeling settled in his stomach. "If you think you're sending me anywhere now that I'm home, you'd better think again."

RoAnn acted as the local sheriff's office dispatcher. Folks kept their band radios tuned to the station frequency just to hear all the local gossip she managed to air over the waves.

"I know it's been a long day for you and I wouldn't ask except Tad ain't got your skill at dealin' with an incendiary temper like Billy Ray Brett's, and besides, he's yankin' old Ruby Kramer out of a ditch again."

"What's with Billy Ray this time?"

"He's mutatin' coyotes into wolves again. Swears he saw one sniffin' at his herd." She snorted. "As if his one mangy beast makes a herd. He needs your reassurance there ain't no wolf-release program active in these parts. Before nightfall—if you know what I mean."

Yeah, he knew. If he didn't handle this now, he'd be up handling it in the dead of night, and he had other plans for his evening.

Resigned, he said, "I'll go soothe Billy Ray."

He found Taryn in the kitchen. She accepted his arms around her, his kiss, but a skin of cool distance had grown between them. "I've got to go talk Billy Ray Brett out of hallucinating wolves. I won't be long."

Her smile had a sad quality to it. "I'll be waiting."

He jostled her hips against his. "It'll give you time to finish your surprise."

She nodded and turned to the chili.

Reluctantly, he stepped into the late afternoon's skin-drenching humidity and into his cruiser.

As sheriff, keeping Gabenburg safe was his job, and Chance took pride in what he did—just as his mentor, Angus Conover, had taught him. He owed Angus and he owed Gabenburg for taking him in, but it wasn't gratitude that drove him to serve and protect as much as a genuine caring for the place and the people. Still, some days, like today when he was bone-weary tired and wanted nothing more than a quiet evening at home with his wife, he yearned for a simple nine-to-five occupation.

He shook his head and mumbled, "You'd go stark raving mad inside a week."

He had a loving wife, a job that fulfilled him and friends who accepted him as he was. What more could a guy ask for? He and Taryn had even talked of making a baby—which would be the icing on an already sweet cake.

She was the blue sky in his life, and his greatest fear was that one day, without quite knowing how, he'd mess up, that the needs of others would take him from Taryn one time too many, that he would lose her and his life all over again.

"Sheriff One." RoAnn's voice squawked over the radio. "Chance, are you there?"

As good as RoAnn was at coordinating calls, he could

never get her to use the proper radio lingo. Chance keyed the mike. "Sheriff One. Go ahead."

"Sam Wentworth just buzzed me. He's out by Gator Park and thinks he's found the safe that was heisted from Leggett's Antiques yesterday."

"Tad can check it out when he's done with Ruby."

"You really ought to yank her license. Ruby's a menace on the road. But does anyone ever listen to me? No. Look, Gator Park's on your way to the Brett ranch, Chance, and Tad's way out on the other side of town. Won't take but a minute of your time. Oh, and since you'll be going that way, might as well stop by Nancy Howell's on your way home and pick up that blackberry jam she's got for Taryn."

Taryn would want the jam to sell at her little Bread and Butter bakery. Might as well give her another reason to smile at him when he finally made his way home again. "All right. Show me en route to Gator Park."

"Don't forget the jam."

"I won't."

Gator Park, the Brett ranch, the Howell farm—then home. He couldn't wait to watch Taryn's face light up at the sight of him, to run his fingers through her soft brown hair, to get his arms around her once more.

Heading north, beyond the Gabenburg town-limit sign, land rolled into gentle hills and patches of pine forests. To the south, the terrain leveled out into grassy marshlands and drifted into the Gulf of Mexico. Ahead in a field, cattle and egrets clustered around a water tank. Here and there an oil derrick pumped. A flock of geese passed over low and honked as they crossed the highway.

The cruiser's air-conditioning was on the fritz again, so Chance drove with the windows rolled down. The air was sticky and heavy with the odor of pine, cow dung and flood-swollen river. He took it all in and smiled. These sights and smells and sounds were all precious to him. Fifteen years ago, he'd been given a second chance at life and he wasn't going to waste a moment of it regretting a past he couldn't remember.

For a while he'd wondered at the blankness of his memory, at his missing childhood. Then, ten years ago when he'd joined the sheriff's office, he'd run a set of his prints through the system. Nothing had matched. He'd felt a measure of comfort in that.

Chance signaled his exit off the highway. The Red Thunder River ran fast and hard in the spring, calmed enough to harvest tourist dollars in the summer, and turned uninviting again in the fall. Sam Wentworth claimed he was born on the river and spent most of his time on the water. If the suspects had dumped the safe in the river, it didn't surprise Chance in the least that Sam would be the one to uncover the fact.

As Chance crested the hill off the ramp, the river appeared. The recent rains had swollen it to the top of its banks and it roared like an awakening giant, churning silt as it rushed to the Gulf. The sun glittered off the racing water, bleeding it red like an open vein. He was halfway down the hill, letting gravity pull the cruiser down, when a flash zapped through his brain.

A picture bolted through his mind. Clear, vivid, horrid.

The sounds, the smells, the sights assaulted him in one overwhelming blow, ripping him from this world and pitching him into another.

Inside this strange realm, everything is tinged red.

Panic surges through him. He's fighting with everything he has, but something bigger, stronger has hold of him and is intent on destroying him.

The smell of death hangs heavy in the sticky air. The taste of muddy water fills his mouth, makes him gag and sputter. The river surrounds him. He's tugged and tossed and tumbled like debris. He tries to swim, but the current is too strong. "Hang on!" His voice? Someone else's? Something catches his foot, drags him under. Black, nothing but black. Hands grab at him. His head is above water once more.

Breath, where is his breath? He's not moving, hanging on to something hard and slippery. A branch. Something bumps into him. He turns. He screams.

A body floats on the water. Bump, bump, bump against his side. Long blond hair writhes on the waves. From a gash on the side of her head pours blood.

Then hands again, tugging, yanking. Pulling? Pushing? Dizzy. Nothing makes sense.

He looks up. Through the water's silver-red surface, he sees his own shimmering face.

Terror engulfs him. He fights with all his might, but the hands only get stronger around his neck. Blond hair flails around him.

He's dying.

He's dead.

THE CHILI WAS HOT. The beer was cold. The green beans were fresh from Ruby Kramer's garden. Taryn had traded for them that afternoon with a loaf of sourdough bread. A cherry pie waited on the counter—a sweet ending to a meal meant to win a man's heart.

All that was missing was Chance.

Taryn flopped into a kitchen chair and straightened a linen napkin. She'd planned everything to the last second.

Then Chance had come home and knocked her best intentions haywire. She couldn't resist him; never had been able to.

The attraction wasn't just that his distinctive cheekbones

made him look at once savage and sexy. It wasn't just that his bottomless dark eyes seemed to take her in and hold her safe. It was also because the bone-deep goodness in him made her believe in the possibility of enduring happiness.

She hated herself for making Chance feel bad about doing his job. His loyalty and his genuine care were two qualities she admired in him.

She'd wanted everything to be perfect, everything to feel right. Determined, she stood up. "It still can be."

The evening was young. Chance could handle Billy Ray Brett in no time. He'd done it often enough. She hurried toward the bathroom and started the shower. This was going to be a special night. One she hoped Chance would never forget. She wasn't going to ruin it with a fit of resentment.

She would feed him. She would seduce him. Then she would tell him their world was about to be turned upside down. As steam started to fill the small room, she stood before the mirror and cleared her throat.

"Chance, I have something to tell you," she said out loud, testing the words she'd practiced all day in her head as she'd mixed and kneaded and baked. Why was her heart beating so fast? Why did her tongue feel so stiff and clumsy? Why did her eyes look so wild with apprehension? She swallowed hard and tried again. "Chance, remember when you said—" She growled at her disappearing image in the mirror. "Chance, I'm...we're..."

A gulp of fear brought one hand to her belly, the other to her throat. What if...? No, she wasn't going to worry. Chance *would* be pleased. Hadn't he said so a dozen times already?

She undressed and stepped into the shower. There she lathered in a shower gel of Chance's favorite summer-rain scent and lingered for a long time under the hot spray of water until the fear and resentment flowed down the drain along with the soapy water. After drying herself, she slathered on a body lotion of the same summer-rain scent. Hair wound in a turban of towel, she headed for the bedroom.

Out of the closet, she took the tiny red dress she'd been hiding for a week—until the time was right. She planned to meet her husband at the door wearing nothing but that scrap of cloth. It left little to the imagination. And this time, she would make him wait before she allowed him to render her mindless in his arms.

A small smile of satisfaction curled her lips as she imagined Chance's appreciation of the dress. She loved the way his gaze seemed to eat her alive when he was aroused, the way his dark eyes glittered with desire. And she loved that little groan deep in his throat as he reached for her. That seductive sound was part warrior's claim, part helplessness—as if he couldn't resist her even if he tried. That made her feel safe and secure and wanted.

Just as she tossed her towel onto the neatly made bed, she heard a car turn into the driveway.

"No, I'm not ready!" She rushed to the window, snapped the curtain open and peeked out. Not Chance's cruiser, but Tad Pruitt's truck. She groaned. Tad was having girlfriend problems and she'd made the mistake of telling him to drop by anytime he needed to talk. He'd taken her up on her offer three times this week already. And what was he doing coming to bother her while he was on duty and Chance was torn from her bed to answer a call?

She'd get rid of Tad quick, she decided as she donned a T-shirt and shorts and stuffed her feet into sandals. Maybe she ought to send him to her grandmother. She shook her head and laughed. Nola Barnes was opinionated enough for three. She'd set Tad straight in no time.

Taryn opened the door. Heat slapped her face, making her suck in a breath. Where was Tad? She couldn't hear his footsteps on the gravel walkway. Frowning, she stepped onto the deck. She lifted a hand against the setting sun and saw Tad sitting in the truck, both hands on the steering wheel. This wasn't good. He'd need reassurance and calming words and all she wanted to do was get ready for Chance.

"Tad? Are you all right?" But something about the way he stared at her wasn't right. An arrow of fear sliced through her heart and razored all the way to her stomach.

The truck door creaked. Tad exited, keeping his gaze toward the ground. In the place of cocky arrogance, he wore a pained expression. His usually straight and tall posture was bowed. His tan uniform shirt sported dark splotches. He fiddled with his hat. Round and round it went. His brown pants were ripped at the knee. His boots were muddy.

"Tad?" Her heart knocked hard. Her limbs felt leaden. She slinked forward, using the railing as a crutch. "Tad?"

"Taryn," he croaked. He took two steps forward, then stopped. His eyes looked desperate. He braced himself as if for a blow. She knew then that her world was about to come apart.

"Chance?"

Tad nodded. "He's had an accident."

Taryn's ears rang. Her heart stopped beating, then made up the lapse in double time. Her legs shook. Despite the heat that slicked her skin, a cold shiver racked her body. She held on to the deck railing with all of her strength. "No, God, no. What happened? Where is he? How is he?"

"He's alive," Tad said in a rush. He climbed the three steps to the deck, started to reach for her, then drew back. "He drove into the river."

"The river?" She frowned, not understanding. *No, no, no. Not the river.* Chance was a cautious driver, an expert diver. No river, not even Red Thunder, could get the best of him. Tad had made a mistake. Chance was too strong, too good to be taken by the river. Then why couldn't she stop shaking? "What happened?"

"We're not sure. They took him to Beaumont." Tad put his hand on Taryn's trembling shoulder. "I'll drive you."

She nodded and let him lead her to his truck.

This was not happening. This could not be happening. *He's mine,* she told the river. *You can't have him.*

As Tad drove, her world unraveled until Taryn's mind became nothing more than a snarl of worries.

She could not lose Chance. Not now. Not with a baby on the way.

"HELLO, darlin'." Garth Ramsey drawled the endearment because he'd learned the ladies liked the sound of his voice deep and gravelly. The performance wasn't so much for the body on the bed as for the staff tending to it. Image, he'd learned the hard way, bought you more than truth.

He handed a plate of oatmeal cookies to Jessie Ross, the night nurse. "I brought a treat for my wife." He smiled and whipped his other hand from behind his back. "And for you wonderful Florence Nightingales, a box of chocolates."

"Aren't you the sweetest man?" Jessie gushed. She placed the plate of cookies on the nightstand beside the bed and the box of chocolates on the dresser by the upholstered glider she was using. A canvas sack with knitting lay beside the chair. Pale blue wool ran from the bag to a set of knitting needles that held what looked like a sleeve for a baby sweater.

"Now you make sure you leave some for the day staff or I'll never hear the end of it," he teased.

"This box is big enough to entertain an army." She smiled at him and he knew he could have her if he wanted. All he'd have to do is ask and she'd fall into his arms. But his taste didn't run to short, skinny brunettes with no figure, even when the room's low light gave her pretty-enough features a soft golden glow. Besides, as part of his image of devoted husband, he'd decided it was best not to fool around with the staff at the Pine Creek Home. Finding a willing partner was never a problem.

"How's she been doing this week?" he asked. He sat on the teal leather chair by the bed and stroked his wife's silky blond hair. They'd wanted to cut it to make it easier to tend, but he'd insisted they leave it long and loose.

"No change really," Jessie said, and popped a chocolate in her mouth. "She's been a little more active during the day."

"How so?"

"She likes to sit outside and puts up a fuss when we take her in."

"Ah, yes, she was always one for the great outdoors."

"She's been more fussy about food, too. We practically have to force-feed her. She's come up a touch anemic on her tests, but don't worry, the doctor's got her on iron. She'll appreciate those cookies. They're her favorite."

"Well, in her case, it's the little things that make a difference."

"You're so good to her. I'll leave you alone and take my break now," Jessie said.

"That would be great. Take your time. My wife and I have a lot of catching up to do."

Smiling and all but batting her eyelashes, Jessie tiptoed out of the room.

They all thought his twice-weekly visits were husbandly devotion. In truth, they were an inspection of his investment. As long as his darling wife was nothing more than a body going through the motions of life, he was free to live as he pleased. Her vacant mind bought him immunity.

He scooted the chair closer to the bed, held her hand in case someone should happen by and peek through the glass window on the door, and whispered in her ear, "Remember, darlin', when you thought you could manipulate me as easily as you did your sweetheart? You learned your lesson, didn't you? I always win."

She turned her head at the sound of his voice and opened her eyes. There beneath the dull veneer in her gray-green eyes was a spark of something that needed to be nipped before it got out of control.

"I've noticed more light in your eyes lately and this longing for the outdoors isn't good. I've got just the thing. My friend says that one extra dose should keep you right where you are."

With his back carefully hiding his activity, he swabbed the crook of her elbow with an alcohol pad and injected a small dose of an experimental drug. The needle was so tiny it left no mark on her delicate skin. She mewled like a kitten in pain, tried to twist away, but she was too weak and there was nothing she could do to stop him.

"That's it, darlin', take it in. Let me take care of you. Let me shelter you from the real world. You were always too good for them."

He returned the syringe and the used alcohol pad to a sunglasses case in his blazer pocket.

As long as Ellen's brain misfired, there was no one to deny any of his claims, there was nothing to stop him. He was on top of the world and climbing higher every day.

"Sleep well, darlin'."

Chapter Two

The gash on Chance's head worried Taryn. The swollen blue and purple mark curved from temple to temple. Five stitches pinched the skin above his left eyebrow.

Watching him so still and white beneath the hospital sheets made her soul wither by inches. The emergency-room doctor had told her Chance had regained consciousness for a while before he'd slipped into a coma and that he might also be suffering from traumatic amnesia. He'd told her not to worry, that Chance's injuries probably weren't life-threatening. But how could she not worry? The man she'd thought invincible was lying in a hospital bed unconscious.

"The chili will keep," she told him, trying to keep up a one-sided conversation to fill the silence that was otherwise too heavy to bear. "Probably taste even better tomorrow. So will the pie. And I'm sure Ruby will have another basketful of beans to sell before the week's out."

Not a muscle moved, not an eyelash twitched. She could be watching a corpse, except that the machinery beside him with its beeps and moving lines told her he was alive.

"Maud came by the bakery this afternoon. Right when I was closing, too. Have you ever noticed she seems to time her every action in a way that will irritate somebody?"

Taryn gave a weak laugh. "She was complaining about the heat as she bought every last buttermilk biscuit I had. Plus a loaf of cinnamon raisin bread. Plus half a dozen sweet rolls. And you know those didn't last until she got home."

Taryn held Chance's hand and stroked the back of it with her thumb. The skin was rough and familiar beneath her finger, but cold. She hiked the blanket over his chest and wrapped both her hands around his to warm him. Her lips trembled and she pressed them tight to hold back a sob.

"Hey," she said, trying hard to inject some lightness into her voice. "Maybe now you'll take the vacation you've been meaning to take—for what?—seven years now. We could go away for a week. Or ask Liz and Jake to join us, and you and Jake could go diving while Liz and I go antiquing."

Wake up. Please wake up. Seeing him like this was killing her. She couldn't bear the thought that he wouldn't come back to her, of trying to live without the man she loved with all her heart. He gave her confidence, made her feel secure. He was always there for her. She needed him now more than ever. She squeezed his hand and willed him to squeeze back.

"I've got something to tell you. I think you'll be pleased. But I want to see the look in your eyes when I tell you my secret. So you'll just have to wake up, you hear?"

She wanted to see the initial shock of her announcement widen his dark eyes, then see the slow spread of his smile. His lips always kicked up a bit higher on one side than the other and lent him a boyish charm she'd found hard to resist since the first time she'd seen him stroll into her mother's diner.

She kissed his fingertips. "Wake up, Chance. Please wake up."

What if the doctor was wrong? What if Chance didn't

come back? What if he stayed in this coma? What if he couldn't remember her? What if he died? Taryn scrunched her eyes closed and swallowed hard. One hand went to her belly and cradled the life growing there. Could she raise this baby alone? The process of single parenting had turned her mother bitter and angry. Was that what she had to look forward to?

No, she wouldn't think about it. Chance would recover. He had to. She would accept no other alternative. She'd waited seven years to start this family; she wasn't going to have her dream taken away from her before it materialized.

"Mrs. Conover?"

The voice startled Taryn out of the loop of her worries. She turned to see a man standing at the door. "Could I speak with you for a few minutes?"

She glanced from Chance to the man and back. "I—I..."

He took the extra straight chair along the wall and dragged it next to her. "I'm Dr. Benton, the staff psychiatrist. I'd like to go over your husband's chart with you."

"Psychiatrist?" She frowned. Dr. Benton had a compact body under a lab coat that somehow reminded her of a cowboy's duster, lank pale red hair that needed a cut, and green eyes that bugged out as if he'd read too many books in less than ideal light. He looked all wrong. A psychiatrist should have a calm, reassuring presence, but this man seemed to have a frenetic energy dancing all around him. "Why does Chance need a psychiatrist?"

"Dr. Gregory, the doctor who saw your husband in the emergency room, believes that the patient's amnesia is not of a physiological nature."

Taryn swiveled her body away from Chance, but still held on to his hand. "But Dr. Gregory said the coma was temporary. That it was helping him heal."

Dr. Benton flipped a page on the chart he was carrying and flicked two fingers on the paper. "Head wounds often look worse than they are because they bleed so profusely. But other than the small laceration on his forehead, there seems to be nothing physically wrong with him."

"But he's in a coma. The knock must have been harder than you think. Chance is strong and healthy. He wouldn't turn into a weakling so easily."

Dr. Benton tried to look sympathetic, but the twist of his features looked more patronizing than concerned. "There's no sign of trauma. The X rays, the MRI all came back negative. There's nothing physically wrong with your husband."

She shot up, placing herself between the doctor and Chance. "Other than the fact that he almost drowned and now he's in a coma! What exactly are you trying to tell me?"

"When your husband came to in the emergency room, he couldn't remember who he was, where he was, what happened to him."

Taryn's heart thudded heavily once in her chest. She hadn't wanted to believe Dr. Gregory when he'd mentioned Chance's probable amnesia. He couldn't forget her. She'd prove that to everyone once Chance woke up. He wouldn't forget the love they had; it was too strong. She squeezed her nape as she ordered her thoughts. "But that's normal. He was in an accident. He'll remember soon. Dr. Gregory said so."

Dr. Benton eagerly bent over the chart. "In his paperwork, it's noted that he suffered a previous episode of traumatic amnesia."

Oh no, God, no. Her pulse jagged fast and hard. She didn't like where this was heading at all. Could Chance have forgotten everything again? How was that possible after all they'd shared? Her legs felt shaky. She sat. "Fifteen years ago."

Dr. Benton licked his lips, his eyes bugged out even more, and he seemed to savor what was coming next. "I believe your husband is suffering through a second episode of traumatic amnesia brought about by the return of a state-dependent memory."

"You lost me."

"The original trauma took place fifteen years ago," he explained slowly as if she were dim-witted. He turned the chart at an angle and pointed. "It says here that his body was discovered not far from where today's accident happened."

"Yes, I know."

A restless energy overtook Dr. Benton as he pointed to a second entry. "The time of the year is the same. Late May for the first incident. Early June for this one."

"Yes, but what does one have to do with the other? The incident happened fifteen years ago."

He scooted to the edge of his chair and leaned forward. "Traumatic events elicit major physiological responses in the body. Memories of the event are biochemically 'attached' to the traumatic physiological state and that produces a state-dependent memory."

"Please, Dr. Benton—"

He held a hand up and rushed on. "I believe that something about the conditions today—something he heard or saw or smelled—brought back the memory he forgot fifteen years ago and it threw him back into that world. Those cues were a match to the conditions that existed fifteen years ago at the time of his trauma and brought back the lost memory. He didn't just *remember* what happened, he *relived* it."

"You're saying that because he remembered what he forgot, now he's forgotten again."

"Exactly!"

"But why would that cause him to forget who he is now?"

He rubbed his hands together as if he were contemplating digging into a juicy steak. "Now that's the mystery I'd like to explore. The brain and how it works is so fascinating."

"I'm not going to let him be a guinea pig—"

"No, no." He patted her knee. "I'd like a chance to help him recover all his memory."

"You could do that?" A flicker of hope sprang up.

"Yes. I know I could. I believe your husband repressed his memories after suffering some extreme stress fifteen years ago. The way he's dealt with his life since then is actually quite remarkable. In all my years, I've never seen such a good case for memory retrieval—"

He stopped as if catching himself about to head into a detour, cleared his throat, then went on. "Amnesia is a coping mechanism—a symptom of post-traumatic stress disorder. I would forward a guess that your husband is a very controlled man."

He seemed to be holding his breath as he paused and waited for her confirmation.

"Yes." Chance kept everything neat and tidy. She'd often thought it was because he was afraid to lose any more of himself. As if by keeping his things in order, he could keep himself in order, too. Sometimes, when he didn't know she was watching him, she could see his internal chaos reflected in his eyes, in the painful gathering of his eyebrows. And he'd been successful at his job because everyone knew that in the middle of turmoil and tempers Chance Conover could be counted on to keep a cool head and bring back balance. No one ever seemed to notice the river of unrest just below the surface.

"He never talks about what happened then," she said, feeling hurt once again that he'd never trusted her with that part of himself.

"Avoidance is another sign of PTSD," Dr. Benton said. "But time alone won't heal him."

"He was doing fine...." Wasn't he? Her mind scrolled back through their time together. She saw it then, the distance, that slight space he kept between himself and everything—even her. Her hand tightened against Chance's, afraid to let him go.

"Internally, things weren't in order," Dr. Benton continued. A slightly manic light gleamed in his eyes, as if her husband's troubles were a treasure to be prospected. "Trauma is stored in the brain's limbic system, which processes emotions and sensations. Just because he's repressed the memories doesn't mean they aren't there and affecting him. What I'd like to do is take him through the steps of recovering those memories and see him through the healing process."

Dr. Benton was practically panting as he waited for her answer.

A headache thrummed at her temples. He was going too fast and not giving her enough facts to make a good judgment. What was best for Chance? "How will you do that?"

He smiled. "There are several techniques we could choose from—hypnotism, guided imagery, dream work, sodium amytal."

"Truth serum! You'd drug him?"

"It's a very safe technique," Dr. Benton assured her, then rushed on. "Once he's retrieved his past, I'll show him how to put these memories in the context of other psychological symptoms, how to live with the feelings the retrieval is bringing back, how to deal with cognitive distortions.''

"Cognitive distortions?" This was all too much.

Dr. Benton seemed annoyed at the interruption, but with quick motions of his hands explained, "There are two forms of memory. Explicit memory is the ability to consciously recall facts or events. Implicit memories are behavioral knowledge of an experience without conscious recall. As an example you can read, but probably can't remember how you learned the skill."

"So you're saying even though he might not remember who he is, he'll remember skills he's learned."

"Precisely. At first he may be flooded with implicit sensorimotor memory. He'll get the picture or the feelings or the terror the memories bring back, but not the explicit memories that could ground or explain the meaning of the sensations or images. He'll need someone to guide him through the process of re-creating the entire scene in order to deal with what happened to him and get on with his life."

Taryn frowned and shook her head. He made it sound so easy. Still, something kept her from agreeing readily. "Chance isn't one to rely on anybody. I doubt you'd get him to agree to therapy of any kind."

The doctor leaned so far forward she feared he would slip right out of his chair. "At the moment your husband is unable to make decisions for himself. You could have him admitted. Once the therapy starts, I assure you, he'll be thankful for your foresight."

"Chance likes to make his own decisions."

"That's understandable, but right now he's not in a position to make an informed judgment. Therapy is his best option for complete recovery."

"I don't know—"

"No."

The word came strong and sure from behind her. Taryn whirled and could hardly contain her joy at the sight of her husband's open eyes.

"Chance!" She squealed and threw herself at him, clasping him into a hard hug. "I knew you'd come back. I knew you'd be all right."

The fact that Chance had turned his head away from hers, that he was holding himself tight and stiff as if her touch was something alien took a moment to register. "Chance?"

The look in his eyes was cool and withdrawn and looked as impenetrable as concertina wire on a prison fence.

"Chance?"

Wanting to hang on to him in any way possible, she reached for his hand. He pulled it free of her grasp and shoved it beneath the sheet.

"Get out. Both of you. Leave me alone."

"Chance?" He wasn't making sense. He wasn't acting like himself. "I'm here for you."

"Out!"

His whole body shook, and Taryn couldn't say whether it was from fear or cold or anger, only that his unseemly behavior scared her stiff. This wasn't the Chance she knew and loved.

Dr. Benton tugged at her elbow. "Mrs. Conover, perhaps—"

"No." She ripped her arm out of Dr. Benton's grasp and took Chance's face between her hands. Short-cropped bristly black hair, slightly crooked nose, sharp cheeks, kissable lips and all, this was the face of the man she loved. He was still there inside that body—*had* to be—and she was going to find him. "Look at me, Chance. Dammit, I said look at me!"

His dark gaze met hers, cold and hard. Like smoke in

the night, specters of torment arose behind the surface. Even as she looked, the man she loved was disappearing inside those tortured shadows.

"Chance."

He didn't know her. He didn't remember their life together. He didn't recall the love that fused their souls, making them one. Right before her eyes, he was turning into a remote stranger. The pain inside her chest was nearly unbearable.

"I won't let you forget, Chance." She cursed her croaky voice, her sniffles, her tears. "I'm your wife. I love you. I won't let you forget who I am, what we had together. We've been through too much for you to just throw it all away. Do you hear me?"

The machinery monitoring his pulse, his heartbeat jumped to life. The vein at his neck throbbed hard and fast. Panic churned in his eyes.

He shoved her away and turned his head. She stumbled backward. Both her hands covered her mouth, holding back her sobs. If he'd taken out his service weapon and shot her on the spot, he couldn't have shocked her more than he had at this moment. Never had Chance lifted a hand to her—to anyone—in anger.

He doesn't know who he is, she reminded herself. *He's not hurting you on purpose. He's confused. He's scared. He doesn't know what he's doing.*

"Mrs. Conover," Dr. Benton said, "it's best you leave now."

"No. I have to stay." She wouldn't let him forget. She'd be here, a constant reminder of his past. He'd *have* to remember.

The machinery's beeps got quicker, the neon lines sharper.

"He needs his rest," Dr. Benton insisted.

"He needs me." Just as she needed him. Just as their baby needed them both.

The machinery beeped faster. The lines jagged erratically. Chance grabbed at the wires connecting him to the monitoring equipment.

"If you don't leave, I'll have to call security."

"He's my husband."

Dr. Benton's grip was unrelenting as he pushed her toward the door. "He's our patient and his welfare is our number one priority."

Two nurses came in. One plunged something into Chance's IV line as the other pinned him down. A rasp between anger and fear grated from his throat.

"Chance!" She reached for him, but Dr. Benton blocked her way. Tears streamed down her cheeks as Chance's face contorted into a mask of sheer terror. "Chance!"

"He needs help, Mrs. Conover," Dr. Benton said, shaking her slightly to get her attention. "Now would be an excellent time to have me admit him to my ward."

Chance's eyes closed. Slowly the beeps and lines on the machinery calmed. And once again, he looked no more than a corpse.

"Chance," she whispered, half in prayer, half in entreaty.

"With therapy," Dr. Benton insisted, "I can bring your husband back. Sign the transfer."

"I have to stay with him."

"To heal, to come back to you, he needs therapy."

"He needs me." Not these white-coated people who didn't care about him.

"He's going to be sleeping for a while now, Mrs. Conover," Dr. Benton said. "Why don't you go home and get some rest? I'll put my therapy proposal together and we can go over it tomorrow."

"I want to stay."

"That's not in his best interest right now." Dr. Benton nodded to one of the nurses. "Call security."

Soon two uniformed guards were leading her against her will to the elevator.

Angus, who'd been in the waiting room, joined her. "What's going on?"

With his graying brown hair, his patrician features just now starting to droop with age and his ever-present camel-colored blazer and matching Stetson, he was a welcome sight. His questioning glance searched the guards' faces, then hers. "You all right?"

"No," she managed to choke out. She wouldn't be until Chance came back to her. "They're making me go home."

Angus wrapped one of his strong arms around her shoulders. "Chance probably needs his rest, sweetheart."

"He doesn't know who I am." She leaned into Angus's barrel chest and the tears flowed harder, numbing her to anything but her own loss.

"I'll take you home, sweetheart."

She could not have said how she got home. Seeing the house all dark and empty was another blow that added a layer of numbness. Angus offered to sit with her. She refused. Like a robot on automatic, she went straight to the bedroom she shared with Chance. Still dressed in the shorts and T-shirt she'd put on after her shower, she slid into bed. She drew the sheet over her head, curled up knees to chin and withdrew into the hard shell she'd escaped to so often as a little girl.

She'd thought having Chance die would be the absolute worst thing that could happen to her. She'd been wrong. Having him alive and looking at her as if she was nothing but a stranger was a thousand times worse.

But as she spent a sleepless night in the dark, alone in

her bed, she knew she could not give up. For her baby's sake, she couldn't let go of what had taken her so long to earn.

She'd help him, just as he'd helped her find her way home again ten years ago. "Together, we'll find you again."

CHANCE CAME TO in a sweat, breath all but choked out of him and coming short and sharp as if he'd been running for hours. His head pounded to a frantic beat. His skin crawled with the need to keep bolting. He tried to blink away the horror flashing behind his lids, but with each flicker, the red haze spread, the blond hair writhed, the hands choked.

Grasping the sheets on the side of the bed into fists, he forced his eyes to stay open until he saw nothing but the white ceiling. And as his breath slowed, as the beating of his heart moderated, he became aware of the anger roiling through him like Class VI rapids. All of his thoughts converged to one overwhelming desire—escape.

"You're awake."

The voice jolted him into hyperarousal, sending the pulse monitor at his side into another wild jangle of beeps. He dragged in a long draw of breath and looked at the man beside his bed. "Who the hell are you?"

He was tall and thin. His features were long and pointed and reminded Chance of an egret. A pink skull showed through the man's close-cropped blond hair. He wore a beige uniform shirt with a gold star above the left pocket and held his hat before him with both hands in a way that struck Chance as a supplication.

"Tad Pruitt." He shifted his weight from one foot to the other. "Your deputy."

Chance looked away, closed his eyes, then jerked them open when the red haze threatened him again.

Tad Pruitt. His deputy.

The name, the man, didn't ring a bell. He almost laughed out loud. Nothing was real anymore. His brain seemed to have been wiped clean of everything except the snapshots of the muddy images running through his mind. His emotions seemed to be able to handle nothing more than the fear running rampant through his body or the anger stirring a fevered need for action.

He fixed his gaze on the acoustic tiles on the ceiling and started counting the holes. One. Two. Three. He was riding a thin line between two nightmares. Any minute now the thread would break and sling him straight into insanity. Four. Five. Six.

"I've got to ask you some questions, Chance." Tad gave a rough attempt at a laugh. "Paperwork's a bitch, but you'll have my head if I don't do it right."

Chance. They kept calling him that, but the name fit about as well as a boot two sizes too small. He sure didn't feel lucky—blistered and bloody was more like it. "The answer to all of them is 'I don't know.'"

"Why don't we give it a try anyway?"

"Why don't you go to hell?"

Tad cleared his throat. "Well, now, I wish I could, but while you're down, I've got an obligation to the town to fulfill."

"You've been here. You've seen me. Your obligation has been fulfilled. Now leave."

"It's not that easy, Chance. Sam Wentworth said he saw you coming down the ramp. Halfway down you accelerated and kept going until you hit the water. They found no mechanical reason for what happened."

No, the dysfunction had been one of his own doing. He

knew that on a level as primal as the fear running through his veins. One hundred seventy-one. One hundred seventy-two.

"That leaves two options, Chance. Did you mistake the accelerator for the brake?"

"I don't know."

The heels of Tad's boots squeaked as he shifted his weight from left to right. "Is there some other reason you'd want to drive into that river?"

"I don't know." Three hundred and one. Three hundred and two. And that was just one corner of one tile. Counting all those holes on the ceiling would surely keep him too busy to think.

"You're an expert diver, but Sam said you didn't even try to get out of the car. You just sat there, staring at the sun while water was pouring in all around you." Tad paused and Chance heard the sound of felt slipping round and round through fingers. The deputy was nervous. "What did you see?"

Blood. Death. Whose? Why? Were they even real? Five hundred and nine. Five hundred and ten. "I don't know."

"You were lucky your rear bumper caught the bank. If it hadn't, the current would have swept you away. Sam got on the horn to RoAnn and got help."

Chance didn't feel particularly grateful for Sam's Good Samaritan act or RoAnn's efficiency at the moment. Whoever they were. Their good deeds had left him swimming in this hell of red and bloodshed and constant dread. Nine hundred and fifteen.

"Let me walk you through what happened right before you hit the water."

"No." He wasn't going there. The best thing to do, he decided, was to walk away and never look back. Escape.

He swallowed hard. The need itched through him strong. Damn! He'd lost count. One. Two. Three.

"You were on the highway heading toward the Brett ranch. After RoAnn gave you the call, you headed toward Gator Park."

Tad paused and seemed to want the silence filled. Chance obliged to cover the quickening whoosh in his ears. "I don't know."

"Sam said you were there pretty quick after he called in the safe's sighting. You climbed the exit ramp. Then what happened?"

"I *don't* know." Twenty-one. Twenty-two.

"Just close your eyes and put yourself back in the cruiser."

"No!" Chance's heart beat frantically in his chest. The monitor's wild beeps only added to his feeling of being out of control. Like a fish out of water, he started struggling for breath. Fisting his hands around the edge of the mattress, he grappled for control. He wasn't going to fall into that red haze. He wasn't going to be carried away on this surge of panic. He wasn't going to drown.

"You're not even trying to figure this out," Tad said.

"I told you. *I don't remember.*" The monitor took another leap and a nurse came in. He saw a syringe in her hands and a fresh wave of terror swept through him. With the drugs, he would be helpless, a bit of debris tossed about with no control. The images would drown through him again.

"No drugs." He grabbed at the IV line. "I'll rip it right out. No drugs."

"Your vitals are off the chart, Mr. Conover. This will help calm you down."

Chance dragged in a long breath, then another. Sweat

soaked him from head to toe. "I'm calm. The deputy irritated me, but he's leaving now. I'm fine. No drugs."

The nurse looked at Tad. "Maybe it would be best if you left."

Hat still in hand, Tad nodded. "I'll be back." His boots squeaked to the slow rhythm of his departure.

"Now," the nurse said as she reached for the IV, "why don't you let me look at that line and make sure you haven't knocked anything out of kilter?"

"Take it out," he ordered.

The nurse clucked at him. "I can't do that without a doctor's order."

"I'm leaving," he said, and started to sit up.

She snorted her disagreement. "And where would you go? You don't even know where you live."

"But I do."

They both turned at the gentle, yet insistent voice. The woman from last night stood in the doorway, one hand braced on the doorknob, the other holding a bag. He couldn't recall her name, but something about her presence sang through him.

She was small, nothing outstanding. All of her features were soft, almost invisible against the pale walls. But her eyes stood out like beacons, warm and welcoming. They were wide, bluer than a summer sky, and had a hypnotic quality to them that kept his gaze riveted and had his throat going dry.

"Do you want to come home with me?" Her eyes were earnest. Her body was braced to handle whatever answer he gave her.

She'd cried for him. She'd said she loved him. She'd told him she wouldn't let him forget. He'd wanted to hang on to that promise. But promises were brittle. They broke like branches on the river and left you drifting still holding on to the thing that had let you down.

Now she was offering him a way out, another scrap of hope.

"Yes."

A whoosh escaped her. Then she went into action, striding past the nurse and standing between them.

"I'm signing him out now." The straight posture of her body dared the nurse to walk through her. If he'd had to take odds, he'd have placed them on the small woman's determination even given the nurse's fifty-pound and five-inch advantage. Did he deserve that fierce loyalty?

"That's against regulations. The doctor—"

"Said there was nothing physically wrong with Chance. There's no reason to hold him."

"Dr. Benton—"

"Isn't the admitting physician."

The woman glanced at him over her shoulder. Her blue eyes revealed a mixture of soul-stirring warmth and utter sadness. "He's my husband. I'm taking him home where he belongs."

He got his wish; he was getting out of this nightmarish place. But as the nurse slipped the IV needle out of his arm, he swallowed hard.

He would be leaving with a woman who was almost as disturbing as the images flashing through his mind.

Chapter Three

Chance had been home for nearly a week and he didn't seem to be making headway. Taryn had tried feeding him all his favorite dishes. She'd tried showing him the pictures taken of their life together. She'd tried taking him out into the community he'd loved. Nothing had made a difference.

He'd eaten with apathy. He'd barely glanced at the photos. Though she'd invited him to make himself at home, he acted as if he were a guest uncomfortably detained against his wishes. Her questions were either ignored or answered with a grunt. He'd refused to go out or to receive visitors—including Angus and his wife, Lucille. They'd been father and mother to him for fifteen years, and being turned away by one they considered a son had hurt.

And always there was an underlying current of anger that seemed to propel him into constant action.

He spent his nights awake, pacing the halls of their small house like a caged animal. Day didn't bring him relief, either. It was as if he had to keep ahead of whatever was haunting him or risk being devoured by it. Not knowing how to help him made her feel as helpless as when she'd been a girl and watched her mother rant and rave at her sorry lot in life.

His blank stare, his restless turmoil, his aloofness toward

her were like a bruise she kept hitting over and over again. She hid the pain with a smile and continued encouragement. But the tenderest ache was knowing that he was home and didn't want to share her bed. So in the bedroom he refused to enter, she cried herself to sleep every night.

Even though every defeat stung, it was up to her to find a way through the amnesia to the Chance she knew. She wasn't going to give up.

Tonight she'd awakened from a light sleep to the quiet. Not hearing the soft footfall of his bare feet on the carpet had whacked her out of drowsiness with a fresh wave of worry. She found him standing in the dark by the sliding glass door in the kitchen. Two hundred yards down the grassy slope of their backyard, the river glistened in moonlight. His gaze was riveted on the water as if it held all the answers.

She went to stand next to him. "It's late. Past midnight. You're exhausted. Why don't you come to bed?"

He flinched as if she'd suggested self-mutilation, and a bolt of panic jagged through his eyes. What was causing the fear? Was he afraid that if he slept he would lose the rest of himself?

"You don't have to sleep," she said, reaching for him then letting her hand fall back to her side. "Come rest." *Let me take care of you.*

He didn't say anything, but kept staring out the window. She hesitated, then stood closer, wrapped one arm around his and twined their fingers as she'd done a thousand times before. Something sighed inside her at the rightness of his hand in hers. He didn't jerk away. She took it as a good sign.

"See the roses by the fence?" She pointed at the dark shape of bushes in the yard. "You planted those for me on our wedding day. You said you didn't want me to live in a home without flowers. The way you said it was so sweet, I cried.''

There was no sign of recognition in his eyes, no shifting of muscle to indicate anything she said was getting through. The tears burning her eyes this time were tears of frustration.

''And the swing by the pecan?'' she continued, proud the rawness in her throat barely wavered her voice. ''You thought we could spend romantic evenings there talking and planning. But we hardly ever use it because the mosquitoes are too fierce. Instead, most nights, we linger over iced tea right here in the kitchen.''

She leaned her head against his arm, heard the sharp intake of breath, smiled and snuggled closer. She could still affect him. That had to say something, didn't it?

''You hate cutting the lawn. You grumbled about it every blessed weekend. I finally got so tired of hearing you complain that I hired the Taylor boy. He's doing a good job, don't you think?''

Chance made a noncommittal grunt. At least he was listening. She'd half feared he was lost somewhere in his own mind, or drowning in the phantom memories awakened by the river.

Red Thunder looked innocent enough tonight. Romantic even, with the moonlight dancing on its wake. The sound of the water through the closed glass door had a steady, soothing quality to it.

''You do love the river. You spend all your free time on it—fishing, paddling, diving.'' She looked up into his dark eyes, wanting to be sure she wasn't pushing too fast into dangerous territory. She wanted to bring her husband back, not drive him farther away. ''You and Jake—''

He stiffened against her as he did every time a name was mentioned. He didn't remember Jake any more than he remembered anybody else, and didn't care for the reminder. She tried to gloss over the ties as if it were something she did every day.

"You went through the police academy with Jake Atwood. He works in Beaumont and we still see him and his wife, Liz, often. Anyway, after your ordeal, you were afraid of the current, so Jake taught you to dive. He was the one who told you that the only way to deal with the fear was to face it. He said you were a natural, that he'd never seen a strong swimmer like you. Must be why you survived."

Chance's jaw flinched.

"It's brought you a great deal of joy, the river has, but it's stolen a lot from you, too, hasn't it? Twice now, it's taken your memory."

He started to turn from her, but she hung on to him. "I won't let it take anything more from you." Reaching across her own body, she placed a hand over his heart, felt the strong thunder of it against her hand. "Talk to me, Chance. I can deal with anything but your silence."

He closed his eyes and swallowed hard.

To evoke memories of their life together, she'd tried feeding him, she'd tried talking to him, she'd tried showing him his world. Maybe what he needed right now was to escape for a while.

She swiveled until they stood chest to chest. Her fingers skimmed his jaw. Afraid to look in his eyes and see rejection, she concentrated on the dark stubble along his cheek, marveled at how the prickly softness showed off the exotic planes of his face, the strength.

With the tip of a finger, she traced the velvet smoothness of his lips, felt them part. His breath blew hot against her skin. She wanted to feel her mouth against his, wanted to feel him devouring her. The sheer power of the desire cut her breath short. Deliberately, she released it. Slowly, she leaned forward. Tentatively, she pressed a kiss against his neck, felt the answering leap of his pulse against her lips.

Chance growled. He captured her wrists in his hands, tore them from his shoulders and pushed them back. Her pulse bounced against the hard manacles of his fingers.

"No." But there was no strength to his denial.

"Yes." She rose on her toes, watched him watch her with his keen gaze, saw his nostrils flare, felt the waft of heat from his body wrap around her, smelled the familiar scent of his musk on that heated wave.

And as her lips touched his once more, there came that delicious helpless-warrior groan low in his throat. Desire flared raw and charged in his eyes.

She could reach him on this primal level. She knew she could. "Let me love you, Chance."

"No," he said, then leaned forward and kissed her with equal ardor.

The rich and warm taste of him sent her blood whooshing through her veins. Her fierce need for him had been a wonder to her since their first kiss. Still was. Longing had her trembling, so she anchored her arms around his neck and brought him deeper into the kiss. Yearning unfurled low in her belly, reminding her what their love had created. A cascade of warmth and lust rippled through her and her kiss turned hard and wild. "Let me love you."

He braced his hands on each side of her hips. The glorious heat of them burned her through her nightshirt. His breath rasped hard against her cheek. For an instant, she thought he would push her away, but his tongue tangled with hers, and the zig to push her away turned into a zag that pinned her against his hard body. Pulse thundered against pulse. Heart drummed against heart. Desire fed on desire.

The Chance she remembered was in there somewhere.

She could feel it in his kiss, in his touch, in his fervor. If it took loving him every night, every day, until she found him again, she would. She wouldn't give up. The power of the love they shared was strong. It would lead him home. Had to.

She buried her face against his neck, brushed her lips against his racing pulse and whispered in a low, harsh voice, "Let me love you."

THE SOFT SEDUCTION of her words, of her touch, jolted through Chance like a sky full of lightning. He wanted to say no, should say no. He was as unsettled as a summer storm and needed to feel in control. But he couldn't help himself. In the heat of her body, in the passion of her kiss, came a strange kind of escape. The world was no longer red, but a blessed, brilliant white. Hands no longer choked; they stroked and stoked. Hair didn't writhe, it seduced with silky slides against his skin.

He wanted the oblivion she offered more than he wanted his next breath, so he let her lead him down the hallway to the room with the queen-size bed. The blue-and-white quilt's windmill design seemed to taunt him, made him dizzy, so he closed his eyes. He let her unbutton his shirt, his jeans, run her hands over his chest, lower, graze her teeth over a flat, taut nipple. He let her soft sweetness infuse him with a desire that was keen and sharp, alive in the minefield of death.

As she stole his breath once again with a kiss, his blood rumbled through his veins, demanding more.

He didn't know this woman who claimed to be his wife, but on a level he couldn't explain he understood the bond they shared, felt the tug of it, soul to soul. Sacred. Frightening. In this world where nothing was familiar, she was his strength, she was his weakness. He could resist her no more than he could stop the storm of his nightmares.

She backed away from him. A fierce growl escaped him at the infinite space, the desperate urgency her departure from his arms left. His body trembled, desperate for a connection instead of the void his life had become. Blood throbbing against his temple, his wrists, his ankles, he waited, could not ask for what he needed.

She smiled at him, her face showing her awareness of the power she held over him. That knowledge so blatantly exposed should have been a turnoff, but it wasn't. The love, the pleasure, the want in her eyes nearly brought him to his knees, had him reaching for her.

With a shake of her head, she stopped him. "Wait."

She grasped the hem of the long pink T-shirt she wore and pulled it over her head. As she looked at him, her eyes were so impossibly blue, so impossibly wide, so impossibly seductive. How could he have forgotten that look when it rocketed through him with such power?

Her mouth was wet and inviting from the sweep of her tongue. Blushing pink, her skin from head to toe was a velvet dream waiting to be experienced. And he wanted it, wanted it all with frightening intensity. Wanted to lose himself in that passionate softness. Wanted the oblivion she offered.

He reached for her. He stroked her back in long, slow glides, let the feel of her skin, her soft trembling rekindle life inside him. Eyes closed, he inhaled the clean, fresh scent of her. Rain on a rose. Sugar. Desire. "You smell good."

She smiled in the crook of his neck, setting an inferno raging inside him. "Summer Rain. It's your favorite scent."

He kissed her, deep and long, thrilled at the hot texture of her. "You taste good."

"Oh, Chance."

She gave. She took. She was real. And for now, she was his. Her body molded to his, blended with his, became his. "You feel good."

With both hands on her shoulders, he held her away from him. Her confused gaze met his, so blue, so deep. The fingers of one hand skimmed his jaw. Her hips pressed firmly into the very center of his need. "Chance?"

Now it was his turn to plead. "Let me love you."

On her sigh floated relief, consent. In her kiss, in the wrap of her body around his, came the escape that had been so elusive since he'd forgotten who he was.

"Always, Chance, always."

ENVELOPED IN HIS ARMS, Taryn fell asleep. The slow patter of her heart caressed his ribs. The softness of her hair against his fingers was a lullaby. Her breath against his skin was hope. Chance wanted to stay in that comforting moment in time forever. His thoughts slowed. His body relaxed. Soon he drowsed.

Then the nightmare came back. Red haze. Blond hair. Dead eyes. He gulped in air, fought the urge to jolt up and run. When his pulse slowed, when the darkness was no longer tinged with red, he gently untangled himself from Taryn's arms. In her sleep, she reached for him.

"Chance?"

"It's all right. I just need something to drink."

"Um. Don't be long," she said on a yawn.

He didn't answer, but padded to the bathroom and closed the door. In the mirror, by the stark light of the bare bulbs on the vanity, his features looked haunted, grim. An unhealthy ashen tint smudged his skin. Dark rings raccooned his eyes. Deep lines etched his forehead, slashed the corners of his mouth. He sluiced cold water over his face, but it failed to erase the haggard man looking back at him from the mirror's surface.

That man, he was becoming certain, had caused a horrible tragedy. Had he killed the woman with the blond hair? He gulped down a glass of water, but could not wash away the dread shuddering through him.

His taste of Taryn had been forbidden fruit. It stirred something deep inside him and filled him with impossible longing. He wanted what she offered. He wanted more. But he couldn't accept anything.

Not until he knew who he was, what had happened to him, what he might have done.

With each passing day, the horrid pictures in his mind grew more detailed and more macabre. Every time he closed his eyes, he saw a young girl's gaze looking blankly back at him, watery blood mixed with her long blond hair. Hands squeezing—killing? The pictures ran one into the other, until they turned into a video on an endless loop.

He had no choice. He had to find out who she was and whether or not he was the cause of her demise.

He opened the bathroom door and paused. Taryn lay in bed, hand on the pillow he'd occupied. The love in her deep blue eyes had stabbed his heart with incredible regret. And now, as he looked at her sleeping, he feared for her. A sense of forewarning told him that who he was, what he'd done, would place her in danger. He couldn't let that happen.

By the light eking through the bathroom door, he searched in the closet of clothes that were supposed to be his. Shirts—white, denim, starched beige. Jeans—from dark blue to nearly white. Neoprene suits. Uniform pants.

He fingered the gold star hanging on the pocket of a beige shirt. Sheriff Chance Conover, Gabenburg County, Texas.

With disgust, he pushed away the unfamiliar star. He wasn't the sheriff anymore. His real name wasn't even Chance Conover. It was a blank—like everything else. Until he found himself, he was nothing. He had nothing to offer to the woman who loved him, to the town he'd once been sworn to protect.

He took a canvas bag from the top shelf of the closet. In it, he stuffed jeans, T-shirts, socks and underwear. He added the shaving kit from the bathroom vanity.

The holster draped over the chair in the corner caught his attention. Though he couldn't remember ever having held the .38 Chief's Special, he knew exactly how to use it, knew without a doubt he could find his mark with deadly precision. Would he need it?

His breathing became shallow. His palms grew moist and clammy. He shoved the gun back in the holster and turned away from it.

Unable to help himself, he stopped by the bed, bent and pressed a kiss on Taryn's temple. She smiled at him in her sleep. His heart hitched. He wanted to deserve that smile.

Wherever the memories had come from, they would cause her harm, and the instinct to protect this woman with body and soul overrode the blankness of his recall of their life together.

With a lingering touch to a strand of her hair, he straightened.

To have any possibility to reclaim his life, to love this woman again, he had to leave Gabenburg. He had to follow the river north and find out why he'd washed down its current fifteen years ago.

Before Taryn awoke, Chance grabbed the canvas bag and a pair of hiking boots. Quietly he closed the bedroom door.

He made sure the front door was locked and bolted. He exited through the back door and tested the lock.

Crushing the keys in his hands until they bit into his palms, he walked toward the black truck parked in the driveway. Whoever Jake was, he'd been right. The only way to deal with fear was to face it.

To get his life back, he had to find himself. And to protect the woman who'd touched his heart, he had to do it alone.

Chapter Four

"He's gone," Taryn said, still not quite able to believe Chance could leave her like that in the middle of the night. Especially after the loving they'd shared. Without really looking at what she was doing, she filled a suitcase with clothes. "Why did he go?"

"I don't think he had a choice, sweetheart." Angus sat in the straight chair in the corner of the bedroom and watched her pace back and forth between the bed and the dresser. In deference to being inside, he held his Stetson in his hands. And though she tried not to notice, she saw a double dose of worry and sadness in his soft brown eyes.

"But why? We were just getting somewhere."

Angus sighed and looked away. "Sometimes you've got to go to find your way back home."

"Not Chance. He's not like that. He sticks around."

"And he sticks to what needs to be done till it's done. My gut tells me he has to do this."

She waved the T-shirt she was holding. "This? What this? Leave me in the middle of the night and disappear? No one's seen him, Angus. He's not anywhere."

"He'll be fine. Let him go."

The sliding glass door in the kitchen rattled closed.

"Yoo-hoo, Taryn!" Her grandmother's call could have deafened half the county.

Angus groaned as he stood and crammed his hat back on his head. "I'd best leave."

"Stay, please. I can't handle her alone today."

Angus nodded and reluctantly sat back down. The bulldog droop of his jowls and the deepening creases around his eyes added years that hadn't seemed present only a few days ago.

"In the bedroom, Grandy." Taryn stared at the half-filled suitcase, but there was no time to hide it. Nola Barnes might be nearing seventy, but she was still quick on her feet.

Nola stormed into the room, the skirt of her chic but well-worn dress swirling around her knees. A white puff of teased hair sat perched atop her head and reminded Taryn of a dandelion ready to seed. Those sharp gray eyes didn't miss a thing, though she'd had to add glasses a few years ago to catch all the details. She kept them attached to a jeweled chain, and when she reached for those specs, Taryn tensed. Of course, Grandy zeroed in on the suitcase.

"Taryn, honey, I just heard about that husband of yours over the radio. Forget that no good son of a gun. I'll take care of you." She hugged Taryn into a too-tight hold, then let her go just as abruptly. "What's the suitcase for?"

"I'm going to find him, Grandy."

"Now, honey," Nola clucked. Her glasses slipped down her nose and hung on the tip. "Why would you want to do such a fool thing?"

"He's my husband and I love him."

Nola picked up Taryn's clothes from the suitcase and started to put them back in the drawers. "Don't go chasing after a man. Haven't found one that's worth the effort yet. Your mother tried that and look where it got her."

Taryn took the clothes out of the drawer and dropped them back into the suitcase. "This isn't the same, Grandy."

"Patsy put her whole stock in one man and it nearly killed her. Killed her spirit is what it did. She was never the same after Earl was through with her."

"This is different."

Taryn wasn't repeating her mother's mistake. She hadn't *had* to get married because she was pregnant. Chance hadn't been forced to marry her against his will. She'd made him wait three years after he asked just to be sure that's what he really wanted. And she'd waited seven years to get pregnant to be sure he'd stick around. This was different. She loved Chance. She wasn't sure her mother had ever known real love.

"Leave the girl alone, Nola. This is hard enough on her without your harping."

Nola turned on Angus and squinted at him down her long nose. "Who asked you? What are you doing here in the first place?"

"Taryn called me."

Nola pushed her glasses up her nose and stared incredulously at Angus. "She called you and not me?"

"I do believe she wanted to hear the voice of reason."

"Reason? Are you telling her this is a reasonable thing to do? Taryn—"

"I didn't want a lecture from you," Taryn said. "And I asked Angus here to help me understand where Chance might have gone."

"I agree with you, Nola. I think she should stay."

"Well, thank you for that."

Taryn intercepted her grandmother and relieved her of the clothes she was carrying. "Can you run the bakery for me?"

"I can't."

Won't more than likely. The woman could be more stubborn than a team of mules when she wanted. "Why not?"

"I'm not as good a baker as you are." Nola plucked a pair of running shoes from the suitcase and deposited them in the closet.

"You taught me everything I know. You'll have to do better than that."

Nola turned around and put both hands on her thin hips. "Okay, then, I won't. I won't help you make the biggest mistake of your life."

Taryn didn't have time for this sulkiness and drama. She reached for the shoes and threw them back into the suitcase. "Fine, then don't. I'll close the store if I have to, but I'm going and that's final."

"You're stubborn. Just like your mother."

"And we all know where they both got it from," Angus muttered.

Nola huffed. "Nobody asked you, Angus." She whirled back to Taryn. "I just want what's best for you."

Taryn closed the suitcase and clicked the latches into place. "What would be best is your support."

"I can't. Not when you're making a mistake."

"The more you press, Nola, the more you're setting her mind."

"Who asked you?"

The one thing about Nola was that bribery worked awfully well. Taryn didn't want to disappoint her regulars while she was gone, but she had to find Chance. Having Grandy take over the bakery's operations for a few days would ease her mind.

Taryn picked up the set of keys from the night table and spoke into the electronic memo-minder Chance had given her two years ago as a Christmas present because she was forever losing her lists of things to do. "Buy Grandy that dress she's been eyeing in Jackson's window as a thank-you for minding the bakery. Although why a grandmother needs a dress like that beats me.''

Nola clicked open the latches on the suitcase. ''I may be a grandmother, Taryn-child, but I'm also a woman.''

''You're seeing someone!'' There was always the hope of derailing Grandy's single-minded track with personal business.

Angus snickered. ''That'll be the day!''

In quick succession, Nola extracted a week's worth of underwear from the suitcase. ''A woman doesn't always have to dress for a man. She can dress for herself. I thought I'd already taught you that lesson.''

''I don't suppose you'd lend me your car?'' Taryn asked.

''Not in this lifetime.''

Taryn ignored her grandmother's sulking and spoke into the memo-minder once again. ''Rent a car. Stop at bank. Put up sign in bakery window.''

''You can borrow Lucille's,'' Angus offered.

Nola pushed up her spectacles. ''Angus! How could you? I thought you were on my side with this.''

''I'm not taking sides. I'm being practical.''

Nola windmilled her hands. ''Then talk some sense into that girl.''

''I've been trying to, but she's determined, and if she's determined, she might as well be safe.''

''Well, a whole lot of good you are!'' She dismissed him with a huff.

''She's old enough to make her own decisions.''

''What right does that boy have to disrupt her life so?'' With jerky motions, Nola refolded a stack of T-shirts into the dresser drawer. ''Came from nowhere and ought to go back to nowhere.''

Taryn hugged the shorts she was holding tight against

her chest and swiveled to face Angus. "Do you think that's where he's gone, Angus? Back to where he came from?"

Angus eyed her sadly, then nodded. "That'd be my guess."

Nola exaggerated a shiver. "He's leading her into trouble. I can feel it in my bones."

Taryn sank onto the edge of the bed. "He never talked about...before."

"I don't think he knows much, sweetheart."

She looked up into Angus's eyes, searching for answers that didn't want to be found. He looked almost as beat as she felt. "How can he go back to someplace he doesn't remember?"

"Look until he finds it. Like I said before, Chance sticks to what he has to do, and if he feels he has to find his past, then he's going to keep at it until he finds it."

"A fool! Like the rest of them, you included, Angus. I thought maybe *you* had some grit, but obviously I was mistaken."

Taryn leaned forward, trying hard to ignore her grandmother as she unpacked everything again. "What happened, Angus? When you found him, what happened?"

"He was just a boy." Angus reached for her hand and held it in his. "Eighteen. Nineteen. He was all cut up, hanging on to a branch with a death grip even though he was beached. Took us a good long time to separate him from that piece of wood. He didn't remember anything."

"Why didn't he try to find out who he was back then? Why didn't you?"

The furrows on Angus's forehead deepened and he suddenly looked uncomfortable sitting in the straight chair. "Because everybody deserves a second chance and he looked like he needed one."

"Angus Conover." Nola stopped her frantic activity. She

adjusted her glasses and stared at the man in the chair. "What do you know that you're not telling?"

"Nola, stop beating on a dead horse."

"What if he had family?" The thought had Taryn's heart beating double-quick. Her fingers curled tight against Angus's leathery hand. What did they know about what waited for Chance wherever he was going? "What if he still does? How could you let him leave everything behind without knowing?" *And let him hurt his family the way he's hurting me now.*

"It was his choice to make." Angus's eyes didn't look so unshakably sure anymore. He slipped his hand from hers and worried the brim of his hat. "Just as it's his choice now."

She should let this go but couldn't. She couldn't believe that someone's decision fifteen years ago was now affecting her on such a deep level. Go. Stay. So simple on the surface. Angus's failure to search for answers then was costing her her world now. She wanted, needed, someone to take the blame for her pain. "But it wasn't an informed choice if he didn't know for sure he needed that second chance."

"Maybe part of him did, sweetheart."

She didn't like the look of pity in his eyes. Maybe Grandy was right and she'd put too much stock in Chance. Except that that also seemed too easy an answer. "If he needed that second chance then, doesn't he still need it now? So why go back after all these years?"

"Because…" Angus faltered and looked down at the floor in defeat.

"Trouble," Nola clucked, and brandished both hands in the air. Her white puff of hair shook from side to side. "I told you from the first day that boy was trouble. And he's proving me right, isn't he?"

"You would have thought a saint was trouble where

Taryn was concerned. You and Patsy never gave the girl enough credit," Angus said. "Chance is a decent man."

A cold, slimy eel of dread wrapped itself around her stomach. Taryn shuddered. "What if he did need that second chance? What's he going to be walking into now?"

Looking at the carpet, Angus shook his head slowly. "No one can answer that question."

"Because nobody bothered to look for the answers when they could have easily been found."

"Taryn—"

"Do you think he's in danger?"

Angus let his head fall forward.

Nola tapped her foot impatiently. "Well, answer the child, Angus."

He exhaled slowly, then looked up again. "No, I think what happened has been long forgotten. He'll find his answers and come home."

Taryn swallowed hard. Chance had allowed her to take him home. He'd depended on her to protect him from the town's well-meaning but curious people. He'd allowed her to love him. That had to say something. The tie between them was loose, but it wasn't broken yet.

"I don't think there's any danger, Taryn," Angus said. "But I do think he needs this time alone."

"There's something wrong here," Nola said. "I can feel it in my bones."

"Hush your mouth, Nola."

"Then there's no reason for me not to go after him," Taryn said. "Two heads are better than one and the searching will go faster."

"You stubborn, stubborn child!" Grandy snagged the holster from the chair and pressed it into Taryn's hands. "Then take this with you. That boy is trouble, I tell you, and this old coot isn't telling you the truth. You need to be able to defend yourself.''

Taryn sprang up and skittered back, letting the holster fall back into Grandy's grip as if she'd asked her to hold a lit stick of dynamite. After a false start toward the dresser, she settled on a path that took her from the bed she'd shared with Chance to the window and its view of the river. As she paced, she rubbed her arms against the chill ghost of the past, bringing back unwanted memories.

"I don't like guns." She hated what their indiscriminate power could do, how the reverberations of one bullet could destroy more than just one life.

"You know how to use it."

Chance had insisted she learn. He'd parroted his best friend's words to her and had not accepted a no. *The only way to deal with fear is to face it.*

"I don't like guns." Never would.

"Take it anyway," Nola insisted, and dangled the holster in front of Taryn. "Or come home with me. I won't watch you waste your life over a man the way your mother did without giving you some way to protect yourself."

"It's not the same thing," Taryn said, knowing Grandy was thinking of her daughter's murder.

"I'll have to side with your grandy on this one, sweetheart. It's best to let Chance find his own way home."

The energy that had driven her to pace wound itself into a weight that was now sinking her down. She stared out the window. Down below, beneath a leaden sky, the river ran fast.

She'd wanted a home, needed a home. This house might not be much, but it was hers and Chance's and they were— they'd been—happy here. She'd felt safe and secure. Chance had seen her through the aftermath of her mother's murder, through the trial where the defendant's lawyer had tried to put the blame for her mother's death on her shoulders. He'd stuck by her through all the tests she'd put him through to reassure herself his words of love were grounded in substance and not simply a passing fancy.

Now he was gone and the house no longer felt so safe, so secure. The walls seemed to be crumbling around her, exposing all her weaknesses for the world to exploit.

Had she, like her mother, put all her stock in one man? Did her happiness depend on Chance?

No, she didn't need a man. The bakery was her own. Her work there was satisfying. She didn't require much; she could live off the profits she made from her business. She didn't have to have Chance or Nola or anyone to support her. She'd been careful in her choices. She didn't need a man in her life.

The pain in her heart was heavy and she rubbed at it with the heel of her hand. Tears welled up, blurring the gray sky against Red Thunder's muddy waters.

She didn't need Chance, but she wanted him.

Maybe Grandy and Angus were right. Maybe she should wait and see if Chance came back to her. He was the one who'd disappeared and left all this turmoil in his wake.

Test him one more time.

Except love didn't work like that. Chance had taught her that with his patience and his care. He'd stayed when it would have been easier to leave.

Maybe this time it was *her* love that was being tested. If she didn't fight for him, for what they had, did their marriage stand a chance of surviving? She circled a hand over her belly. And there was the baby to think of. This precious child deserved to know his father.

She closed her eyes against the sight of the ever-flowing river. It had given her her husband. It had taken him away.

"You can't keep him," she whispered. "I won't let you."

"Taryn?" Angus placed a gentle hand on her shoulder.

"I love him," she said to no one in particular. Staying would be easier, but for all he'd given her, he deserved more. "He needs me."

"Let him go, sweetheart."

"Leaving will only cause you more grief, Taryn-child."

Taryn turned to look at them both. In her grandmother's tears, she suddenly realized that Grandy was afraid for herself. If Taryn left, Grandy would be all alone. She'd lost a husband, a daughter and feared losing a granddaughter, too. Taryn got up and hugged her grandmother. "I love you, Grandy, but Chance needs me right now. I have to go."

She looked at Angus. "Will you look after Grandy for me?"

Angus hesitated, worrying the brim of his hat as if it helped him weigh the pros and cons of the situation. Then he nodded once. "Don't you worry. Lucille and I will take good care of her."

"If you could just make sure she eats. She forgets unless I remind her."

Nola buried her face in her hands and shook it from side to side. "I can't go through this again. I can't. If you go, Taryn, don't you come back."

Angus wagged a finger at Nola. "Enough." He turned his gaze back to Taryn. "We'll hog-tie her and spoon-feed her if we have to. And she'll be waiting for you when you get back. Though why you'd want her interfering hide back, I don't know."

Taryn smiled through the tears swimming anew in her eyes. Grandy would be in good hands. She could let that worry fall aside. "Thank you."

Angus reached into his jacket pocket and took out a cell

phone. "Here, take this. There's a charger in Lucille's car. I want you to call me every day and let me know where you are. If you need anything at all, you give me a holler. Anytime, you hear?"

She nodded. Tears dripped onto the backs of her hands. "Thank you."

"Take the gun, Taryn," Nola insisted. "I know you don't care for firearms, but I'd feel better if you had it with you."

Reluctantly, Taryn accepted the holstered gun and burrowed it deep into the suitcase. She wouldn't need it, wouldn't use it, but she'd take it—for Grandy's peace of mind. She swiped her tears, closed the suitcase and secured the latches. Dropping the bag at her feet, she looked at her grandmother who was busy closing drawers. "Grandy?"

"I won't do it, Taryn." Nola's voice was strained as she busily straightened the already neat picture frames. Against the dresser's top, she flattened the silver frame holding a photograph of Chance on his graduation day from the police academy. "I won't give you my blessing for this fool's errand."

"I'm sorry you feel that way, Grandy." She turned and searched Angus's face. His expression was pained and resigned. "Where do I start?"

"Follow the river."

THE AIR SEEMED to be thicker, staler around the small town of Ashbrook. The clouds were heavy with the promise of rain and the air crackled with expectation. His or the storm's? Chance inched the truck down the near-deserted main street. Nothing looked familiar, but something had his gut knotted with tension.

Time to stop and refuel. He'd been on the road for two and a half days, crisscrossing the river to cover both sides.

At each small town, he'd visited the local library and searched records for a report of an incident that matched the picture in his memory. He slid into a space in front of Driller's Good Eats and took stock.

The architecture of the town's commercial center seemed to be right out of a page of history—stuck somewhere around the 1920s. The street was redbricked, the buildings simple yet solid. Like most of the towns he'd come across, there wasn't much to this one, either—just an odd collection of stores, a town hall and a couple of churches. And a library—which he'd check out after lunch.

As he stepped out of the truck, he heard a gasp. An old woman wearing a cotton-candy-pink muumuu clutched her straw handbag with both hands and looked at him as if she'd seen a ghost.

"You're alive!" She crossed herself and hurried away, making the plastic bluebonnets on her hat bounce with each of her lumbering steps.

For a moment he was stunned. She recognized him. This woman knew who he was. Heart thundering in his chest, he trotted across the street. "Ma'am! Ma'am!"

She sped up and entered a building before he could catch up to her.

He knocked on the door but got no answer. He turned the knob, but it was locked. When he looked up, the blinds on the window snapped shut.

Someone had thought him dead, someone who knew who he was. The image of the dead girl's eyes floated through his mind. Had he killed her? Was that why the old woman feared him?

He wiped a hand over his face, then squeezed the building tension out of his nape and turned to look down the street. If one person knew him, someone else was bound to recognize him, too. Trepidation needling his skin, he entered the diner.

Inside, he was met with curious and cold stares. Conversations stopped. Food was forgotten. All eyes seemed to follow his progress as he walked to the counter. The click of his boots against the tile sounded like thunder. The red stool at the counter squealed a protest as he sat. The swirl of air-conditioning against his sweat-slicked skin pearled goose bumps along his forearms.

"Coffee, please." He glanced at the menu on the blackboard behind the counter. "And the brisket platter."

The thirty-something waitress in the green-and-white uniform didn't acknowledge his order. She stared at him as she poured him a cup of coffee. He stared back, but nothing about the brunette clicked a memory. Did she know him? Had she been a schoolmate? "We're out of brisket."

"Give me a burger, then."

"We're out of burgers."

"Chicken-fried steak?"

"We're out of steak."

"What do you have left?"

"We're just about to close."

At the height of lunchtime business? "Thanks, then."

He dropped some coins for the coffee and drained the cup.

"Do you know who I am?" he asked before he got up to leave.

She took a step back. Her eyes rounded. "N-no."

"Chance Conover," he said. "I'm visiting from Gabenburg. Where can I find a place to spend the night?"

Her gaze blazed into his and she hesitated a bit too long before she finally answered. "Your best bet would be Lufkin. Take Farm Road 255 to 63 and follow the signs. It's about fifty miles up the road."

"Much obliged," he said, nodding once.

At the general store, he was met with the same cold reception. The middle-aged clerk accepted his money for the beef jerky, crackers, cheese and apple, but seemed to do so reluctantly. The bed-and-breakfast at the edge of town claimed it had no vacancy. For the number of rooms being taken up by visitors, the streets sure were quiet.

Good thing he'd found a tent in the workbox at the back of his truck. It looked as if he'd need it tonight. Just as well, he thought as he bit into the apple. He had no idea what the limit was on the credit card in his wallet.

Maybe it was the heat that was turning this business district into little more than a ghost town. Chance made a gruff sound. Or maybe it was something less pleasant. *What did you expect? That they'd welcome a killer with open arms?*

The thought wasn't reassuring. *Don't dwell on it. Get the facts.* Wasn't that what the hospital shrink had told Taryn? That the pictures and feelings needed to be grounded with facts. That was his training, too, getting the facts. He swallowed back the bitterness burning in his throat.

He threw the apple core into a trash bin.

He'd once been a sheriff, but instinct told him to avoid the local police station and not to count on professional courtesy. He didn't want to end up in jail before he was ready.

Part of him wished Taryn were with him. Holding her hand would ground him in this place where nothing felt real. An ache lodged itself in his chest. A sense of loss as deep as his amnesia faltered his step. He could smell the freshness of her scent, hear the sweetness of her voice, feel the passion of her touch.

These new memories were nearly as strong as the old ones driving his search.

Both tugged him in different directions.

He stuffed his hands in his jeans pockets and forged ahead, trying to push the image of Taryn out of his mind. He had to find the truth of his past to know where his future lay.

An unseen series of gazes seemed to follow his progress down the street. The hot, unbreathable air was once again replaced with the cold slap of air-conditioning when he walked into the library. The smell of burnt coffee, dust and neglect didn't do much for his tense stomach.

"Where can I find your newspaper records?" he asked the young man sitting behind the checkout desk. His dark mustache was thin. His black hair was cropped short. His white shirt seemed brand-new. With his bulging biceps and flattened nostrils skewed to one side, he looked more like a boxer who'd taken one too many punches than a librarian.

Shaken out of his boredom, the man eyed him up and down. "That'd be back in the reference area. The reference librarian's on the phone right now. Can I help you?"

"I'll wait."

"And your business?" There was a hopeful note to his voice, as if anything would be more interesting than calling patrons to tell them the books they'd placed on hold were in.

"Personal."

The young man quirked an eyebrow. Disappointment drooped his mouth. "Around the corner to your left."

Was the boy old enough to recognize him? Did he know what Chance had done fifteen years ago? The look in the focused gaze was curious, but not afraid like the old lady's or the waitress's at the diner.

Chance wandered through the reference stacks. He kept an eye on the two elderly patrons sitting at the long wooden table with magazines, and the other on the reference librarian. She wore a white blouse embroidered with red, a long denim skirt and red cowboy boots. Her white hair was tied in a ponytail with a red-and-white bandanna. Her laughter was pleasant, her voice helpful, her eyes friendly. The name on the placard said Joely Brahms.

After she put the phone down, she looked up at him. One eyebrow shot up. Recognition? "Can I help you?"

"I'd like to look through your newspaper records."

She led him toward the machine and pushed the On button. "Are you looking for anything in particular?"

"Your local paper going back about fifteen years."

Wariness clouded her dark eyes. "You won't find anything."

"I won't?"

"A fire twelve years ago burned down the library. And I'll save you the trouble of going over to the *Ashbrook Herald*. Their records went missing when they moved from Marshall Avenue to Green Street about eleven years ago."

"I see."

"You'd have better luck finding what you're looking for in Lufkin." She flicked off the machine and started to walk away.

"Why Lufkin?"

She gave him a wry smile. "Size does matter."

With a grandmotherly hold on his elbow, she ushered him toward the door. "If I were you, I'd head on that way."

"Why is that?"

She shrugged. "It's a matter of economics."

He stopped and studied her lined face. "Do you know who I am?"

"How can I since you haven't told me your name?" Her small laugh tried to dispel the current of anxiety stirring between them.

"Chance Conover."

"Oh, that's a fine name." She seemed relieved. "Lufkin is about fifty miles northwest of here. Good luck with your search."

Chance found himself dismissed and the library's side door closing behind him.

Outside the building Chance paused. It was as if they all knew him and hated him. Once more he wished for Taryn, for the unwavering trust in her eyes. He looked down Main Street at the slow bustle of activity. The contents of his stomach turned. In the roll of nausea one thing became clear.

He'd come head-on with his past.

IF THERE WAS ONE THING Garth couldn't stand it was someone who couldn't control his emotions. He had little respect for the man who'd broadsided his way past his secretary and into his office, but instead of telling him how he felt, Garth welcomed the sheriff and offered him a drink. He was nothing if not the perfect host.

"I don't need a drink. I need to wring the bastard's neck."

"Who's neck would that be?" Calmly, like a man who knew he had all the time in the world, Garth poured two generous fingers of his best scotch into a cut-crystal glass from the wet bar along the wall before he turned back to face his unexpected guest. The liquor went down smooth and easy.

Carter Paxton ran a hand over his bald head, wiping perspiration as thick as the lava of anger that had brought him fifty miles out of his way. His bull shoulders were rounded forward as if he was going to charge at any second. Heated breaths shot out of his nostrils just short of a snort. Red was creeping up his neck at an alarming rate. "He's back."

"Who's back?" These conversations with his father-in-law were never easy, but were part of the price he paid for his freedom.

"One of the Makepeace brothers."

The cut-crystal glass stopped halfway to his lips. One of the Makepeace brothers? They were both dead. He'd seen them with his own eyes being swallowed by the river. "Are you sure?"

"Saw him plain as day walking down Center Street. So did half the town."

"Are you sure?"

"You don't think I'd recognize the men responsible for my daughter's condition?"

"Facts—"

"*Fact,*" Carter punched a fist at the paneled wall, rattling the oil portrait of Garth's Royal Legacy Ranch, "I *know* what I saw. And what I saw was a Makepeace."

"Which one?"

Carter stopped tromping the Persian rug and glared at him. "Does it make a difference?"

Hell, yes, it did. Garth took his place behind the massive walnut desk. Either one could destroy the kingdom he'd built. The difference was that one could be bought; the other would have to be dealt with by using a firmer hand. Buying was easier than killing. And he believed in taking the path of least resistance.

How could the sheriff go off half-cocked like this? What was the point of coming all this way if he didn't have the facts that would be needed to make a decision? But Garth already knew the answer. "Details make the difference between winnin' and losin'."

"Ellen is the way she is because of them." With each of his steps, Carter's heels dug half-moons into the plush burgundy-and-navy pile. He'd have to have the carpet raked overnight.

''So why didn't you wring his neck when you had the chance?'' *And saved me the trouble.* Garth leaned back into his chair, cherishing the creak of butter-soft leather beneath him.

''Ellen.''

With Carter it always came down to Ellen. Ellen and all the soup of emotion she stirred in her father. That's what happened when someone built their world around one person. How many favors had Carter bought to insure Ellen's welfare? Too many to count. She was her father's weakness, and in this case, his weakness was greater than his strength.

Soon Carter would outgrow his usefulness. Careful plans would have to be made when the time came to put the sheriff out of his misery.

''You owe me this one,'' Carter said. His nostrils flared more rapidly as his hold over his temper lessened.

''I owe you nothing. I take care of Ellen the way you want me to. I buy her the best of everything.''

Carter tried to stare him down. ''I want him out of my town.''

''Then escort him out.''

''It's not that easy.''

''Why not? You're the law in Ashbrook.''

Carter's gaze wavered. ''Elections—''

''The town would praise your diligence.''

''I want him dead.''

''Who would fault you for takin' down a dangerous element?'' *For acting on your foolish impulses?*

Garth despised weak men. Success took planning, and planning required logic. There was no room for emotions. Only when all the precautions were in place could a man afford to indulge himself in the pleasures life had to offer.

Carter had never understood that, and that was the true reason he was here today.

"I don't want to spend my retirement behind bars," Carter said, and it sounded like a pitiful whine from such a bull of a man.

"No, you'd prefer I do." Garth drained the glass and poured himself another. He knew his limits. He'd stop at three.

"You owe me."

"I owe you nothing."

Carter rounded the desk, leaned down and jabbed a finger at Garth's chest. He brought his red face close enough for Garth to see a capillary pop along Carter's temple, to smell the scent of fury and fear, to hear the rasp of helplessness with each fetid breath. "Take care of him or I'll take care of you."

"Then what would happen to your precious Ellen?"

"I've kept records."

"So have I."

Once again bested, Carter could do nothing more than retreat. "For all the tight spots I've helped you out of—"

"I've taken care of Ellen."

"Then do it for Ellen. She deserved a better life."

She deserved exactly what she got. He rose and turned his back on the sheriff. "I'll think about it. In the meantime, find out why he's surfaced after all these years."

The heavy oak door rattled at Carter's exit, but Garth's attention was already elsewhere. A tendril of anticipation unfurled. He'd built himself an empire. Oil. Lumber. Cattle. Real estate. Racehorses. Everything his father had tried and failed. His fortune now measured ten times the one his father had lost. But it had been a long time since anything had been a real challenge.

Kyle or Kent?

Who knew him better than the Makepeace brothers? Who could appreciate how far he'd come more than one of them?

Garth stared out the window at the downtown buildings and the lightning storm reflected in their windows. Trees, in their carefully planned urban landscape, bent and swooped, whipped in all directions by the storm winds.

Kent or Kyle?

How long had it been since he'd felt the thrill of drawing a pat hand out of a stacked deck?

Chapter Five

Taryn had stopped at each small town along the river, shown Chance's picture to anyone who would look at it and asked about him. Her inquiries had been met mostly with shakes of the head. A time or two, someone had pointed north and she'd moved on, following his crooked trail back and forth across the river.

As she crossed the bridge into Ashbrook, her eyes burned, her head ached and the ginger ale and peanut butter crackers she'd downed while she'd filled up Lucille's compact car in Magnolia Springs were long gone. Not to mention the driving rain was making it hard for her to see where she was going.

She hated to stop before she found Chance, but she would have to rest before she went on. She couldn't risk getting into an accident.

Through the gray veil of rain, Ashbrook appeared deserted. No one walked the sidewalks. Hers was the only car moving on the main drag, although there were vehicles parked along the street. Given the nasty weather, that wasn't surprising.

She stopped at the general store. A clerk with a crown of white hair looked up from his crossword puzzle and gave her a smile. The smile faded as soon as she showed him Chance's picture.

"Have you seen this man?"

"No." The answer came too quickly. The clerk turned back to his crossword puzzle and worked hard at ignoring her. To the peppering of rain against the building, she walked the aisles for a few minutes, but found no one else shopping.

Her reception at the antiques shop next door was nearly identical. Showing Chance's picture had brought her a firm no. Further questions were met with a cold shoulder. The few patrons were all tourists and couldn't help her.

The experience left her with a bad feeling. Chance had been here. She could sense it. But if any of these people had seen him, why wouldn't they say so?

As she walked out onto the sidewalk, the rain assaulted her anew, drenching her T-shirt and shorts. As a wave of dizziness swept through her, one hand tightened around the strap of her purse, the other cradled her belly. Getting back into the car, she decided she needed to eat for the baby's sake.

The red neon sign at Driller's Good Eats bragged it was open, so Taryn headed toward an empty parking space. There she could regroup and plot a strategy. And if Ashbrook was anything like Gabenburg, the place should be filled with diners at this time. Someone might be willing to talk.

As she glanced in her rearview mirror, a sheriff's cruiser flashed on its lights. Instantly, her pulse sped and her heart raced. She'd passed no stop signs, no lights and she knew she'd been going below the speed limit. Why had she been stopped?

With Chance a member of the law enforcement community, she shouldn't be reacting to being pulled over with sweaty palms and a sense of dread, but she always seemed to shake in the face of authority. A uniform, any uniform—even the mailman's—put her on the defensive. As the officer called in her tag, she wiped her clammy palms along the front of her wet shorts and tried to calm her nerves.

"Afternoon, ma'am." The officer's voice was deep and authoritative. The pelting of rain against his black slicker added a note of menace.

"Good afternoon, Officer." Hands on the steering wheel, she waited to be told why she'd been pulled over. She hoped her state of anxiety wouldn't provoke suspicion. She'd done nothing wrong.

The officer leaned an arm over the car's roof and peered into the half-opened window. There was no heat or humor in his steel-colored eyes. "I'll need to see your license, registration and proof of insurance."

His voice was cold enough to draw a shiver. With slow movements so as not to startle the officer into reaching for his gun, she dug the requested documents out of her purse and handed them to him.

"I hear you've been asking questions—" He looked at her license. Rain sluiced down the front of his hat, soaking her documents. "—Ms. Conover."

"I'm looking for my husband." God, that sounded so pathetic. What would he assume? That she was a jilted wife trying to hang on to her man? Was that so far from the truth?

"He's missing?"

"Not exactly." She groaned silently. That wasn't helping her cause.

"Well, now, you either know where he is or you don't."

"I—I'm not sure where he is." She hated that the officer made her so nervous with his hard eyes and unvoiced accusations.

He examined her documents, looking, it seemed, at every period to find a misplaced one. One square hand with its stubby fingers dangled from the car's roof, dripping rain onto her thigh. The wide brim of his hat accentuated his broad face and short neck. His slicker strained over his shoulders and chest. Every now and then he gave a cross between a grunt and a snort that reminded her of Billy Ray Brett's aging bull. Aging or not, though, she wouldn't want to be cornered by Billy Ray's bull. He was mean through and through.

"This car is registered to a Lucille Conover," he said, leaving no doubt he wanted an explanation.

"My mother-in-law lent me her car." Chance had taken the truck and they had no other vehicle.

"Uh-huh. What's your husband driving?"

"A black Ford pickup."

He pointed toward the picture on the passenger's seat. "Let me see that."

She handed him the snapshot of Chance taken at the last Memorial Day picnic held at the fire station, and silently blasted the slight shake of her hand. She had done nothing wrong. There was no reason for her to be so nervous.

"That him?" the officer asked.

"Yes, that's my husband."

"What did you say his name was?"

She hadn't. "Chance Conover. He's the sheriff down in Gabenburg County."

"Uh-huh. What's he doing so far out of his territory?"

Was there a good way to explain what had happened to Chance? She'd been there and she still couldn't quite believe it. "He was in an accident about a week ago."

"What kind of accident?"

"The doctors say he has traumatic amnesia." The explanation sounded lame even to her. And if she hadn't known Chance so well, she might be doubtful, too. "He can't remember who he is."

"Uh-huh. Trau-ma-tic amnesia." He rolled the words in his mouth as if to weigh their truth. "So he ran away?"

"No, not exactly." She hated the way the officer was making her feel like a fool. On top of that, she didn't trust him one bit. There was something malicious in the narrowing of his eyes, in the pinching of his features. He was working too hard at hiding the feelings rippling right under his skin. "He's trying to find out who he is."

"What makes him think he'll find the answer here?"

Taryn perked up. "He's here? You've seen him?"

He handed her back the photo and the sopping documents. "We don't need that kind of trouble here."

Something wasn't right. "Trouble? No, he just—"

"I'll let you go this time."

Let her go? This time? He hadn't even told her why he'd stopped her! For Chance's sake, she swallowed her temper and forced herself to speak evenly. "That's very kind of you. Chance—"

He tapped the roof with the flat of his palm and pushed himself off. "If I were you, I'd take your husband and leave the area before you regret you ever crossed into Ashbrook."

There was nothing more she wanted to do than to get Chance safely back home. But if he'd seen the reaction of the people of Ashbrook to his arrival, he would have to stay. He would have to find out why he was being shunned. And if he stayed, she feared no good would come of the answers he'd find.

"I'll take your suggestion under advisement," she said, and turned the key. The engine sputtered to life. The wipers flapped a fast tempo. The cold air blasting through the vents aced goose bumps over her arms. "You mentioned you aw my husband."

"Try the state park outside of town. I'll let you have one ight. Then you'd best be on your way."

"Why?"

"Because I'm a fair man."

Fair was the last word she'd have used to describe this nan. "What is it you think Chance has done?"

He leaned toward her until she could see the cold steel f his eyes tempered with hatred. "He destroyed my life. f I find he's a Makepeace and not Chance Conover, sheriff f Gabenburg County, I'm going to destroy him."

"IT'S NOT SAFE for you here." The rain had gone from rog-strangling heavy to dribs and drabs. In the wake of the fternoon downpour, humidity rose in ghostly snakes from he ground. The air was thick with the scent of wet pine, oaked loam and muddy river. Raindrops bombarded the round in staccato bursts whenever the hint of a breeze rifted through the trees.

Chance wished Taryn hadn't found him. He was aware f her so close to him in the cab of his truck, of her hair, f her skin, of how much he wanted to touch them, touch er. And the need evoked a fierce sense of protection he idn't need right now. It was too confusing to an already nuddled mind. "Go on back home."

"That's what I'm trying to tell you." She twisted in the eat. Her knee bumped against his thigh, sending an electric harge through him. He jerked his leg away and covered he awkwardness by opening the cab door. "It's not me nat's in danger. It's someone named Makepeace. Someone e thinks is you. You should have seen the look in that heriff's eyes, Chance. He's got it in for this Makepeace omething fierce."

"I can handle him." He could handle anything that wasn't steeped with emotions. The sheriff and his claim meant nothing to him, except maybe a window to his past. But he wasn't planning on doing anything as stupid as confronting an angry man. Not without ammunition. Now that he had a possible name, finding an answer should prove easier.

She followed him outside and stood on the other side of the truck. Rain plastered her hair and soaked through her T-shirt, revealing the lace edging of her bra. He had to look away.

"We'll handle this together," she said. "Like we've always done."

"I'm moving on tomorrow. Going up to Lufkin." Chance rummaged through the truck's workbox and found the tent and the blue ground cloth he'd spied earlier.

"Lufkin? Why Lufkin?"

"Everyone seems to be in a hurry for me to get there, so I'm going to see what there is to see."

She dogged his steps as he searched for a flat piece of ground among the loblolly pines of his assigned campsite. Their hands touched as she took one end of the ground cloth. He let the touch linger for a moment before spreading the cloth on the ground.

"There's nothing but trouble waiting for you here." Taryn held on to the bottom of the tent bag while he pulled out its contents.

"Which is why you should go home. This is my trouble and I don't want you hurt by it."

"I'm already hurt. Every second you're gone, I'm afraid for you. I need you home."

He could hear the wound in her voice. He could see the anxiety of uncertainty in the choppy way she extended the shock cording of one of the tent poles. Their movement were mirrors as each ran a pole through opposite guides. "I've got to figure out who I am."

"You're Chance Conover, husband, friend, sheriff. You belong in Gabenburg where you're loved."

He said nothing. Inside him, emptiness rattled in the darkness. A cold sweat bathed him. The dome tent popped into shape. Then she was next to him, handing him a corner of the rain fly.

"If you won't come home with me, then I'm staying with you."

The blue of her eyes was clear and true. The determined set of her mouth almost had him smiling. He wanted to say yes. He wanted to know he wasn't alone in the quagmire his life had become. But he didn't want to have to worry about her when his mind was already full with a past that preyed on him.

"No."

"I'll help you look for whatever it is you're looking for."

"No."

"Two sets of eyes can cover ground twice as fast."

"No."

It was her turn to be silent as they, each on one side, pushed in the stakes to anchor the tent. She wiped the rain from her face and looked up at him. "Have you had supper yet?"

"No."

"Any chance you can start that grill?" she asked, jerking her chin in the direction of the concrete contraption at the campsite's edge.

"Got charcoal?"

"Charcoal and a couple of steaks."

She handed him a bag of charcoal, then lifted a Styrofoam cooler from the trunk of her car and placed it on the ground near the concrete grill. One more trip to the car, then she stood shielding him with a red-and-white golf umbrella as he bent over the grill. As he removed the grate, the rain pattered around them harder.

She twirled the umbrella in her hand, blurring the red and white into a swoosh. "I've got a story to tell you."

"I don't want to hear about Chance Conover. He's not real." He walked away from the dry circle to a nearby trio of pines and snapped off squaw wood.

"It's not about him. It's about me."

That wasn't much better. He didn't want to care for her any more than he did now. But he didn't say anything and she took his silence as a green light to start talking.

"My mother fell in love when she was seventeen. His name was Earl Truman Douglass the Third. He was from Houston, working a summer job out in the oil fields. She called him a blue-eyed devil on her good days, a son of a bitch on her bad. I never knew his real name until after she died and you helped me find him.

"She fell for him hard, let him sweet-talk her into believing he loved her, too. She gave him everything—her heart, her body, her soul."

Chance dropped the wood into the concrete nest.

"Then she got pregnant."

Before he could search for matches, she handed him a box and a stack of restaurant paper napkins. The river flowed. The rain fell. The gloom of the gray sky seemed to permeate everything around them.

"His parents decided that Earl had pulled their strings once too often and insisted he take responsibility for his actions. They forced him to marry my mother. She thought she had it made."

He concentrated on his task, on striking the match, on

watching the napkins catch and spread the flame. When the kindling was burning well, he added charcoal.

"But marriage only made things worse. Earl found Patsy's changing body repugnant. He couldn't bear to touch her anymore and satisfied his passion elsewhere. And though she was disappointed, Patsy accepted Earl's behavior. At least she had social standing and security. Something that wasn't hers waitressing at the family diner in Gabenburg."

Without missing a beat, Taryn handed him the umbrella and went to the car. She came back with a roll of foil, handed it to him, then took back the umbrella. He scrunched a ball of foil in his hands and scrubbed the grate.

"Then Earl died one night. Plowed his car right into a utility pole. He was drunk and he wasn't alone. A woman died right along with him."

The fire was going well. He was running out of things to do. He wanted to hide from the sadness of her story, but couldn't move away, so he fiddled with the kindling, with the coals, with the grate.

"Barbara couldn't get over her son's death and blamed it on Patsy. If Patsy had been able to hold on to her man, her son would still be alive. She turned them out, Patsy and her two-year-old kid, and refused to acknowledge them. Patsy was forced to run home, her tail between her legs. Her father had just died a few months before. Her mother was still a mess. There was nothing else for Patsy to do but take over the running of her parents' diner. She grew into a bitter woman."

What happened to you? he wanted to ask, but didn't want to know, didn't want to weave another invisible thread between them.

"Patsy didn't want her daughter to become any man's fool, so she kept a tight rein on her. Dates weren't allowed, parties forbidden, friends discouraged. She kept her too busy working to have a social life of any kind.''

Taryn handed him the umbrella once more. Over his shoulder he watched her dig into the car's trunk and come back with two potatoes. "Think the coals are hot enough?"

"Should be."

She wrapped foil around each potato. He placed them on the coals.

"As careful as Patsy was to protect her daughter," Taryn continued, "nothing could save her from the real world." She crouched beside him. Their shoulders touched. The contact felt good. He didn't move away.

She picked up a wet stick and stirred the rusty pine needles at their feet. "One night as we were closing, a man came in, ordered a meal, then instead of paying the check, he asked for the day's receipts. I was about to comply when Patsy grabbed the money and told the man to get lost. He insisted. She argued. He pulled a gun and shot her.''

Her hands shook at the memory. She flung the stick into the fire. It hissed. She wrung her hands as if that could crush the unpleasantness. Tears sprang into her eyes and flowed freely down her cheeks. Chance wanted to hold her, but found himself cemented into place.

"I couldn't do anything except watch the shock cross her face, the blood flower on her chest. I was standing so close, droplets sprayed all over me. I couldn't get the smell of gunpowder and blood off me for weeks. I'd scrub and scrub and scrub and still I'd see the blood freckles on my skin. I'd smell that smell. And every time I'd close my eyes, I'd see Mama fall.''

She shivered. He took the umbrella from her and wrapped an arm around her shoulder. She leaned her head against his shoulder.

"I think I screamed. I don't remember really. It was all

slow-motion, but kind of unreal, too. I was reaching for her and I saw the man's gun turn toward me. I remember thinking I was dead. Next thing I knew, the man was on the floor moaning and someone was holding me.''

The fire glowed orange in front of them. The umbrella was a cocoon around them. His throat was tight.

"This deputy—who I had seen but never talked to—didn't let me go. He saw me through all the questions. He saw me through the trial when the gunman's lawyer was trying to make it look as if my mother's murder was my fault. He helped look for my father and put that missing part of me to rest. He saw me through all the horror and never asked for anything in return.''

She looked up at him, the blue of her eyes soft and watery.

"I fell in love with this man and came to trust him with mind, body and soul.''

Him. She meant him. And he couldn't remember a second of the story she was telling him. His hand fell from her shoulder. She took it into hers and twined their fingers together. A knot. Her white fingers woven with his sunburnished ones.

"I love you, Chance. You stuck by me when it would have been easier to leave. You showed me the way home. You showed me how to love. I can't go home and let you face whatever you're going to find alone. We're a team. I've got to stay.''

Feeling mired in the bog of his memories, in the town's cold reception, in the warmth of Taryn's presence, Chance yearned for an anchor. That was what she was offering him, what she'd offered him every day since he'd woken up with his mind a blank slate save for the nightmare.

All the blood she'd already experienced, all the blood in

the frantic video playing itself in his mind told him she should leave. If she stayed, she would get hurt.

"I don't know what I'm going to find."

"Whatever it is, we can handle it together like we've done for the past ten years."

Determination shone bright in her eyes. She would stick by his side like a scuba tank on a dive. She wouldn't leave him unless he cut the line between them.

He stood up and walked to stand at the edge of the riverbank.

The river ran strong, undulating in black and gray snakes, reflecting a slate sky. The race of it rumbled a warning. He didn't feel better with his back to her, with distance between them. He felt confused and lost. All he knew were the memories playing on an endless loop every time he closed his eyes. All he knew was the drive to find the facts to blow the nightmare apart. For now that was all he could handle.

"I killed someone."

She shot up and once again shielded him from the rain, from the water. "No, not you. It's not in your nature. The man I know could never kill. Not without a good reason."

"But I'm not the man you know. I'm not Chance Conover. I don't know who I am."

"It doesn't matter. Whoever you are, you didn't kill."

He closed his eyes and let the loop play. "There's a girl with long blond hair. There's blood in the water. A gash on her head. Her eyes look dead. Through the water's surface, I can see my face, my hands holding her down, drowning her."

Taryn touched his cheek. "Look at me."

He ground his teeth and opened his eyes. True blue met the terror rumbling through him. "How can you see from the victim's point of view? It doesn't make sense. It's not real, Chance.''

He'd told himself the same thing time and again, but the pictures didn't change. He viewed the murder over and over, saw his face, his hands through the water's silver-red surface.

''I want you to be safe,'' he said. *From what I did. From me. From what I could do.* ''I don't want you to pay for my mistakes.''

''You stood by me. I'll stand by you.''

A strange kind of silence filled the woods. With the rain stopped, he was more aware than ever that they were alone. He suddenly wished for the noise of other campers, for the blare of a radio, for the growl of a motorboat on the water. For something, anything, to shatter the singular aching need in his chest.

He reached for her, pressed her head against his chest, placed a kiss on her soft brown hair. Her arms wrapped around his waist. Her sigh sank into him, trailing a deep sense of satisfaction.

He was walking the edge again. Getting to know her, to like her, was a mistake. Needing her like this could not be good.

But what else could he do? If she wasn't going to go home where she'd be safe, it was up to him to see that no harm came to her. If he kept her by his side, then he could at least see the danger coming and deflect it.

''It's like someone took a picture and ripped it up,'' he said, not knowing quite why he was so suddenly willing to share the abomination crowding his mind. A last-ditch effort to repulse her? ''Then threw all the shreds up in the air. Except this picture has sounds and smells and feelings and it keeps moving. I kill her over and over again.''

"It's the feelings that scare you."

"I don't want you hurt."

"We'll get the whole picture, Chance."

But what would they find when they exposed the truth?

Chapter Six

"We should get going."

Taryn hadn't slept well. The *plink plink plink* of bugs hitting the side of the tent and Chance's restless rustling had kept time with the river's thunder and left her staring at the dark. An owl had planted himself overhead and entertained them for what seemed an eternity. Then a faraway coyote had taken over and barked and howled. At dawn, the repeat and repeat of a chuck-will's-widow had started a chorus of birdcalls and squawks. The hard ground hadn't helped much.

Neither did the nausea.

This morning, the queasiness seemed stronger than any day before. Every slight movement seemed to make her stomach pitch and heave. While Chance had been out to the shower house, she'd inched her way to the cooler in the trunk of her car and nibbled half a dozen saltines to settle the morning sickness. She hadn't heard him return and the sound of his voice nearly undid the good the crackers had done.

There had to be a way to cut to the heart of things and get her life back to where it belonged in Gabenburg.

"I think we ought to ask a few questions around town before we go all the way to Lufkin." She stuffed the crackers back into the trunk and took out the cooler. At the picnic table by the grill, she got out some ham and cheese for a sandwich that would have to pass as breakfast. "Why drive all the way over there, if we can get what we need here?"

Chance turned from the pickup where he was stowing his towel and toiletry bag. His gaze assessed her. She hoped she didn't look as green as she felt. If he started worrying about her, things would drag on for too long.

"You said the sheriff warned us to get out of town."

Taryn considered her answer carefully as she piled ham onto the bread. "He told me I had a day."

"Do you think he's the type of man who's going to split hairs like that?"

Probably not. But she really didn't feel up to a drive to Lufkin when home was pulling on her so strongly. What she wouldn't give to have everything back the way it was. Chance. Her marriage. Her home. Everything. "Now that we have a possible name, we'll be done before he gets wind we're even there."

She offered Chance a sandwich. He accepted the food without really looking at it. His piercing gaze reminded her of the looks he used to give her after her mother's murder as he was trying to judge how strong she was, how much she could take before falling apart. Those looks had made her feel safe then; now they unnerved her.

"I'll go and you can stay here and rest," he said. "You didn't get much sleep last night."

And now, just like then, he was ready to play the role of protector. She gave a small smile. *You and me against the world.* Did he remember, or was the action one of instinct by a male toward a female? "Neither did you."

"The sheriff warned me off, not you. I don't want my troubles to visit you."

They already have. She contemplated a couple of slices

of bread and decided against the ham and cheese. Maybe they could stop for ginger ale before they left for Lufkin. "He warned both of us off. Where you go, I go. I really think we can find the answers here and go on back home."

He came closer, put his sandwich down on top of the cooler and stuck both his hands in his jeans pockets. His gaze was narrow and his expression blank. "Did you ever stop to consider that the picture I see may be real?"

"You didn't kill anybody." There were many things about this Chance she didn't understand, but on this point she was certain. A man's basic nature remained true. "It would take a mighty good reason for you to take anyone's life. You won't even let me kill spiders in the house. You insist on shooing them outside."

He shook his head. The sunlight ribboned blue highlights in his black hair still wet from the shower. "This isn't the same thing."

She rose from her seat at the picnic table and faced him. The shadows beneath his eyes gave them a haunted look. The only way to get him to change his mind was to show him proof. "I think we should give the library another try."

"The newspaper records were destroyed."

"There are other ways. Remember when you helped me look for my father?" His eyes clouded and the tendon along his jaw tightened. No, he didn't. That was the whole point. She sighed and looked away at the flowing river. "I'm sorry."

Their search then hadn't ended on a positive note. Barbara Douglass had served her tea, then politely told her never to come back. This time it had to be different. She loved Chance. She hadn't known Barbara enough to let her grandmother's rejection truly crush her.

"Why are you so all fired up to stay in Ashbrook?"

"I want you to find your answers as soon as you can. Then I want us to go home."

His hand rested lazily against her neck. The tender touch shivered delight all through her body. With his thumb, he turned her chin until his dark gaze could drill into hers. She swallowed hard, wishing to see something warmer, more intimate in his eyes.

"You might not like the answers," he said.

The feel of him this close made it so easy to get distracted. She wanted to lean her head onto his chest, let his arms gather around her and hold her, make herself believe everything would be all right. But she also didn't want to make things harder for Chance than they already were. She wouldn't be weak or pathetic. She would be as strong for him as he'd been for her.

She broke the contact, swept up the leftover bread and stuffed it in the cooler. "You're determined to think the worst, aren't you?"

"I'm trying to stay realistic."

"Realistic is that this town has the answers," she said as she put away the ham and cheese. "Realistic is that we can find them. Realistic is that the sooner we find them, the sooner we can go on with our lives."

"I'd feel better if you stayed here where you can be safe."

"I'd feel better if you came back home with me." She looked up at him. "I guess neither of us are going to get our way."

She held up his uneaten sandwich. "Want this?"

He shook his head.

She wrapped the sandwich and put it away, then picked up the cooler and headed toward the car. He intercepted her, took the cooler from her and stowed it in the back of his truck. "Then we'd best get out of here and get this business out of the way. We'll take the truck."

They drove in silence, Taryn as close to the door as she could manage without feeling as if she was going to fall out. He was a stranger, this Chance. The smiles she knew and loved were no longer part of his silent vocabulary. The tender kisses, the hungry touches, were locked away in an unreachable part of his mind.

Yet, the single-mindedness of his purpose was familiar. Chance stuck to things and saw them done right. His protectiveness was familiar, too.

But not the deliberate remoteness, not this wrong belief he had purposefully caused anyone harm. Chance protected—always had. That was his true nature.

A couple of days, she told herself as the loblolly pines flickered by her window, and everything would be back to normal. He would have his identity. He would have his answers. They would go back home, and she could tell him about the baby.

They had a whole rich life waiting for them. She wouldn't let anything steal that from her.

THEY DROVE through town, avoiding the main drag until a parking space opened up on a secondary street. There was no avoiding walking past a few shops to reach the mustard-colored brick building that was their destination. There was no avoiding the stares, the silent condemnation, the barely disguised hatred.

Taryn was used to having people treat her husband with respect. At home, wherever he went, Chance inspired confidence and goodwill. Watching people turn from him as if he were an evil creature was disconcerting. She wanted to take Chance in her arms and shield him from their scorn.

She wanted to shout back at each silent accusation, "He's a good man."

As they entered the library, the scent of burnt coffee made her stomach roll. The librarian at the circulation desk looked barely older than the preadolescent girl who stood on a small stool having her books checked out. Chance led Taryn around the corner to the reference section. There a white-haired woman looked up from her desk.

"You're back."

She wore a turquoise shirt, a black skirt and black cowboy boots. Her hair was tied back into a ponytail with a black velvet scrunchie. Turquoise dangles jangled at her ears. And if it weren't for the painful frown etching her forehead, Taryn would have described her as friendly-looking.

"Yes, ma'am," Chance said, offering her a crooked smile. He could still charm a snake if he put his mind to it.

"I told you. The library burned. The microfilm files were destroyed."

"We thought we'd look through a few of your other resources. That all right?"

Joely hesitated. "Can't be any harm, I suppose."

Chance took Taryn's hand and led her toward the stacks. Though she sensed the action was more for show than from desire, she cherished it.

"Where do you want to look first?" he asked once they were hidden from Joely's view.

"The phone book," she said. "We have a name, now, remember?"

He nodded. "Makepeace."

They gathered phone books for this and the surrounding towns and took them to a table. In one after the other, both

Yellow and white Pages, they found no mention of anyone named Makepeace.

From her desk, Joely Brahms watched them, but offered no help.

"Do you have Internet access?" Taryn asked when Joely's gaze lingered on her. Two terminals waited, cursor flashing, in the back of the room.

"Not unless you have a library card."

"Okay, how do I sign up?"

"You've got to have proof you're a local resident. Utility bill, deed to a house, rental agreement."

The awkward silence between them was filled with the murmurs of patrons at the circulation desk, the ring of the telephone, the beeps of the computer entering checkout data into its memory.

"Do you have any of the high-school yearbooks?" Chance asked.

"No." The answer came too quick and the slight look toward the shelves told him exactly where to look.

As Chance went to retrieve the books, Taryn edged to Joely's desk. She leaned in close as if she were looking at Joely's terminal for an answer to a question. "What are you afraid of?"

"What is there to be afraid of?" Joely asked, but her laughter was strained and she glanced to her right to see if anyone was looking at the exchange.

"We don't mean anyone any harm," Taryn insisted. "We're just looking for answers to help Chance."

"Are you his girlfriend?"

"His wife," Taryn said. "He's a good man."

"This here's my life." Joely spread her hands to encompass all of the library as if she was afraid to lose what she had.

"He's mine."

She turned to include Chance in her line of vision. He was feeding dimes into a photocopy machine. A burst of light exploded from beneath the cover at regular intervals. What had he found?

"Then take him and go back home, honey. Nothing good will come from disturbing dust that's long been settled."

"I don't understand."

"The sheriff. For fifteen years he's been looking for someone to take the blame—"

Taryn leaned closer. "The blame for what?"

But no more answers would come from Joely today. Her face blanched as an officer strode toward them. The gold star on his pocket read Sheriff Carter Paxton.

Taryn stood tall, but her insides quivered. "Good morning, Sheriff."

"I do believe I issued you a fair warning yesterday, Ms. Conover." He stood square and solid, his bald cranium shining in the glare of the fluorescent lights overhead.

Stuffing the folded photocopied pages in the back pocket of his jeans, Chance came to stand next to her. She drew strength from his presence. "You gave me a day, Sheriff. I decided to take it."

"My patience is short for impertinence."

His patience looked short, period. If he were a bull out in pasture, she was sure he'd be stamping his hoof and lowering his horns.

"And mine is short for threats," Chance said, twisting his body to protect hers. "Have you got any reason to harass innocent citizens making use of public facilities?"

A hushed silence fell over the library. Patrons stood watching, hugging books to their chests like shields. Joely seemed to shrink behind her desk.

The sheriff drew up to his full height, meeting Chance eye to eye. His gaze narrowed. His nostrils flared. "My reports should be in soon, and I won't hesitate to grant you intimate knowledge of the county jail if I'm not satisfied with their contents.''

"Just what is it you expect those reports to tell you?"

"Why did you come back?" His eyes were hard steel. "Didn't you do enough harm the first time around?"

"An explanation, Sheriff, that's all I want."

"Makepeace," the sheriff said, spittle flying as if the name was a curse. His face was turning red and hatred blew from him as strong as a norther. "Sorry excuses for human beings, the lot of them. Couldn't stand up to what you'd done. No, you just left someone else to clean the mess behind you."

Taryn sensed the tension stringing Chance's body tight, feared its release.

"You stole her from me," the sheriff said.

They were going to come to blows right here in the middle of the library, she saw it in Chance's tightening fists, in the sheriff's pressed lips and bared teeth. The last thing she needed was to have Chance end up behind bars for assaulting an officer.

Taryn took Chance's arm and jiggled it to get his attention. "Did you find what you needed, sweetheart?"

Chance nodded, but he didn't take his gaze away from the sheriff's face. "What happened?"

"Now you're pretending amnesia." The sheriff snorted. "Of all the low-down tricks you've played, this is the dirtiest."

"Let's go have breakfast," Taryn said, desperation coloring her voice. "I'm hungry."

Chance didn't move.

"Chance, please."

He ignored her. "What do you want from me?"

"I want you to jump when I say frog." The sheriff dug a finger into Chance's chest.

"Chance, let's go." She tugged harder on his arm.

The sheriff poked again. "I want you to pay for what you've done."

"Chance." She squeezed between the sheriff and her husband and caught the next poke on the shoulder. The cruelty of the blow expelled her breath and shoved her against Chance's chest. He steadied her and spun her out of harm's way.

"I want you to rot in jail for the rest of your natural life."

Chance caught the sheriff's hand as it arched for another jab. The sheriff was deliberately trying to provoke him.

In a low and measured voice, Chance said, "You got a beef with me, you take it up with me. If you've got cause to arrest me, then do it. If not, I'll thank you to leave us alone. Good day, Sheriff."

Holding on to Taryn's hand tightly, Chance brushed past the sheriff, deliberately accosting his shoulder.

"I'm a fair man," the sheriff said as the gathered crowd opened up to let them pass. "When I put you behind bars, I want to be one hundred percent damn sure I've got the right man. I'll give you the equity you never gave Ellen."

Taryn didn't release her breath until they were outside. When she let go of Chance's hand, she was shaking all over.

"You shouldn't have pushed him," she said. "You could have ended up in jail."

"Could be I'll still end up there."

"Don't say that." She rubbed her arms at the sudden chill shivering through her. "You don't belong there."

"I do if I'm the monster the sheriff is making me out to be."

No, she wouldn't accept that. Chance did not belong in jail with the rest of society's scum. He belonged with her in Gabenburg.

"What did you find?" she asked, striding forward onto the sidewalk to keep herself from falling flat on her face.

"Sixty-six graduating seniors from fifteen years ago. Including Kent and Kyle Makepeace."

Her heart bumped hard against her chest. She stopped short, turned to face him and grabbed both his upper arms. "Which one are you?"

He unfolded the photocopied sheets and handed her one page. Justine Lassiter. Christine Lloyd. Mark MacDonald. Taryn sucked in a breath. Kent Makepeace. Her shaking hands made the page flutter.

The black-and-white face looking back at her was so familiar. The sharp cheekbones, the black hair, the dark eyes, the full mouth. So familiar, yet unlike anything she'd seen before. She'd seen no evidence of Chance's life before he'd washed up in Gabenburg. No baby pictures, no gap-toothed six-year-old smile, no graduation portrait. Looking at this picture was like creaking open a door to something she hadn't acknowledged existed.

Twice.

Because next to Kent's picture was one of Kyle. Except for the different shirt collars, they could have been a Xerox copy of each other.

"Twins?" she asked when she found her voice again. She looked up at Chance and found a reflection of the same confusion pinging inside her.

Chance raked a hand through his hair. "Or brothers. Or cousins."

"Wow."

"Yeah, wow." He took her hand and squeezed it hard.

She could feel his excitement, his fear all the way down to her toes.

"We've got a lead," he said. His eyes were bright with hope. "Two of them."

Kyle and Kent. And Ellen. Was she the girl from his nightmares?

Even though this new development would take her farther from home, she knew she could not deny him the right to know himself. "Let's follow them."

"WANT COFFEE?" Chance asked.

Taryn shook her head, placed a hand over her stomach and turned an unhealthy shade of green. "Sprite," she croaked.

They went through the drive-through of the fast-food joint on the edge of town, then sat in the truck in the parking lot. Taryn was sipping her Sprite and ignoring the ham and cheese sandwich they'd retrieved from the cooler.

This woman was supposed to be his wife, but he knew little about her. He should know if she liked coffee. He should know how she took it. He should know she preferred Sprite with her breakfast. But he knew none of those things. He chewed on his own sandwich and stared out the window. "How long have we been married?"

He heard the swish of her hair as she turned her head to look at him, wanted to feel its silk graze his skin.

"Seven years come September. We've been together almost ten."

After ten years with a woman, he should know her inside out. He didn't know anything about her, except that her touch made him forget the horrid vision growing stronger every night, that her loyalty to him made her overlook his amnesia and fight for him with the ferocity of a wolverine, that the feeling he would hurt her wouldn't leave him.

The sheriff's goad, intended for him, proved that. What if it was only the beginning? Would she regret standing by him?

The distance between them suddenly seemed canyon deep and unbreachable. And the sense of loss the feeling brought echoed eerily inside him like the coyote's call in the dark last night. Lonely, he remembered thinking, and hollow.

Yet he was conscious of her presence by his side, of the subtle scent of her, feminine and sweet, of his need to bring her closer to him, skin to skin, of her liquid blue eyes looking at him, studying him. Most of all he was keenly aware of his curiously strong hunger for the missing years of intimacy with her that were locked away in some dark corner of his mind.

He knew the memories of their life together still existed in her mind. The last thing he wanted to do was hurt her by following instincts that seemed awry at best. She wouldn't deny him. He knew that, too. But he couldn't take advantage of her memories, of her willingness to awaken his through physical expression. He wanted to come to her a complete man, not one lost between two worlds he couldn't remember.

The need to protect her from himself was as strong as his need to hold her close and draw comfort from her unconditional belief in his inherent goodness. A goodness his vision told him was nothing more than illusion.

That, he told himself as he finished his sandwich, was a dangerous direction for his thoughts. Focus. He needed focus. And facts. Drawing conclusions before he had the facts would only drag him deeper into the quagmire of emotions flooding his frustrated brain.

If he was going to find the truth, if he was going to

protect her from the ills he was stirring with his search, he needed to stay sharp.

His gaze worked a grid of the mirrors and the surrounding area. A sheriff's car was parked down the road. The man inside was shorter than Sheriff Paxton. A deputy assigned to keep track of them? Another reason to increase his vigilance.

"What do we have?" Chance asked, wanting something other than his dismal thoughts to keep him company.

"Two names," she said, picking at the crust of one slice of bread. "No, three. Kent Makepeace, Kyle Makepeace and Ellen Paxton."

"No identifiers. No date of birth." He'd used the day Angus had found him on the river as a birthday for the last fifteen years. "No full name. No social security number. No previous address."

"We know you were set to graduate from high school."

"But we're not likely to get help from anyone here in town." He was silent for a while, contemplating the large black blotches between the patches of information. "We need facts."

"I know."

He heard the sigh of regret in her voice, but sensed that bringing up the question of her going home would be useless. The loyalty she felt toward the man she thought she loved was too strong to abandon him. And arguing he wasn't her husband wouldn't get him far. She saw the same exterior she'd seen for ten years.

What was different was the unseen part of him.

"We'll have to go to Lufkin," he said, hoping to discourage her.

"I know."

Chapter Seven

Joely Brahms had been right, Chance thought. Size did matter.

The Kurth Memorial Library in downtown Lufkin dwarfed the library in Ashbrook. There they found the unexpected boon of a collection of newspapers from the region, including the *Ashbrook Herald,* and a treasure in the Ora McMullen Genealogical collection, including a history of the Makepeace family.

Of Caddo and Scot roots, the Makepeace forefathers had settled in the area generations ago. But the spiderweb of ancestry, which should have led to an increasing lattice of names, dwindled instead to a few broken threads. Conflict between father and son, it seemed, was as much a legacy as blood.

Cutting cords. Cutting ties. What had happened to sever Kent and Kyle from *their* family? The genealogy didn't hold that answer, only a series of dates of births, marriages, occupations and deaths that stopped in 1900.

Chance perused the newspaper microfiche files while Taryn worked her way around the World Wide Web at a nearby computer station. His eyes were burning and his head was aching from the concentration, but eventually his morning of dedicated focus was rewarded. A headline caught his attention. He straightened in his chair, then stilled. ''I found something.''

He waved Taryn to come close. She hunched over him. The scent of her shampoo cascaded down to him. He held on to the edge of the table to keep his hands from reaching for a strand of her silky brown hair, his arms from reaching for her, his body from stretching up to kiss her cheek.

''Two Missing In Local Tragedy.'' She read over his shoulder:

ASHBROOK, TX—Two local teens are missing and presumed to have drowned. A third teen is suffering from critical head injuries sustained when the river drove her into a boulder. She was rescued by Fish and Game officers.

Captain Julio Arcaro said the teens were trespassing on the Woodhaven Preserve late yesterday afternoon. A full search will resume in the morning for the two missing boys.

A witness told authorities that the teens had gone by the river to share some burgers and Cokes, then gone swimming to get relief from the heat. An argument ensued and the boys were carried away by the current. Trying to rescue the boys, a third victim was also swept up by the current.

''People need to take responsibility for their actions,'' Arcaro said. ''If these kids had obeyed the law, this tragedy wouldn't have happened.''

Names of the victims are being withheld pending notification of their families.

An argument. Temper. The same slow sickness of anger that had been eating at him since he'd woken up in the hospital. What had they argued about? Was he responsible for this disaster? Had his anger caused Ellen's death?

As he moved the microfiche file forward, the images of his vision crept back in. Blond hair. Dead eyes. Blood, so much blood. And those hands pushing down.

"Here's another," Taryn said, putting her hand over his to stop the page. The warmth of her touch eased the chill icing his insides. They read:

Local Teens Presumed Drowned

ASHBROOK, TX—Two brothers, Kent and Kyle Makepeace, are presumed drowned in the Red Thunder River. Three days of searching by the Fish and Game Department, as well as local volunteers, has not yielded either body.

"The river runs fast at this time of the year," Captain Arcaro said. "They could be all the way out to the Gulf of Mexico by now." He added that with the debris floating on the current, the bodies had probably been torn apart and were unlikely to be recovered.

The third victim, Ellen Paxton, daughter of Sheriff Carter Paxton of Ashbrook, is still unconscious, but doctors expect a full recovery is likely.

"No wonder the sheriff is so emotional." Taryn glanced down at him. Her eyes were shining bright. Her smile could make him believe just about anything. "She's not dead. Ellen's not dead. See, I told you you were wrong. You didn't kill her."

"She could have died later. The sheriff's attitude implies she's either dead or not herself." The printed story and his vision didn't match. "He said he lost her."

"What you're seeing," Taryn insisted, finger accelerating the microfiche through the scanner once again, "is not reality. The psychiatrist at the hospital said that your emotions might not be grounded in facts. These are facts."

But were they? Nothing felt real anymore. He had no routine to ground him, no order, just a mass of chaos. And the more they uncovered, the more adrift he was feeling, the more the sensation of corruption stalked him. How could something so vivid be so wrong? If it was right, how could he make peace with it, make amends for his actions?

"Wait," he said. "Go back."

She sucked in a breath. "An obituary."

Chance tapped the screen. "Two."

"'Kent Aaron Makepeace,'" she read, "Seventeen, of Ashbrook, died last Friday. He was born on November 22, 1970.

"'Mr. Makepeace was active in the Vocational Agriculture program at the Ashbrook Area High School. This spring, he took part in a volunteer program to inventory the Woodhaven Preserve. An avid saxophone player, he was a member of the marching band. He was also a member of the cross-country team and ranked thirteenth in the state.'"

Taryn paused. "Any of this spark a hint of recognition?"

He shook his head. Emptiness, as keen as a coyote howl, wailed inside him.

Taryn read on, "'He was the son of the late Lloyd Makepeace and the late Sarah Jordan Makepeace. He is survived by his paternal grandfather, John Henry Makepeace, of Ashbrook.

"'A memorial service will be held on Thursday at 4:00 p.m. at the Makepeace home on Twin Oaks Road.'"

Taryn crouched beside him and rubbed the stiffening triangle of muscles between his shoulder blades. Maybe he wasn't Kent. Maybe that was why none of this information was clicking any memories into place. He scrunched his eyes and read the next obituary.

"'Kyle Bryce Makepeace, seventeen, of Ashbrook, died last Friday. He was born on November 22, 1970.'"

"Look, Chance. The age and birth dates are the same. Kent and Kyle *are* twins." Taryn squeezed his shoulders and nudged her cheek against his. The energy vibrating through her echoed inside him.

Twin. He was a twin. He had a twin.

A lump formed in his throat, but he read on, "'Mr. Makepeace was an exceptional horseman, excelling in saddle-bronc riding and bareback-bronc riding. Named all-around champion for the season by the East Texas High School Rodeo Association, he was set to start a job at the Triple Z Ranch, in Ropestown, near Lubbock.'"

The rest of the copy was the same as Kent's obituary.

Still nothing stirred his memory to life. Just the thought of getting up on a bucking bronc made his bones ache. If he were Kyle, wouldn't he be drawn to the beasts?

But with the pictures accompanying the obituaries looking so much like him, he could not deny that he was one or the other of the Makepeace brothers.

His parents were long dead. But he had a grandfather. He had a twin. Somewhere out there was a man whose face matched his own, if that man was still alive, too. He was no longer a nameless nobody who'd washed up all grown in Gabenburg. He had a history, a family, a brother. Had his twin survived the river, too? Where was he? What had happened to him?

As he scanned more pages of the *Ashbrook Herald*, the feeling of tempting fate trickled through him, burning like acid. He was resurrecting ghosts. Was he throwing away the second chance Angus had given him fifteen years ago? So far, there was nothing pretty about this family's history. Would he regret digging deeper?

Horror movies always had a happy ending, he reminded

himself. The monster was always beaten. But not before it had killed off most of the cast. What was he sacrificing to learn the truth?

He turned to Taryn who was focused on the microfiche files, and a new wave of apprehension, buffeted by yearning, surged through him. His two unremembered pasts were colliding like waves on a beach, eroding, chafing, eating away bits and pieces of him. He wanted her. But what could he offer her without the truth? In the next painful heartbeat, he feared he would have to give up one for the other.

As the files flowed forward, the microfilm scanner sounded like the flap of wings in the dead of night, threatening to blind him with his failures.

"Ha!" she said, pointing at the screen, stilling his hand over the knob. "There it is. Ellen's still alive. She was transferred from the hospital to a place called the Angelina Rehabilitation Center."

"That was fifteen years ago."

Taryn looked at him and shrugged. "It *is* a long shot."

Kent or Kyle? He had to know. He had to know what had happened that day fifteen years ago.

He flipped backward to the obituaries. "We've got an address. Maybe John Henry Makepeace is still alive. If anyone knows the answers..."

"He would," Taryn finished, smiling brightly.

Chance was also beginning to understand that he was damned no matter what he decided.

Just as he felt the anger of resentment rumble through him once more, Taryn's hand reached for his, connecting him to the present. Another wash of emotion swamped him, warm and comforting. His grip tightened against the edge of the table.

If anything happened to Taryn, he would have another

ghost haunting him. And this time, he knew, even amnesia would not save him from the torment.

"Chance?"

"Let's go back to Ashbrook." He swallowed hard. "Let's find my grandfather."

THE PHONE'S JANGLE was an irritation in a field of aggravation that day. The financial statement for the small oil company he was considering buying kept drifting out of focus. Garth let it flutter to the desktop and yanked the receiver off its cradle.

"Ramsey."

"They're up your way."

Garth spun his chair to face the window and scoured the downtown area. The noon sun cut stark shadows across the buildings and blistered heat from the asphalt in waves. The sculpted trees stood still, limp and unmoving without the aid of a breeze. Flowers drooped, their gold and orange heads resting on the mulch trying to extract remnants of moisture from the morning's sprinkler shower.

Instant excitement coursed through him as he watched pedestrians move along the sidewalks, searching for a familiar profile. That, he decided, was what he'd been waiting for. Playing a chess match with someone who wasn't there wasn't as fun as watching a face when it was put in checkmate and realized there was no way to win. He'd always been one for being up close and personal.

"Let 'em come," Garth said. He returned his attention to the financial statement on his desk. Every line was now in clear focus. "Oh, and Carter, make sure the welcome committee leaves our guests a token of our esteem."

"I don't think that's a good idea. When I confirm he's a Makepeace, I want him where I can find him."

Already concentrated on the bottom line, Garth dismissed Carter. "If he's here, there's something he wants. He won't leave till he gets it. The trick is to make sure he doesn't get it till you have him where you want."

AT LEAST they were headed in the right direction, Taryn thought. Toward home. She studied the map they'd printed off the Internet. "Turn left at the next road."

They'd found no phone number listed for John Henry Makepeace. Chance hadn't wanted to call anyway, hadn't wanted to give his grandfather a chance to reject him out of hand.

Taryn rubbed a hand over her stomach. Morning sickness had extended all day today and she longed for some ginger ale to settle the nausea. Maybe she was coming down with something. She shivered. She didn't want to think about that. For now, she had to focus on Chance.

Bright tangerine clouds streaked the purpling sky. Pines fanned their limbs lazily in the light breeze. Evening was starting to throw shadows, creeping darkness across the land. A crooked mailbox appeared around the bend of the road. The faded number on the rusty box stirred a bevy of butterflies in Taryn's stomach.

They were here.

She glanced at Chance, but saw no expression cross his face—just the same stony blankness he'd worn since they'd left Lufkin. She hoped for both their sakes John Henry Makepeace would hold the answers Chance sought—and would be willing to part with them.

Chance turned onto the dirt road as instructed. Two deep ruts formed a narrow path. As the truck rocked and rolled its way down the incline, the tires fomented puffs of dust, cloaking the landscape around them in a reddish haze.

Chance brought the truck to a halt in front of a small log house. As the cloud of dust settled, age and neglect became apparent. An old magnolia in dire need of pruning scratched at a window. No fragrant blooms garnished its branches. The barn to the left of the house stood empty. The skewed top half of a Dutch door creaked in the breeze. The pens beyond were overgrown with sandspurs and hadn't seen a horse or cow in years.

No flowers bloomed in the clay pots on the sagging gray porch. No light shone at the windows. No life seemed to stir within.

"Stay," Chance said as he exited the truck. "I'll go take a look around."

Taryn ignored his directive and followed him, shadowing his steps as he walked around the building, peeked through windows and rattled the doorknob, offering him her silent support.

"No one's been here in years," he said, disappointment heavy in his voice.

"Someone's still managing the land, though." She pointed at the cleared woods on the other side of the small pond beyond the animal pens. Stumps blistered the view like acne on a teenager's face. Beyond the scar on the property flowed the river. "He might have moved."

"Or he might have died."

She took his hand in hers, laced their fingers, wanting desperately to put her arms around him and hug him. She didn't want her actions misinterpreted, or worse, for anything she did to add more confusion to Chance's situation, so she simply held on to his hand and hoped it would be enough for him to know he wasn't alone. "Tomorrow, we'll go to the county courthouse and find out."

Not taking his gaze off the blight of shorn trees, he nodded. "Let's grab some supper and get some rest."

That sounded like a good plan. "Drive through?"

"Unless you want another taste of Ashbrook hospitality."

"I've had enough excitement for one day, thank you."

He looked at her then, traced the puffiness below her eyes with his thumb. "You look tired."

"I'm holding up okay."

"You should go on home."

"Not without you."

He nodded again. Wrapping an arm around her waist, he led her to the truck and tucked her into the seat like an invalid. And he had the nerve to think he could harm another human being without provocation. She shook her head. When was he going to listen to her?

By the time they found their campsite, night had fallen hard and fast. As she exited the cab, Taryn scrunched her nose and almost heaved her supper. "Smells like someone hit a skunk."

"Or two," Chance agreed.

His gaze narrowed. His body tensed.

"Chance?"

He held her back. "Get into the truck."

"What's wrong?"

He didn't answer, but grabbed the flashlight from the glove compartment. He shone the beam onto their tent. The teal sides breathed listlessly with the night.

"Stay."

This time, the tone of his voice was strained and she gladly remained within the truck's protective armor.

WITH EVERY NERVE on high alert, Chance unzipped the tent opening. The burnt-rubber smell of skunk musk had him covering his nose and mouth with his free hand. The beam of his flashlight caught the dark streak on the gray light weight sleep sacks. This stain wasn't normal, not unles this particular skunk had a bladder problem. And even if it did, he didn't think it had found its way to his tent by accident.

He backed out and played the light in widening circles around the tent. Footprints, almost invisible in the fall of pine needles, led a crooked path toward the water. On the river's edge, caught between brush and a rock, was an empty vial that smelled of skunk scent.

Not natural at all.

His first instinct was to leave, but one look at Taryn's pale face told him he couldn't. He'd noticed her lagging energy as the day wore on, the way she cradled her belly as if she wasn't feeling well. She needed rest.

To find a motel that would take them in, they might have to drive all the way back to Lufkin, and Taryn didn't look as if she could last that far. She hadn't complained. She wouldn't. But he wanted to spare her the added trauma of another long ride.

Sheriff Paxton—or one of his minions—had made his point. He wasn't likely to strike again that night. More than likely, he expected them to have moved on.

After dunking the musked sleep sacks into the river and anchoring them there to soak, he escorted Taryn to the shower house, stood guard while she bathed, then made a nest in the truck's bed with the blankets he found in her car. He sat by her side until she fell asleep.

The river's rush pounded his pulse faster and faster through his veins, making sleep impossible. Striking a balanced stance, he surveyed the woods for any shadow out of place. He remembered the Chief's Special hanging on the chair in Taryn's bedroom, and for the first time since his nightmare had started, he wished he'd brought it along.

All he had to do was wait till morning, he decided, then

he'd see Taryn home. It was the best thing for her—for both of them.

THE VIDEO IN CHANCE'S MIND was enhanced by sleep. The reds and silvers and blacks became sharper, the emotions keener, the desperation more acute. He awoke from the drowning nightmare gasping for breath, more sure than ever he'd killed the girl in his memory. How else could he explain his own face reflected above the water's silver-red surface? But why was he seeing the drowning from the victim's point of view? And, according to the paper, Ellen had been alive after the accident.

It didn't make sense.

Taryn wrapped her arms around him, pressed her body against his, placed a soft kiss against his neck. "It's all right. Everything'll be all right."

She kissed him again and his pulse slowed. On the whisper of the breeze, he heard words that struck fear into his heart. "I love you."

"Don't," he said, scrambling away from her.

"I know you. I know your spirit. You didn't do anything wrong."

In the conviction of her kiss, he could almost believe she might be right. He wanted to believe she was right. But the memories still reeled too strong for him to trust. He could not keep her at his side with a clear conscience.

Chapter Eight

"You can do what you want," Taryn said. She was ignoring him as she straightened the campsite.

Despite the unhealthy paleness of her skin and the fact something she'd eaten wasn't agreeing with her, she refused to listen to common sense.

"Kick, scream, order till you're blue in the face," she said, shaking pine needles from the blankets. "I'm not ready to go home, and there isn't a damn thing you can do about it."

"It's for your own good."

She pointed at the tent. "I don't think it's salvageable."

"I don't give a damn about the tent." He grabbed the blanket she was folding and threw it into the truck bed. "I want you to go back where you belong."

She had the nerve to smile at him. "Then I'm already there."

Once at the car, she shuffled things around in the trunk. "If we're not coming back here tonight, I suggest we just pitch the tent in the garbage, along with the sleep sacks. There's enough money in the budget for a couple of nights at a motel. I'll park Lucille's car at the campground office till we're ready to go home. It should be safe enough there."

"*You're* not going anywhere but home."

She hiked her suitcase into the truck bed. Then, dusting her hands together, she turned to face him. "I suggest we hit the courthouse first thing before the sheriff realizes his surprise didn't scare us away."

He was losing his cool and was having to use his last shred of patience to keep himself from giving her a good tongue-lashing.

"Well, what are you waiting for?" she asked as she got into the truck.

"A miracle," he muttered as he climbed into the cab.

Had Taryn always been this stubborn? The hell of it was, in any other circumstance, he might have found this spunk admirable. Now it was just complicating his life to no end.

This was a battle she had no plans of letting him win. Even if he dragged her all the way back to Gabenburg, she'd just follow him again. He didn't even want to admit there was a piece of him that found comfort in her presence.

And he couldn't give up on his quest. Not when he was so close to the answers.

THEY HADN'T HIT the courthouse early enough, it seemed. The surly clerk at the counter, wide-awake and her system overstrung from the twenty-four-ounce cup of take-out coffee at her elbow, would not budge from her position.

"There's nothin' I can do for you. Darryl Hager is on vacation. Won't be back till next week."

"We just want to take a quick peek at some of your records." Taryn smiled at the clerk, but it was having no effect. Might have worked better, Chance thought, if the clerk had been male. As it was, the thin woman with the bad perm and overbleached hair wouldn't make eye contact with him. She answered only when Taryn spoke to her.

"Won't take but a minute." Taryn inched a twenty-dollar bill along the desk's polished surface.

The clerk slurped her coffee. Never taking her gaze from Taryn's face, she dragged the Jackson toward her with a long, manicured nail. The bill disappeared into her pocket. "Ain't got the key to the records room, honey. I'm just the receptionist here."

"Well, is there someone else I could talk to?"

"There's Darryl Hager, but like I said, he won't be back till next week. And Judge Frasier's not due to make his rounds till next Wednesday."

Chance tugged on Taryn's sleeve. Why didn't anyone want to just up and spit out the truth? Did the sheriff hold that much power over the whole town? Or did it go deeper? Frustration hummed along every one of his nerves. If he didn't get out of here, he'd explode and do something he'd regret—like hike that skeleton of a clerk against the wall and rattle her till the key he knew she had on her clunked to the floor. "This isn't getting us anywhere."

"But she has to let us look. This is public information."

"And we can probably get it elsewhere."

Taryn sighed and gave the clerk one more shot. "Do you know where we could find someone named John Henry Makepeace?"

The clerk tapped her long nail against the desktop. Eyes scrunched, she appraised Taryn. "Try Gum Springs Road."

"Any specific address?"

"Look for the white gate. Can't miss it."

The phone rang, and the clerk pointedly turned her back on them.

Taryn followed him outside. Heat slapped at them from every direction. The breeze kicked up dust on the street, stinging their exposed skin. Sun beating down on them, drawing beads of sweat on every inch of them, they walked back to the truck.

"Think she was telling the truth?" Taryn gamely tried to keep up with his ground-eating strides. He slowed half a beat, compromising between blowing off some steam and accommodating Taryn.

"I guess we'll find out." He started the truck and turned the air-conditioning on high, then grabbed the map and searched for Gum Springs Road. "There, east of where we are, on the edge of town."

In silence, they made their way to Gum Springs Road. After the initial two houses, there was nothing but pine lots on the road until a white picket fence shot into view half a mile away. Chance slowed down.

"Oh, wow," Taryn said, twisting to get a better view out the window.

The truck idled, rumbling the seat beneath him. He should feel something, shouldn't he? Sadness? Relief? He tried to assess what he was feeling and found nothing.

"Want to go in?" Taryn asked.

He nodded. They went through the gate, followed the asphalt path past the gatehouse, hiked alongside the slimy creek running nearly dry. Taryn slipped her hand in his, and he was immensely grateful for the sense of connection.

In a neglected corner of the cemetery, near a statue of an angel green with moss, they found what they were looking for—a granite marker memorializing John Henry Makepeace. He'd died ten years ago. Beside the grave of his grandfather were those of his parents, and beside them were two small plaques bearing his and his twin's names.

"Someone still cares," Taryn said, fingering the fresh bouquet of red, pink and white roses on John Henry's grave.

But who? And how could they find out? His parents were dead. His grandfather was dead. His twin was also missing.

"So what do we do now?" Taryn asked, squeezing his hand.

He led her away from the graves holding his family. With those worried blue eyes, she was evaluating the effect this find was having on him. What would she think if he said he felt nothing about the grandfather he couldn't remember? Would it drive her away? For whatever reason, he wanted to hang on to her trust. He swallowed the bitter feelings rising with the slow burning anger.

"The best plan would be for you to go home—"

"I told you—"

"But since you're insisting on being so stubborn," he said, "let's move to plan B."

"Which is?"

Chance held the passenger door open for her. One other person had witnessed that awful day fifteen years ago. "Finding Ellen."

"And how do you propose we do that?"

Trapping her in the truck, he leaned one arm against the roof and one on top of the door. "We're going to find a phone and you're going to call the Angelina Rehabilitation Center. Then you're going to pretend to be a long-lost friend of Ellen's trying to locate her."

"No." She shook her head, hugging her purse to her stomach. "I can't do that. You know I'm not good with lies. My face turns all red and I start stammering."

"Nobody's going to see you on the other end of a phone, and we'll practice before you make the call."

He stared hard at her. A twinge of guilt twanged through him at the naked fear in her wide blue eyes. But if she was going to play stubborn, then he'd make her see the foolishness of her ways. The facts they were uncovering were telling him he was not the man she thought he was. "Or you could always go back home and let me handle this on my own."

"You're not playing fair."

"Sweetheart," he said as he pushed himself away, "nothing in this situation has been fair from the get-go."

Dropping her gaze, she nodded. "Okay, so what do I say?"

TARYN WAS GOING to throw up. She just knew she would. She was shaking so hard, she could hear her insides rattle. Chance was driving, heading toward Lufkin, but she saw none of the scenery. All of her attention was on the small black object in one hand and the piece of paper with the phone number of the Angelina Rehabilitation Center in the other.

"I can't do this, Chance. I just can't."

Looking for Ellen wasn't such a good idea, she suddenly decided. If Ellen was even alive. Fifteen years was a long time. She might be dead by now. For all they knew, if she was still at the rehab center, then she might not be in any shape to answer questions. Hadn't the newspaper article mentioned critical head injuries? That could mean brain damage. How could she possibly help them?

"I think we should look for whoever's still caring for your grandfather's property," she said, staring at the phone.

Chance didn't say anything. It was so unlike him to just leave her hanging like that, wallowing in her own misery. Yet she knew, that in the past, she'd also grown from pushing to overcome her own fears. If she didn't follow through, she'd be disappointing not only Chance but herself, too. And knowing Ellen's fate would at least relieve part of Chance's nightmare.

Taryn was sure that Chance wasn't to blame for whatever

had happened fifteen years ago. The only way to prove that to him was to talk to Ellen. And to talk to Ellen, she'd have to get over her own fear and place that call.

"I'm not very good at lying," Taryn said in one last desperate bid to have him move on to plan C.

"We *are* looking for Ellen. It's really not that far from the truth."

Taryn nodded. Not a strict lie—just a smudging of the truth.

Pressing one button at a time with slow precision, Taryn initiated the call. When someone answered, not hanging up took everything she had.

"Can you connect me with Ellen Paxton's room?"

"One moment, please." The distant voice came back on. "I'm sorry that patient is no longer with us."

"Ellen died?" The prospect horrified Taryn. Chance's gaze cranked toward her. Already guilt hardened his eyes.

"Oh, no," the voice said quickly, seeking to reassure. "Miss Paxton was transferred to another facility."

"I'm so glad to hear that." Taryn gave a huge sigh of relief that really didn't take much acting. If Ellen was transferred, then she might still be alive. "When did she leave?"

"I'm not sure. Before I was here, so that'd be at least eight years ago."

"I'm an old friend from high school and I was driving through, hoping to visit. Can you tell me where she is now?"

"I'm sorry, but it's against our policy to give out patient information."

"I'm just passing through Lufkin on business. I'm an old friend. I was so hoping I'd be able to see her. Can't you look at her file or something?"

"What did you say your name was?"

"Oh, I'm sorry, I should have said." Taryn racked her

mind, picturing the yearbook pages Chance had photocopied. Heat burning her face, she silently prayed that small town tendencies kept true in Ashbrook as they did elsewhere and that she wasn't stepping in too big a pile of troubles. "Justine Lassiter."

Over the line, Taryn heard the clicking of computer keys.

"Miss Paxton's no longer current, so her file isn't available on this system. Someone would have to go down to the file room and that request has to be made in writing."

"Oh." Taryn didn't have to feign her disappointment. "Well, is there someone who was on staff then who's still on staff now who could help me? I'd really hate to be so close and not be able to say hello."

"Er," the receptionist hesitated. "Let me see what I can do."

In the tuneless elevator music that followed, Taryn could hear her own heartbeat drum against her ear. "She's looking," she said to Chance. "Ellen was transferred to another facility."

Chance nodded. "You're doing great."

The brief upward kick of his lips and his encouragement warmed her.

"I'm sorry," the voice said. "It's against our policy to give out patient information."

"Even for a friend?"

"I'm afraid so."

"Well," Taryn drew out the word, giving herself time to think. "I thought maybe a picture of the old gang might have cheered her up."

"I'm sorry," the voice said. "But really, how many private facilities are there in Lufkin? I hope you find your friend."

Taryn smiled. "Thank you for all your help."

She signed off and turned to Chance, beaming a smile

f triumph at him. "When we get to Lufkin, we need to
nd a phone book and look for a private rehabilitation
ome."

ARMED WITH ELLEN'S ADDRESS, Chance and Taryn made
heir way through the maze of streets in Lufkin to the Pine
Creek Home.

As its name implied, the nursing home sat overlooking
he slow-moving Pine Creek. Magnolias and old oaks
culpted the manicured lawn, lending the estate an aura of
alm. Accompanied by nurses in crisp white uniforms, a
ew patients in wheelchairs enjoyed a shady garden.
roomed flower beds here and there added to the portrayal
f serenity. A wraparound porch surrounded the enormous
ictorian-like house painted in proper white with black ac-
ents.

Despite the outward appearance of tranquillity, some-
ing about the place made Chance uneasy. Taryn held his
and as they climbed the front steps. A discreet sign on the
oor read Entrance. Chance tried the knob and found it
cked, so he rang the doorbell.

Why secure the front door? To keep patients in or in-
uders out? Neither scenario did anything to calm the alarm
nsing his body.

After a moment, the door swung noiselessly open and a
eerful face peeked through. An old-fashioned white cap
orned the nurse's dark hair knotted at the nape. "Can I
lp you?"

"Yes," Chance said. He felt Taryn's hand squeeze en-
uragement. "We're looking for Ellen Paxton. She's an
d schoolmate of my wife's and she wanted to visit while
e were passing through."

"Oh." The nurse frowned. "I'm afraid that won't be
ssible."

"We won't stay long," Chance insisted.

"We just want to say hello," Taryn added, smiling. "It' been a while and we're just passing through."

The nurse looked apologetic. "I'm sorry, but it's agains the rules."

"Visiting hours are over?" Taryn asked, frowning and glancing at her watch.

"Yes," the nurse said, but Chance got the distinct im pression she'd snagged Taryn's suggestion to mask deeper truth. What exactly was going on behind thes locked doors? "Our patients thrive on routine."

"When can we come back?" Chance asked.

"It would be best if you checked with her husband first He's very protective of her and won't allow visitors unles he's aware they're coming."

"Husband?" Chance asked. How could someone who' lived in a nursing home for fifteen years have gotten mar ried? The uneasiness inside him stirred to hornet frenzy His grasp on Taryn's hand tightened and it was all he coul do not to wrap her in his arms and shield her...from what She shot him a worried glance.

"I didn't know Ellen had married," Taryn said.

"Yes. If you went to school with her, you might knov him. Garth Ramsey."

"She married Garth?" Taryn's surprise seemed genuine She was getting good at pretexting. "I would never hav pictured that match."

"Oh, he's so good to her. After all this time, it woul have been easy to lead his own life and forget about he, but he visits her twice a week, every week, without fai And it's not just a quickie visit, either. He sits and talks the for hours."

"He sounds devoted."

"He is. It's too bad more of our patients don't have amily as caring as he is."

"Where can we find him?" Chance asked.

"You *have* been out of touch for a while, haven't you?" he nurse gave a small smile. "Mr. Ramsey is probably at ne of his offices in town. Try the Ramsey Oil Company, e Ramsey Cattle Company, or the Ramsey Land Comany."

COME ON IN. Come on in." Garth ushered the two people aiting for him into his office. For once Carter had been ght. Seeing this man in the flesh left no doubt as to his lentity. The Caddo cheekbones. The Scot stubbornness in e set of his mouth. The dark eyes that seemed to reflect light. He thought he'd been ready to face the past, but wasn't. The sight of Kyle Makepeace looking at him all rk and angry was enough to turn him into a seventeen-ar-old—for a second. Then the familiar drive kicked in d the game was on.

The missus by his side was pleasing on the eye. But then, yle had always had good taste in women. Ellen had that y quality about her with her long blond hair and witch-een eyes. They'd once made him yearn for the promise moonlight magic of her and him on a blanket by the ver. His fingers lingered on Taryn's shoulder as she shook s hand while they introduced each other. This woman's ue eyes and velvet skin had him thinking of slow satis-ing sex by a roaring fire. Fire was more appealing these ys than fey magic.

She looked around his office with open curiosity while yle sat in his chair ramrod straight and looked about as mfortable as a pig at a pork sale.

As she spied a framed picture of him at the White House, r eyes widened. "Is that the president?"

Garth smiled. Making an impression was so easy. "…sure is. I was invited to a state dinner and got to spend the night in the Lincoln Bedroom."

She arched her eyebrows and part of him purred at the caged pleasure he thought he saw in her eyes. "Impressive."

If you think that's something, wait till you get a gander at the rest of my assets. He let his gaze slide down her front, pause at her peach-perfect breasts, then skim down her curves. A figure like that needed silk. The clothes had to go. Now, *there* was a thought. *Oh, yeah, I'm gonna get me some of that.* "That is the least of my accomplishments."

"I can see that," she said as she glanced at the signs of success he'd displayed across the walls. "You seem to have accomplished quite a lot in fifteen years."

The leather of his executive chair creaked as he leaned back and studied her with delight. She'd be feisty. The soft, sexy look was a ruse for the vixen beneath. She'd be a real conquest for a change, not just the plastic variety so ready to throw themselves at him. He was up to the challenge. "You want to know my secret?"

She shrugged, but the dismissive move didn't fool him.

"Real estate," he said, barely able to contain the need to reach for her skin and taste it. "I've got so much passive income comin' my way with property investments that I can finance any project I want." He turned to Chance. "Remember that summer when I was going to work for my uncle?"

Chance's gaze narrowed and his jaw tightened. Makepeace was still a hard-ass when he wanted to be. "No."

"I saw the possibilities. But Uncle Weldon was too conservative. He didn't understand the difference between risk and risky."

"And you did," Taryn said, deflecting his attention from Kyle.

I got Ellen. I'll get you, too, darlin'. "If you've done it, it ain't braggin'," he said with his best drawl.

"You can't argue with success." She reached for Kyle's hand, but he ignored her. "Chance and I would like to visit your wife."

"Chance?" God, that was good. Chance. Like the guy needed any more luck. Kyle had really gone and fooled the girl. He'd kept up the facade for fifteen years. Why break it now? "When did you change your name?"

Worry turned her eyes so big and the blue so watery deep, his pulse actually kicked up a notch. When was the last time a mere woman had raised his blood pressure?

"When I washed up downriver without a memory." There was an edge to this new Kyle. His fists were tight by his side. Anger bubbled right below the skin. And Garth wanted to make it boil.

"Amnesia? You've got to be kidding." Garth leaned over his desk and pierced Chance with a gaze. "This is me, Garth, your old pal. You can be straight with me."

"I don't know you from a dog on the street," Chance said.

Garth's eyebrows rose. "Well, now, that is interesting, considerin' you've told me all of your secrets. I know it was your fault Kent got caught in a drainage ditch when he was five. I know where you stole your first bottle of cheap whiskey for your first drunk. I know who your first lay was."

"That's enough. We came to talk to you about Ellen."

"But you want to know more."

The tightening of his features was a victory.

"Will you let us talk to Ellen?" Taryn asked. Her voice

was too thin and quick. He had her on edge, too. How far would she go for her man?

"Why would you want to do that?" Garth asked. Ellen could tell them nothing. Of that, he was sure.

"I want to know what happened fifteen years ago."

Could Kyle really be suffering from amnesia? The medical report he'd acquired indicated so, but Garth had thought the condition a ruse. If the memory loss was real, he wouldn't be able to buy either brother. Here was his chance to keep everything he had. And if a convenient accident should happen down the road, well, who could possibly blame him? Kyle's driving record was public record. "What happened is that you and your brother were stupid."

"Stupid in what way?"

Garth narrowed his gaze. "I was there, you know."

Taryn gasped. "At the river?"

Without looking at her, he nodded. "You and Kent—"

"He's Kyle?"

Garth shrugged. "Kent couldn't swim." He pointed at Chance's face. "Then there's the crooked nose. Kyle had his broken a couple of times."

"The nose doesn't mean anything. Chance was really beaten up when he was found."

"Let it go, Taryn," Chance said. "What happened?"

"You took out your frustrations about Ellen on Kent and it went too far. Couldn't quite manage to keep that temper of yours in check."

"That's not like Chance at all." Taryn swallowed hard and shook her head. "The newspaper said they'd gone swimming."

"Kent never went swimmin'. His brother pushed him in the river."

"We were fighting about Ellen?"

Kyle seemed to be barely breathing. He looked so tense

one good blow could shatter him. Taryn reached for her husband's hand. He snatched it away. Trouble in paradise. Wasn't that a shame?

"Kyle had dumped Ellen and she'd come beggin' for him to take her back," Garth continued. "Kent interfered and ended up in the river for his troubles."

She was mad now. The little lines around her eyes looked like lightning. Was she like lightning in bed, too? A storm, he imagined, a whole damn sky full of bolts to electrify a man right where it counted.

"How did Ellen and Kyle end up in the river?" she asked.

She was distracting him. Kyle was the one who was a danger to him, not her. He needed to find out exactly where the memory had fallen into a black hole. "Ellen jumped in to save Kent. She was always one for the underdog. Kyle went after her to prevent her from rescuing Kent."

Taryn jumped up. "I can't believe there was so much hatred between two brothers that one would let the other drown."

"You don't know the half of it."

"Tell me," Chance said. His voice was so dead, Garth knew he was making his point.

"And where were you when all this was taking place?" She braced a hand around her middle.

The thought of her beloved as a killer was surely making her sick. *That's all right, darlin', I'll make you forget.*

"I heard the argument as I was comin' up to the clearing. By the time I got there, it was too late to do anything but call for help."

He kept his body language relaxed, his face genial. He was, after all, the good guy in this little drama.

"Kyle always had a temper," Garth added. "He'd gotten himself in more trouble than I can say. He lost his license barely six months after gettin' it because he got so many speeding tickets. He probably still holds the record for after-school detentions because of all the fights he got into.''

Garth laughed, watching Kyle. Not even a blink of recognition. Oh, yeah, this was going to be good. ''Once he even put the rodeo mascot in the principal's office overnight. Mr. Talberg wasn't amused. Took Kyle a whole day to scrub all the calf sh—, er, droppings off the carpet.''

''What happened to Ellen?'' Taryn asked.

Garth turned to her. The smile he sent her was one that spoke of challenge, of the thrill that came with it, of knowing he held the winning hand. *Might as well face it, darlin', you've been hangin' with a loser.*

''Ellen was hurt bad. She didn't die that night, but she's been trapped in her mind since then. Accordin' to the doctor, there's nothing physically wrong with her. She couldn't handle the trauma of bein' nearly drowned by the man she loved, so she's stayed shut in her own world since then.'' With a little help.

Taryn closed her eyes. For a second, he thought she'd heave all over his clean carpet. Instead, she went to stand behind her man—loyal like a she-wolf—and placed her hands on his shoulders. Kyle tensed at her touch.

''Why did you marry an invalid?'' she asked, still throwing daggers at him though she was beat. He had to give her points for guts.

''Because you see, I love Ellen. That's why I was goin' to that preserve that night. I was goin' to protect her from Kyle.'' Garth speared Kyle with his gaze. ''And I'm always goin' to protect her from Kyle.''

''He's not Kyle. He's Chance Conover, sheriff of Gabenburg County.''

Such devotion. So archaic.

''I do admire your loyalty. It's a rare quality these days.

But I've known the Makepeace brothers since they were babies. If anyone is ornery enough to survive Red Thunder, it's Kyle. I won't have him disturb Ellen's peace after all these years." *I won't have you ruin all I've worked so hard to earn.*

Taryn planted her fists on the desk and leaned to look him in the eye. "Even if he was Kyle all those years ago, he's a different man now."

"Let it go, Taryn."

"How different can he be when he's pretendin' he doesn't remember who he is?"

"He's not pretending."

"That's enough!" Kyle said.

Garth released her gaze and challenged Kyle. "You think you're walkin' in tall cotton with your faked amnesia? You may have fooled her, but for me, my friend, that blanket is mighty thin. I was kind enough to see you for old time's sake, but I will protect what's mine."

Kyle rounded the desk and grabbed Garth's shirtfront. Leaning into his face, Kyle spoke in a low, dangerous tone. "Why would I pretend amnesia?"

Garth sneered. "To avoid payin' for the charge of attempted murder on your head."

"Attempted murder!" Taryn shook her head. "No, not Chance."

As if punched, Kyle stumbled back. His fists flexed by his sides.

"You destroyed a brilliant mind that day," Garth pressed. "Did you know she'd been accepted at Texas A & M? She was goin' to be a vet."

"Let's go, Chance."

Garth rose and met Chance nose to nose—the desk between them. "Did you really think Carter would forget that? Did you really think he'd let you get away with murderin' all of his hopes? There's a price on your head, Kyle. And because we were once friends, I'm givin' you the chance to disappear before Carter catches up with you.''

Taryn grabbed Chance's arm and pulled him toward her.

In the mirror over Kyle's shoulder, Garth adjusted the cuffs of his shirt, centered his tie. Oh, yeah, he had him right where he wanted him. Now to put on the finishing touch.

"You know, I think it might be good for you to see Ellen after all. Maybe once you've seen what your temper created, you'll be ready to take responsibility for your actions.''

He pressed the intercom button on his desk. "Mary, cancel all of my afternoon appointments.''

Chapter Nine

A few minutes later, fingers tight against the steering wheel, Chance forced himself to concentrate on the lunchtime traffic snaking down Chestnut Street. The red brake lights on the car in front of his truck flashed on and off with the ebb and flow of the stoplights. He didn't need the cold blast of air-conditioning to cool the sun's heat. His thoughts were enough to chill him to the marrow.

The images in his mind whirled at tornado speed, lifting new debris with each passing second, thickening the funnel of his broken memories. All this time, deep down, he'd hoped the nightmare was, as the doctor had said, an exaggeration brought on by past trauma. Secretly, he'd hoped there was a logical explanation for the blood, the dead eyes, the hands pushing down, drowning.

And there was.

The nightmare was real.

He'd let his own twin drown. He'd kept the woman he'd loved from saving his brother. He'd almost killed her, too.

The colors. The feelings. The pictures. All real.

And the anger. It swelled and crashed inside him in unending breakers. He'd almost lost his control in Garth's office, almost beat the man raw for giving him what he'd sought all along—the truth.

"You're accepting all this as if it were gospel," Taryn said in a mist-thin voice.

Dulled with clouds of worry, her eyes begged for a retreat that had become impossible. Her skin looked too pale and blended in with the hot, white sky outside the window. The wrinkles on her forehead shouldn't be there. That full mouth of hers should be open with laughter. Her skin should have the pink glow of happiness. And her eyes should be shooting sparks of joy.

I will protect what's mine. Chance bit down on the sour taste filling his mouth.

He'd almost forgotten she was sitting next to him in the truck. Another trick of the mind? If he didn't acknowledge she was here, then he wasn't responsible if anything happened to her? Taking the easy way out again?

"He knew me." Chance hadn't wanted to believe Garth, but each new detail brought cohesion to the random fragments of his memory, giving weight to Garth's words.

"That doesn't mean he's telling the truth."

"He knew things only someone who'd been there could know." *Kyle went after her to prevent her from rescuing Kent.*

The frown lines deepened on Taryn's forehead. "He's not telling the truth."

"What reason does he have to lie?" *Kyle had a temper.*

"I don't like him."

"You don't like him because you don't want to hear the truth. It doesn't match with your idea of reality." *Ellen couldn't handle the trauma of being nearly drowned by the man she loved...*

"You're the one who's not paying attention to reality—"

His jaw ached from clenching his teeth. "Reality is that Kyle tried to stop Ellen from saving Kent. The picture in my mind shows me pushing someone underwater. There's no way Garth could have known that unless he'd been there and witnessed it.''

She twisted in the seat to face him. One palm lay protectively against her stomach. One fist pounded on her thigh. ''No! Your nightmare showed *you* being pushed under.''

Breath, where is his breath? Bump, bump, bump. Long blond hair writhes on the waves. From a gash on the side of her head pours blood. Hands pushing down. Drowning.

''Watch out!''

Shaking off the ghostly images, he stomped on the brakes to avoid colliding into a minivan's rear end.

''The truth isn't always as pretty as you want it to be,'' he said. Hollowness rang inside him. He'd wanted to deserve her fierce loyalty, but he knew he didn't.

She reached out for him, then drew back. Afraid? She should be.

''Dr. Benton said the feelings can skew—'' she started.

''I don't give a damn what a two-bit country shrink said. I know what I see, and what I see is death.''

Taryn shrank back against the seat and looked out the side window. ''I don't think you should see Ellen.''

Was Taryn so bent on preserving the image of who she thought he was that she would try to prevent him from seeing the truth?

''I have to.'' How else could he start to make amends?

Garth was right. He had to face up to what he'd done. He'd tried running away. He'd tried forgetting. But his deeds had found a way to come back and haunt him.

''Verify, Chance. That's what you'd do if you were yourself. You wouldn't take anyone's word on the surface. Especially a total stranger's.''

He sneered as he braked for a red light. "Chance Conover, sheriff of Gabenburg County, Texas, doesn't exist."

"Chance—"

He flexed his fingers against the steering wheel. His foot on the gas pedal revved the engine. When the light turned green, he shot through the intersection. "I'm not a cop, Taryn. I'm not sure what I am anymore."

The soft entreaty of her gaze rippled against his conscience, but he refused to meet it. Ever since he'd woken up in that hospital room, he'd sensed he'd bring her nothing but heartache.

"You're my husband and my best friend. I won't ever let you forget that."

The cop, the husband, the friend. All were built on lies. Now was the time to face the truth. "Seeing Ellen *is* verification."

"I won't let you give up." She seemed to wither into the seat, becoming small and fragile like a delicate flower on the edge of a well-traveled path. If he wasn't careful, he would trample her, too. Part of him wanted to throw his head back and howl the lonesome echo baying in his soul.

"I'm not giving up."

The time had come to finally stand up and do the right thing.

Whatever the consequences.

THE FRONT DOOR of the Pine Creek Home opened as if on cue. The same black-haired nurse from this morning stood waiting with a smile. "Good afternoon, Mr. Ramsey."

The nurse looked at Garth as if he were a god. Taryn almost gagged at the unwarranted adoration.

She'd fallen for the charm, too. For a minute. Garth's polished good looks had reminded her of a golden retriever groomed for the showring, oozing with reassuring allure.

Then she'd realized by the exhibition of success tacked up on his walls and his braggadocio that he *was* mostly show and little substance.

And that had frightened her. Not for herself—she had nothing to offer this man. But for Chance. A man with no substance had little regard for another man's worth. In Garth's currency, Chance was expendable. Especially when Chance was so ready to accept a blame he hadn't earned.

The guilt was there in every tense line of Chance's body. The worst part was that there was nothing she could say to reassure him. The distance she'd hope to bridge by standing by his side was instead growing wider. She was losing him to his faulty memories.

What if he chose to become Kyle? What would happen to her? What would his decision mean for her baby?

"This way." Garth led them into a second-story hallway where the plush burgundy carpet muffled their footsteps.

The Pine Creek Home didn't exude the impassive institutional atmosphere she'd expected. Instead of glaring white walls, the hallway wore comforting cloudlike swirls of cream and pale pink with a rich burgundy trim. Only the undertone of freshly cut flowers scented the air.

If it weren't for the small window in the door, Ellen's room would have looked like a bedroom straight out of a decorating magazine. Gauzy fabrics in watercolor shades of teal and blue covered the window and draped the canopy of the fairy-princess bed. Muted sunlight filtered through the sheers and danced rainbows on the collection of crystal horses on the dresser.

Taryn gasped at the figure who sat at a small table by the window. The translucent skin, the frail body encased in a flowing white robe and a shawl of the palest green, the long blond hair curling down to her waist gave the woman an ethereal look. A Rapunzel dreaming of her prince.

As the woman was fed a spoonful of soup by a nurse, the distressing vision of vacant green eyes shattered the romantic notion. For all the pleasure her face showed, she could have been a china doll eating dirty rainwater.

"Ellen, darlin'. I've brought you some company."

She didn't look up. She didn't acknowledge their presence, just accepted another mouthful of soup.

Garth crouched beside her and took her hand in his. With a finger, he turned her chin in his direction. Her eyebrows scrunched and a strange mewling sound escaped her.

"It's all right, darlin'. Look who's here." He guided her head until her line of sight included Chance.

Chance looked like a prisoner facing execution. He seemed poised between two breaths, accepting, dreading the bullet that was coming. Yet when the shot rang out, neither of them was prepared.

Ellen bleated like an injured calf. Her spastic attempts to rise resulted in the scattering of soup, bowl and utensils in every direction as if she were an animal caught in a snare and panicking.

Garth stood beside her, supporting her. "It's all right, darlin'. He can't hurt you. I won't let him."

The echo of Ellen's cries tore at Taryn. She leaned forward to help, but Garth shook his head. The nurse and Garth exchanged a look and she disappeared.

"Maybe it would be best if you left now," Garth said.

Taryn nodded.

But Chance was rooted to the spot as if that bullet had found its mark and blasted all remaining spirit from his body. Tortured ghosts darkened his face.

Tears burned Taryn's eyes and choked her. No, this couldn't be happening. Garth was confirming Chance's nightmare. She wanted to rush across the room and strangle the man who was killing her dreams, her future, with his thoughtless actions. Instead, she went to stand next to Chance and took his arm. Tension strung him tight and the pain in his eyes wrenched her heart.

"Chance, let's go."

His gaze fixated on Ellen, he didn't move. The woman twisted in Garth's grasp, reaching her stick arms toward Chance. Her features contorted into a grimace of pain. Her mouth opened. Tears streamed down her cheeks. The scream that finally pierced through was inhuman. "Kyyyyyyle."

Chance jolted back as if slapped.

"Kyyyyyyle. Kyyyyyyle."

Her agitation increased.

"Leave," Garth said, holding her hard against him.

The nurse rushed back in and plunged a syringe into Ellen's arm.

The scream became a whimper. "Kyyyle."

She collapsed into Garth's supporting embrace.

Through blurred vision, Taryn shoved Chance out of the room, down the hall and into the truck. She wanted to let her tears fall, wanted to collapse from the grief swirling inside her, wanted someone to tell her everything would be all right.

Go home, go home, a small voice inside her insisted. *Grandy'll take care of you. You're pregnant. You need to take care of yourself, not run around on a fool's errand. No man is worth losing yourself over.*

No, she wasn't her mother. She wasn't going to run home like a rejected mongrel. She wasn't going to suffer silently and let everything she believed in fall apart.

This wasn't the Chance she knew. He was confused. He was hurt. But the man she loved still existed somewhere in that buried memory and she would find him.

If he couldn't do his job, then she would.

Leaning against the truck while Chance sat unmoving inside, she wiped her tears with one hand, and dug through her purse with the other. She found the cell phone Angus had given her, then dialed.

"Hello."

"Angus, what was Chance wearing when you found him?"

"What's this about?"

"I'll explain later. What was he wearing?"

"Taryn, sweetheart—"

"Angus, please."

There was a heartbeat of silence. "Not much. Just jeans and those were pretty much in tatters. His whole body was bloody and beat."

"Was he wearing a belt?"

"No."

"Boots?"

"No."

"Shirt?"

"No. Taryn, where's this going?"

No rodeo belt buckle, no cowboy boots, nothing that clearly identified him as Kyle. That didn't prove a thing either way, but it didn't confirm anything, either. Suddenly, she was at a loss. Even after watching Chance do his job for ten years, she didn't have a clue where to go next to find the evidence she needed to prove him wrong.

Angus would know what to do and she desperately needed someone else to make the hard decisions.

"Chance thinks he's Kyle Makepeace, a boy who might have caused his brother to drown and a woman to end up in a nursing home. But he's not. I just know it. He's not anything like that. Angus, what should I do?"

Angus hesitated again. "I think you should come home."

Leaving only causes grief.

"I can't leave Chance."

"He needs to work this out on his own."

Leaving her exactly where she'd started—alone and pregnant. Would her heart grow hard and cold like her mother's? What would happen to her child if she went back home and became the passive creature her mother had raised?

Grandy would take care of her. But that wasn't the life she wanted for herself. And if she didn't fight for what she wanted, then she'd regret her decision. Just as her mother had.

"Can you do me a favor?" she asked Angus. Her heart was beating fast and her stomach was rolling again. She had no idea if she was heading in the right direction. What if she took a wrong turn? She swallowed hard. At least she would have gone down fighting. For her baby's sake, she couldn't give up.

"Anything, sweetheart."

"See what you can find on a John Henry Makepeace. He's dead, but someone is managing his property and I need to find that person."

"Taryn, sweetheart, I don't think that's such a good idea."

"Please, Angus. Chance needs the whole truth, not just the mismatched bits and pieces he's getting now."

There was another uncharacteristic hesitation on Angus's part. "How is Chance?"

She glanced at her husband. Shock still etched his face in acid clarity. But he was strong and so was his will to survive. Why else would his brain have wiped his memory clean, not once, but twice? She wouldn't let him judge and execute himself. She would, as the doctor had suggested, re-create the whole scene for him and prove to him how wrong he was. She would find the explicit memories he couldn't recall. Basic nature didn't change. And Chance was a good man.

"He'll be okay." She hoped. She prayed. "Oh, and Angus, is there a way to find out if there's an outstanding warrant for Kyle Makepeace for attempted murder?"

"You're rocking a chair in a roomful of long-tailed cats."

"What's that supposed to mean?"

"It means I should have gone with Chance and left you home."

"I would have followed."

Angus sighed. "I know."

CHANCE COULD NOT ESCAPE the endless loop of his mind. Death, dying, drowning trapped him on a never-ending roller coaster. He was Kyle. He had allowed his brother to drown. He had rendered a promising young woman into nothing more than a shell going through the motions of living.

"I've still got those pages you photocopied from the yearbook." The rustle of pages, Taryn's voice, and the noises from the diner reached him through the blackness of his thoughts. "We could look up some of the names, see if any of them live here in Lufkin. Ask questions."

Her blue eyes came into focus. The hypnotic quality of her gaze centered him, made him swallow back a knot of distress.

He wanted to reach out to that trusting calm. But he wasn't Chance Conover, the man she knew. He was Kyle Makepeace, a man whose rage had hurt the people he supposedly loved. He didn't want to hurt her, too, but as long as she stayed by his side, that result seemed inevitable. He had to drive some distance between them.

"You want to confirm. Let's confirm."

He signaled a waitress scurrying by and asked for a phone book.

An hour and two ginger ales later, Taryn had talked to three of Kyle and Kent's schoolmates. All of them presented a less than ideal portrait of life at the Makepeace home. Two of the three had been on the receiving end of Kyle's short temper—one for making fun of his horse, the other for disparaging his grandfather during one of John Henry's frequent absences. Both could still remember the sting of the blow. Kent was mostly a blur in all of their memories. Two more classmates had refused to even discuss the Makepeace brothers and hung up.

"Are you satisfied?" Chance asked Taryn after she relayed the gist of her last conversation.

"One more." She flipped through the phone book and sipped on ginger ale.

"What's wrong with you?"

Frowning, she looked up at him. "What do you mean?"

"First you eat like you've missed a week of meals, then you look sick."

She shrugged and slid a finger down a phone-book page. "There are two Talbergs listed."

"Talberg?"

"The principal Garth Ramsey mentioned."

"You've been looking peaked for the past couple of days."

"I'm not sick, okay. I'm…" She rubbed her stomach in a soft circle.

"What?"

"I'm a morning person and I shouldn't skip breakfast. I was hungry and ate too much, that's all."

But the sheen of tears dampened her eyes as she punched numbers into the cell phone. He wanted to slide in next to her and hold her, tell her everything would be all right. But given the facts they were uncovering, that was one promise he couldn't make. The further he stayed from her, the better off she would be.

"Mr. Talberg's out fishing," Taryn said, "but his wife says he'll see us."

"You sure you want to do this?"

She nodded and looked down at the straw she was swirling in the glass. Sweat fogged the sides even though she'd asked for no ice. The swish of the soda matched Chance's own internal hiss.

"Even if you talked to the whole class, the story's not going to change." Why couldn't she see that?

"To get the whole picture, we have to see as many facets as we can. You're too willing to take the blame."

She thrust her chin out, but some of the determination was waning from her eyes. The dimming of that light hurt in ways he couldn't explain. He resisted the urge to reach out and take her hand, as she'd often done to comfort him. If he touched her, he couldn't let her go, and that wasn't fair to her.

For her sake, he wished the truth was different. She'd already seen so much heartache in her life and he would add to her grief. She deserved a happily-ever-after ending. She wouldn't find it with Kyle Makepeace. "And you're too willing to deny facts when they stare you in the face."

He pointed at her glass. "Are you done?"

She nodded. He paid the bill and they returned to the truck. Traffic lightened as they reached the edge of town and found the small ranch-style house where the principal of the Ashbrook Area High School had retired.

Barely a ripple flowed in the narrow creek where Doug Talberg had dipped his line. Oaks arched over the water. Sun spotted through the ends of the branches, giving the surface a mosaic alligator-skin appearance. The breeze stirring the branches lent the shade-drawn reptile creeping life.

Mr. Talberg leaned against an oak, a wedge of cheese and a peach spread out on a kerchief beside him. A beer in one hand, a book in the other, he seemed to be adapting well to retirement. By the neglect the ex-principal was offering his line, Chance guessed the point of this exercise wasn't catching fish so much as relaxing.

"Mr. Talberg," Chance said, bracing himself against the expected cold reception, "your wife said you wouldn't mind the interruption."

"You'd think that after thirty-five years of marriage she'd know I like to fish alone." He put down his beer, then plucked a weed and marked his place in the book.

"We won't disturb you long," Taryn said.

Steadying himself against the trunk, he rose. "You boys always did know how to ruin a good day." He looked up. His gaze narrowed beneath his bass-adorned cap as he studied Chance's face. "Which one are you?"

"I was hoping you'd tell me."

Mr. Talberg's bushy gray eyebrows rose. "So the rumors are true."

"What rumors?"

"That you're claiming amnesia."

Chance spun on his heels and headed back up the small incline to the house. He could do without being called a liar for the second time in a day. His amnesia was the one truth he was certain of.

"I never did believe the river got you," Mr. Talberg called after him.

Chance stopped and closed his eyes. "Why not?"

Everyone else seemed eager enough to believe he'd been swallowed whole by the river. Everyone seemed to think he deserved his fate. Slowly he turned back to face Mr. Talberg.

"As nasty as you were, it would have spit you out."

Chance laughed. "Just Kyle or Kent, too?"

"Most likely Kyle."

"I'm told your office reeked of calf manure for a while."

"And the cafeteria floor still has a spot of grease from the time you and your friends decided to park my car in there. I won't even go into the pep rally–bonfire incident." Mr. Talberg smiled. "I do believe I saw more of you than your grandfather did. Sometimes I got the feeling you misbehaved just for the opportunity to talk."

"Doesn't sound like he was a happy boy," Taryn said, hands in front of her like an obedient schoolgirl.

Mr. Talberg reeled in his line. "Kyle wasn't a bad kid. He just didn't know how to deal with all the anger inside him. The rodeo helped, but…" He shrugged. "He needed someone to ground him."

"Lucille and Angus Conover took him in like he was their own."

Mr. Talberg nodded. "A fresh start, that's what I hoped he'd found."

"He did. Now he needs to find it again."

Mr. Talberg emptied the beer bottle and placed it on the kerchief with the cheese and the peach. "Then take him home."

"I don't want a fantasy," Chance said, itching to leave. None of these details were making him feel any better about being Kyle Makepeace.

"Then you're not the boy I remember." Mr. Talberg knotted the kerchief around the end of his fishing pole.

"What did Kyle want?" Taryn asked.

Mr. Talberg slung the fishing pole over his shoulder and bent down to grab his book. "He wanted it all—the fame, the glory, the girl. But I think when it came down to it all, what he really wanted was to come home to a house with someone waiting for him.'' He turned to Chance. ''Seems like you got your dream. Why risk it all for a past you gave everything to escape from?''

''What good is a dream that's built on lies?''

''Ah, well, that's something you've got to decide for yourself. If you'll excuse me, I think the fish are done biting for today.''

Taryn thanked Mr. Talberg for his time.

Anger returned and now burned inside him hot and spuming, crushing his hands into fists that ached to lash out at someone, anyone, to relieve the pressure. Chance powered the truck back onto the main road and gunned the engine.

''Where are you going?''

He didn't answer.

''Chance. Stop. Don't you see what Mr. Talberg was trying to tell you?''

That he'd sacrificed everything to fulfill a selfish dream? This wasn't exactly a moment of redemption. ''Stay out of this.''

''I can't. Not when you're this upset.''

''I told you to stay home.''

''My place is here with you.''

''You can't handle the truth.'' He rounded on her. ''I am Kyle Makepeace. We've more than verified the fact. I've already ruined one woman's life. What makes you think yours won't be next?''

''Because it's not in your nature.''

He gritted his teeth. She was right. Basic nature didn't change. And his legacy was one of anger and violence. ''There's nothing in my heart except anger.''

He jerked the map spread between them. After studying it, he cranked a U-turn on the road.

"Where are you going?"

"Back to Ashbrook." He'd put her in her car and send her home. For his own peace of mind, he needed to ensure her safety. That meant distance. A moment of grief now would save her from a harsher disaster later. She wasn't going to end up like Ellen. He would sacrifice no one else to fulfill his selfish quest.

"Good idea. I want to find the spot on the river where the accident took place."

"No—"

He cut his retort short when the smell of gas twitched at his nostrils. Scanning the instruments, he looked for something out of place.

"What's wrong?" Taryn asked, too in tune with his mood change for him to dismiss.

"Probably nothing."

The gas gauge needle hovered at the halfway mark. None of the warning lights shone. Steady traffic moved on the road, but three car lengths stood between him and the Lincoln in front of him. "When was the last time I had this truck serviced?"

"A couple of months ago. You're real picky about maintenance."

He could see nothing wrong, but something didn't feel right. "There's a garage at the light. I'll pull over."

The engine revved by itself. It sputtered and coughed. Chance applied the brakes. No response. The stoplight turned red. The engine died. The steering wheel froze. He couldn't brake. He couldn't steer.

A plumbing-supply truck coming the other way leaned on his horn.

"Chance?"

''Hang on tight.''

Brakes squealed. Seconds before the truck smashed into them, Chance threw himself against Taryn. He covered her with his body, protecting her from the force of the impact. Metal ground against metal. Plastic popped. Glass crushed.

The sound of buckling metal soon gave way to the hiss and pings of mangled engines. Shouts and sirens filled the air. The reek of burnt rubber and spilled gas soaked the cab.

The body beneath his was much too still. ''Taryn?''

His voice seemed to come from another dimension. He moved as if in slow motion. His arms and legs felt heavy and thick. He took the too-pale face in his hands. The eyes were closed. From a gash on her forehead, blood poured.

Chapter Ten

"From what I hear, you're a lucky man," the doctor said as he put the finishing touches on the reopened wound over Chance's left eye. "If that truck had hit another foot down, you and the missus might not have gotten off so easy."

Chance hadn't been aware of the bleeding. His only thoughts had been for Taryn. His gaze had been fixed on the blood streaming down the right side of *her* face.

When her eyes had fluttered open, relief had made him kiss her again and again. Though she'd insisted she was fine, he'd carried her to the strip of grass on the median separating the gas station from the road and made her lie still until a paramedic had examined her.

Then the cops had arrived and the chaos of questions and fixing blame had started. Worried about Taryn, he'd accepted a citation for reckless driving and followed her to the hospital. The truck, the insurance, the blame, they could all be sorted out later.

"How's my wife?" Chance asked. Wrapping his tongue around the word *wife* felt odd. How could someone he didn't remember be his wife? Except that she wasn't such a stranger anymore. Over the past few weeks in Gabenburg and here, she'd become part of his life again—part of his being. He looked forward to seeing her in the morning, to having her close by during the day. He'd come to count unconsciously on her unwavering support. Her absence now filled him with dread. "Is she all right?"

"Everything's fine. She's just having her cut cleaned. She won't even need stitches."

The door behind Chance opened and the doctor smiled. "There she is now. Right as sunshine."

She looked whiter than the cemetery gate guarding his grandfather's grave. "Are you sure? She doesn't look good."

Taryn's eyes widened. The doctor chuckled. "There's nothing wrong with her time won't take care of."

"She's been feeling sick lately, too. Maybe you should keep her overnight for observation."

"Son, your wife is the healthiest civilian who's crossed that door today. If it's all the same to you, I'm gonna keep those hospital beds for someone who really needs one." He taped a protective bandage over the stitches. "There, that should do it."

The doctor reached for Taryn and brought her next to Chance and touched the bandage on her right temple. His burly laughter filled the room. "A matched pair. Why don't you go home? Is there someone you can call to pick you up?"

They took a taxi to a motel a few blocks away. Chance insisted Taryn take a bath to relax, then lie down for a nap. After his own shower, he fingered the fogged mirror, tracing the features that were both alien and familiar. At least the image confirmed he was concrete, not the hollow ghost he feared he was becoming.

Emptiness whistled through him. As he dried himself, a useless train of questions chugged in his mind. Who was he? Kyle, the angry teen? Chance, the sheriff, the husband, the friend? He felt like neither.

What did he believe in? What did he want out of life? What made him *him?* Drained of memory, he had no more substance than the shower mist clouding the mirror.

The only thing anchoring his shadowed self was the woman on the other side of the bathroom door. Her faith in him was both a burden and a balm.

But his quest to give himself an identity had nearly cost Taryn her life. If she'd been hurt in that accident, he could never have forgiven himself.

The towel stilled in his hands. *You're real picky about maintenance.* Accidents happened. Parts failed. *Did you really think Carter would forget?* Was Carter's need for revenge strong enough for him to resort to tampering with the truck?

He pulled on jeans and strode out of the bathroom. Instead of taking a nap, Taryn was dishing out Chinese take-out onto paper plates. She blushed when she caught his gaze drifting to the mound of fried rice piled on her plate. "I'm hungry."

Her embarrassment, her hunger, soothed him in a way he couldn't understand. Both were so normal in the mess his life had become. "Where's your cell phone?"

She nodded toward the dresser where the phone sat in the charger. "Who are you calling?"

"The garage where the truck was towed."

The mechanic took his time coming to the phone. Chance paced a tight circle from the door to the table. The scent of soy sauce, chicken and vegetables made his stomach rumble.

Taryn's curious gaze added a layer of tension. Those mesmerizing blue eyes followed his every move. Then he caught the hunger of her look as she took in the anxious flexing of his bare torso. Warmth spread through him, thick and needy. He tried to shrug off the sudden desire, but it clung to him, kicking his pulse up a notch. The blue of her eyes darkened. Her lips wrapping around the straw of her drink caused a jolt of anticipation so strong he had to turn his back on her or he'd regret his impulsive action.

When someone spoke in his ear, for a second he forgot why he'd placed the call.

"I'm glad you called," the mechanic said.

Chance cleared his throat. "What's the damage on the truck?"

A pneumatic drill whined in the background. Something clanged to the floor. The mechanic listed a handful of parts that would need replacing. "Now here's the interesting part. I found a pencil lead blocking your fuel pressure regulator valve."

"A pencil lead?"

"The kind you'd find in a mechanical pencil."

"How did that get there?"

"Well, now that's an interesting question. Know anyone who'd want to tinker with your truck?"

Was Carter desperate enough? Did he have the mechanical knowledge? But Lufkin wasn't his territory. *I will protect what's mine.* Did Garth feel Chance was a threat to Ellen? Chance didn't see him as the kind of guy who'd get his white shirt soiled with grease. "How long would it take to tamper with the valve?"

"About thirty seconds under the hood, if you know what you're doing."

"How long before the engine shuts down once it's started?"

"Ten, fifteen minutes."

Exactly the bracket of time from when they'd left Mr. Talberg's home to when they'd reached the intersection. Mrs. Talberg had seemed more than eager for them to talk to her husband. Did she have a stake in Kyle remaining lost? Did the ex-principal? Chance hated the way everything and everyone was now suspect.

They spoke for a few more minutes before Chance hung up. His bare foot grazed Taryn's ankle when he sat down to eat. The touch set off a chain reaction of need so strong, he pushed back his chair to avoid a repeat performance.

"The truck's going to be out of commission for at least a week," he said, focusing on the food on his plate. It wasn't doing much to fill the hollowness growing wider inside him. "We'll have to rent a car to get back to Gabenburg."

The fork she held paused in front of her mouth. "We can't go home yet."

"The truck was tampered with. You could have died."

She put the fork down and tilted her head. "Doesn't that make you wonder why?"

"It makes me want to get you where you'll be safe. I think we should leave tonight."

She stared at him for a long moment, making him wonder at the thoughts whirling in her mind. "We have to stop in Ashbrook."

"I'm not taking a chance Carter Paxton will play out his plan for revenge or you getting caught in the middle of it."

"Lucille's car is still at the campground in Ashbrook."

"I'll send someone to pick it up later."

She toyed with the last remaining forkful of fried rice on her plate. Her face colored. She squirmed in her chair. "Um, your service pistol is in Lucille's car."

"What's it doing there?"

She shrugged. "Grandy made me take it. It was easier to just pack it than to argue with her. I'm sorry."

"Your grandmother let you go when she thought you might be in danger?"

"Not exactly," Taryn said, but didn't elaborate. She

started picking up the empty food cartons and sweeping them into the trash can. "And we've also got to stop by the river."

He frowned. "The river? No. Who I am doesn't matter anymore. What matters is getting you home safe."

As he said the words, he wished they were true. He'd already found out enough of his background to know there was nothing positive to be gained from staying. But if that was all there was to him, why wasn't the emptiness filled?

Wringing a napkin in her hands, Taryn sat down. "Chance, you know that's not going to work. You can say it doesn't matter, but it does."

He stood up, turned his back to her and raked a hand through his hair. How could she read him more clearly than he could read himself? "Adding more details to what we've already found isn't going to make a difference."

"You'll be restless until you find all the answers." She came to him, slid both arms around his waist, pressed her head against his back. Contentment sighed through him. "That's not what I want from you."

Her arms around him felt wonderful. She was warm and soft and so comforting. The scent of her wrapped around him like a spell. If he closed his eyes, he could almost imagine himself playing the role she wished for. But it would be a lie and lies had already cost him so much.

"I'm not Chance, Taryn." *Who am I?* "I can't give you what you want."

"Which is why you have to finish what you started."

"No, not if it means you'll get hurt in the process."

Arms still looped around his waist, she turned until they stood face-to-face. "Remember when you were in the hospital in Beaumont?"

The blue eyes staring up at him so frank and sure had

him swallowing back regret. He didn't deserve that trust. "I try not to."

"The doctor said the reason you lost your memory was because the conditions were the same as when the accident happened fifteen years ago. Something about the river jogged your past back to life." Her fingers skimmed his chest, his neck, then rested alongside his jaw. His throat went dry. "I've been thinking that maybe if we go to the river, to the place where the accident happened, it'll jar your memory again."

Temptation was sweet on his tongue. "Taryn—"

The bleating of the cell phone on the table cut short his retort. She let him go, answered the phone, listened. Then she looked at him. "That was Angus. There's another reason we need to stop in Ashbrook."

"Why?" he asked, suddenly feeling so adrift without the warmth of her against him that he wasn't quite sure what to do with his arms, with his body. He was mist again, twitching this way and that at the whim of his forgotten past. Taryn was right. Without all the answers, he would forever be nothing more than a ghost of himself.

"J. D. Brahms is the trustee of the property once owned by John Henry Makepeace."

THE NEXT MORNING, rain beating down from a sky as bleak as his thoughts, Chance drove back to Ashbrook. He'd spent a restless night haunted by the unending horror looping in his mind, by the sweet torture of Taryn's body spooned to his.

Taryn sat beside him, entertaining him with stories from their past. The soft sound of her voice was as close to a caress as he dared to take.

He wanted to credit the headache jackhammering inside

his head to the cold front coming through. But he knew the origin was something darker.

Urgency forked inside him so intensely, he felt split by it. Part of him had to find the whole truth about that day fifteen years ago and make amends where they were required. Part of him had to bring Taryn home to safety. The last thing he wanted to acknowledge was the needle-sharp need to find where he belonged. If it wasn't by Taryn's side...

"There's a spot," Taryn said, pointing at the curb a block from the Ashbrook library.

"Stay," he said as he turned off the engine. "I'll go talk to Joely. No sense in both of us getting wet."

She ignored him. Chance sighed. She was as stubborn as a two-year-old—and as persistent. He found himself smiling. Life with Taryn would never be boring. With his faltering step came a heartbeat of regret. As best he could, he shielded her from the rain with the morning's paper.

Joely sat at her desk, squinting at her computer screen. Her red layered skirt and vest were paired with a white blouse and a bloodstone bolo tie. A red scrunchie held her white hair back into a ponytail.

"Morning, Ms. Brahms."

A blaze of fear zapped in her eyes before she could quelch it. "Please leave. I don't need any more trouble."

"Why didn't you tell me you were the trustee of my grandfather's property?"

She stood up so fast, her chair rolled back and clanked into the set of metal shelves behind her. A dictionary splattered to the floor. Looking toward the front desk, she scurried around her workstation. "You've got to leave."

Standing between him and Taryn, she urged them toward the side door. Then her footsteps hesitated. She stopped, raced back to her desk and picked up her purse.

In the stairwell, she stopped again and rifled through her purse. Her voice echoed in the narrow space. "Here, take this."

She slapped a key into his hand. "It's to your grandfather's place." Her gaze darted up and down the stairs. "I can't talk now. I'll meet you there after I get off work."

"Why not get it over with?" Taryn asked.

Did she fear, like him, that Joely wouldn't show if she was given too much time to think?

Joely's fingers shook as she zippered her purse. "I can't."

She turned to leave. Chance caught her elbow. "You'll show?"

Licking her lips, she gave a nervous nod. Her footsteps clanged on the metal stairs and she was gone.

"We've got to stay," Taryn said.

Chance folded his fingers around the key. Its teeth bit into his palm. His gut tightened. Was he afraid of the answers or of something else?

"You're so close," she insisted, taking his arm.

So close he could almost taste the truth.

"Let's stop by the supermarket and get some lunch fixings." She opened the door. "We'll take a look around the cabin. Maybe something will spark a memory."

Rain pelted his scalp, his face. It ran down his face like tears. And he couldn't shake the feeling he would regret this decision.

"HELLO, DARLIN'." Rain slicked the windows of Garth's office, blurring the world below him in liquid silver. The patter of drops against the glass soothed him in a way a mother's lullaby never had.

"What do you want, Garth?"

"Now, Joely, is that any way to greet your dear cousin?"

"Second cousin. Twice removed." Her words were girdle tight.

"Family nonetheless."

"What do you want?"

"I'm just checkin' up on you. Seein' how you're doin'."

"I haven't said anything."

"That's good."

"You said I'd be protected."

"And you are—as long as you keep your mouth shut."

He was comfortable with the silence, patient enough to let her fill it in her own time.

"You'd run over anyone in your way. Family be damned."

He didn't like the note of resignation in her voice. Beaten people had a way of thinking they had nothing left to lose and made even bigger mistakes.

Garth didn't put stock in anyone but himself. Sentimentality was far too flimsy to be trusted. Family ties were the least of his concerns. Loyalty, he'd learned, had to be bought—and he'd paid Joely well for hers. "I don't take kindly to betrayal."

Over the line, the stirrings of Joely's emotions filled the static.

"Neither do I," she finally said.

The line went dead.

Garth spun his chair to face the wall across his desk. Hands tented above his lap, his gaze met the glassed shadow box in the corner. There, a frayed blue ribbon resided. The token was the only thing of his childhood he'd taken with him when he'd left Ashbrook.

One year, his mother had decided he needed a positive male role model and enrolled him in the elementary school's Boy Scouts program. He'd hated every second of the ordeal, but he had gained something from the experience.

When he'd won that blue ribbon for top popcorn sales— above all the do-gooders of the troop—he'd seen his destiny unfold before him. *He* was the master of his own fate.

He never had to learn a lesson twice.

Garth picked up the receiver and dialed. "I've got a deer that needs stalkin'."

Chapter Eleven

Where the sand had washed off the red subsoil, rain had deepened the ruts on the driveway to his grandfather's house into little gullies. Behind the house, the woods were razed and the land looked odd without its green cloak of forest. Chance gazed at everything except the cabin.

He'd felt nothing before. Not the tender-sweet sentimentality one should have for his childhood home, not the expected awakening of memory, not the flash of his teenage self moving with familiarity across pictures of the past.

Having exhausted the landscape, his gaze finally settled on the house. Breath held, he waited.

He felt nothing still.

Inside, the cabin had been more or less maintained. A thin coat of dust dulled the wooden surface of the dining-room table, two chairs and coffee table. With no people living and breathing in the space, must had found a home and scented the air.

When Taryn sat, a faint cloud of dust rose from the plain brown cushion on the chair. Elbows braced against her knees, she watched him stalk the perimeter of the rooms.

Was she feeling sick again? She hadn't sipped through a gallon of ginger ale as she had the past few days. Her skin had a rosy blush. Her eyes practically glowed with life. Spending the night at the motel had proved a good decision. She looked rested. Or maybe taking turns feeling blinky was one of those unwritten rules of marriage. And he certainly felt rode hard and put up wet.

In one of the bedrooms, he found a pair of twin beds separated by a window. Serviceable denim comforters covered both. Two sets of shelves nailed to the wall served as headboards. One side contained field guides of all kinds and several trophies topped with a running figure. The other was filled with horse books, ribbons and rodeo buckles.

From the chest of drawers, Chance picked up a framed picture of a boy—thirteen? fourteen?—and a black horse. *Me?* Caught on the mirror's frame, faded and yellowed, were two tickets to the senior prom.

He sat on Kyle's bed. The bedsprings squealed. Something. He should feel something. But he didn't. He tried lying down. Staring at the ceiling, just as his teenage self might once have, he waited for the flash of a picture, the pulse of a memory. Nothing came. Hollowness blustered in the disturbed silence.

What dreams had he dreamed? What thoughts had he thought? All those years, sleeping in this bed, what feelings had he felt?

Taryn came to him, sat beside him on the bed. With fingertips, she brushed the side of his face. A trickle of warmth seeped through his skin. "The rain's almost let up. Why don't we open the windows to air the place and eat lunch by the river?"

Because he couldn't bear to remain in the stale atmosphere of his unremembered past, he agreed.

From his grandfather's cabin, an old dirt logging road led to the abandoned remains of a sawmill. Branching off to the right, an unmarked trail led to the Woodhaven Preserve and the Red Thunder River.

The rain had released the fragrance of nature. Chance inhaled the fresh smell of pine and hickory, enjoyed the soft padding of leaf litter under the soles of his boots. The distant crash of a dead oak limb seemed natural and right. So did the sharp disagreement between two squirrels. The white corsage of a sweet bay magnolia softened the green of the woods like a smile. Wilderness infused itself into every part of his being, tickling at his memories.

He put down the blanket he'd taken from the truck and the bag of sandwiches and fruit they'd picked up at the supermarket. Feeling lost, he stared at the river rushing by, willing it to divulge its secrets.

"What are you thinking?" Taryn asked.

She wound her arms around his waist and the intimate caress grounded him. She'd done this before. Not just last night, but a thousand times. The contentment her embrace brought seemed familiar somehow. Why could he remember nothing of something that touched him soul deep?

"I'm thinking this might not be the right spot."

"It's not sunny or late afternoon or as hot as it's been the past couple of days. Give it a chance."

He scowled at the water. Ribbons of gray wove in and out of the hurried surface, rippling a race downriver. Nothing stopped the water. Relentlessly, it pushed at whatever blocked its path. One hand over Taryn's, he reached for a pencil-thick dead branch and broke it off the pine. He tossed it into the water and watched it being carried away and swallowed. Closing his eyes, he tried to sweep away the tide of dread punching into his gut.

Then Taryn's hug tightened around him.

He turned in her arms, brushed a strand of hair from her temple. In her arms, he could forget everything. Her hypnotic eyes were a draw stronger than fear. He wanted to be who she thought he was. He'd reinvented himself once. Couldn't he do it again?

He didn't want to lose this. He didn't want to lose her.

Looking down at her darkening eyes, at her mouth parted in invitation, he leaned down and brushed his lips against hers. She yielded to him as if he were water. The current of his desire surged and he lost himself in the riptide of her kiss.

After a while, her gaze met his, and her eyes brimmed with emotion. Love. Love for him. His chest tightened. In the all-encompassing embrace of her dazzling smile, suddenly nothing mattered except her and him and the magnetic pull between them.

Her willingness to trust him, to surrender her whole being to him, created a magic as primitive as the woods in which they stood.

He wanted her. He needed her.

"Taryn…"

"The first time we made love," she said as her fingers tugged the hem of his T-shirt from his jeans, "was on a day like today." Her hands glided over his bare skin, palms flat on his stomach, then they followed the contours of his chest. His blood rushed downward, pooled in his groin, pulsed. "Fourth of July weekend. It had rained all day and cleared up just in time for the fireworks." Her fingertips played havoc on the sensitive nerves at his nape. She nipped at the lobe of his ear. His pulse roared like surf. "We never did quite make it to the park." She slanted him a wicked smile. "But the fireworks were definitely explosive."

"You're a witch," he said, smiling and pulling her down with him until they tumbled onto the blanket.

She laughed, a deep, sensual laugh, and the sound was delicious…a salve to his shipwrecked soul. The curve of her hip pressed against his thigh. She toed off her shoes and ran her foot along his leg, inciting a flood of need. "That's what you said then, too."

While she worked the buttons of his jeans, he shed his T-shirt. As he watched her unlace his boots, he licked his lips. With a provocative light gleaming in her eyes, she drew his jeans down over his legs agonizingly slowly. Nothing could look more sexy than this woman's eyes. Nothing could possibly feel better than this woman's hands over his skin. He was going to explode right here, right now.

He pulled her back up to him, played with a tendril of her hair as he fought for control. "What do you like about Chance?"

"I like everything. I like the way your mouth kicks up a little higher on this side when you smile..." She touched the left corner of his mouth. He drew her fingertip into his mouth and savored the warm flesh. "Ummm. I like all the little ways you take care of me. The foot rubs after a long day standing at work. The rosebush in the backyard. The swing." Her fingers moved lovingly on his shoulder. "I like the way you listen when I talk. The way you care about everybody around you—not because it's your job, but because it's your pleasure."

She pushed herself onto her elbows and looked at him deep and true. "I even like the way you try to keep everything neat and orderly, even though it drives me crazy because I can never find anything after you tidy up." She placed a hand over his heart. "I love that groan that seems to come from the deepest part of you when you hold me. It makes me feel..." She shrugged and lowered her gaze. Her dark hair veiled her face. "Like I matter."

He lifted her chin until their gazes met. "You matter."

If nothing else, he was sure of that.

With precise deliberation, he set out to cherish her. He kissed her long and slow, then kissed her again. He relished the dark heat of her tongue—sin laced with sweetness. Leisurely, he unbuttoned her shirt, favoring the newly exposed skin with licks of his tongue. An intriguing mixture of clean summer rain and feminine musk wafted from her desire-heated body. Irresistible.

He unclasped her bra, grunted his appreciation as his fingers glided around her rib cage and found the erotic weight of her breast. Taking one ready peak into his mouth, then the other, he savored her moans of pleasure. He drew her shorts and underwear down her legs with one hand.

"Have I told you before that you're beautiful?" he asked.

"A time or two." Her voice was breathy, her smile teasing, her eyes pure sexual heat. "And I never tire of hearing it."

He kissed the valley between her breasts. "You're beautiful." He kissed the crook of her elbow. "You're beautiful." He kissed the palm of her hand. "You're beautiful."

Her laughter rippled in his ear. He'd never felt so good in his life. Alive. Solid.

Then panic seized him. His heart galloped. He was drowning. He couldn't breathe.

"Chance?"

He rolled onto his back and put his arm across his eyes. He was water flowing, ever moving, ever changing, rushing blindly to nowhere. No memories, no past, no identity grounded him.

He wanted to be somebody. Not the fame-and-glory kind of somebody, but the kind of somebody who knew who he was, what he wanted, where he belonged. He wanted goals and chores. He wanted the comfort of a routine. And Mr.

Talberg was right—he wanted someone waiting for him when he got home at night.

More than anything, he wanted to deserve someone like Taryn.

HAD SHE DONE SOMETHING wrong? Had she said something to hurt him? The tortured shadows in his eyes had writhed with his pain before he covered them. "Chance—"

"Would you still want me if I was Kyle?"

"Oh, yes." God, yes. She would want him always.

"Even if I never remember who I am?"

"Yes." The certainty of her answer surprised her, but it felt right.

"Why?"

"Because you're a good man."

He shook his head and opened his mouth, but before he could speak, she put a finger on his lips. "It's there, Chance. There's a bone-deep goodness in you. No matter how you try to run from it, it's there."

"I'm not Chance."

"Look at me." She pried his arm from his eyes. "I don't care what name you use. Call yourself Chance. Call yourself Kyle. Give yourself a brand-new name. It doesn't matter. It's *you* I love."

He was the one person who made her feel whole. He was her best friend. He was the father of her child. She could not imagine a future without him.

"Always."

She tangled one leg around his, pressed her body against his and reveled in the solid masculinity of his form, in the strong, hard lines of taut muscles, in the smoky fire burning in his eyes. Even the scars on his back, shoulders and ribs could not mar her pleasure in simply looking at him. The barest touch of his fingers could arouse her beyond endurance, and it thrilled her that she, too, could make his powerful control shatter.

She slid her hand down his torso, enjoying the warmth, the silk of it. She sampled his salty skin, inhaled the seductive spicy scent of him. Then she strayed lower and wrapped her hand around the boldness of his arousal. His gasp of pleasure kicked her own into overdrive. She kissed him the way he'd kissed her—long and hard and deep.

He lifted her until she straddled him, then eased himself into her, filling her completely. The soft sound escaping her mouth seemed far away in the ripples of desire, bliss and utter rightness. He clasped her hips, silently demanding a more urgent rhythm.

"Oh, no. Not yet." Joy rippling through her, laughter bubbling out of her, she took his hands, laced their fingers and planted their joined fists on both sides of his head. She kissed him until he groaned and squirmed pleadingly beneath her. Then letting him see through her eyes just what he could do to her, too, she let his hips meet hers once more. With excruciating slowness, she filled herself with him then withdrew. Never once did her gaze stray from his as she repeated the torture again and again. Spiraling tension built. In him. In her.

"I love you, Chance. I will always love you."

She gave herself to him with every atom of her being until her body tightened around his, until she shuddered in wave after wave of sheer ecstasy, until she was nothing more than a pool of sated flesh.

With a warrior's cry, he rolled her onto her back. His fierce gaze told her she was about to get retribution for her bold seduction. And as always, her body responded to his keen desire, making her ache for him all over again.

In the intensity and the complete concentration of his lovemaking, in his whispered words of need and passion and desire, she found her husband again and she was not going to let him go. She would not let him give up—on himself, on her, on their marriage.

After he was spent, she held him tightly, heart beating against heart.

"This is the way it always is between us," she said, and hoped he understood the tie between them went deeper than memory. The solid weight of him blanketed her with warm satisfaction. Absently she stroked slow circles in the perspiration slicking his back, relaxed for the first time since Chance's accident. "We belong together."

Bodies tangled, they rested until the sky opened and rain started pouring down again. In the midst of squeals and laughter, they dressed. Giggling like teenagers, they raced back to the car parked by the trailhead.

Yes, she thought as she ran with her husband's hand in hers, with his laughter in her ear, *this is the way it should always be.*

And soon, when they were home again, she could tell him about the baby their enduring love had created.

"I DON'T KNOW where to start," Joely said. She sat on the edge of one of the chairs in his grandfather's living room, her purse on her knees, both hands clutching the leather trim of the southwestern tapestry bag.

In the soft light of the hurricane lamp burning on the coffee table, her skin looked sickly yellow. Her darting eyes, her choppy movements, her hurried speech infected the atmosphere with a nervous energy he couldn't shake off.

Rain fell with renewed vigor and sounded like a stoning from the gods against the roof. The relaxation Chance had felt alone with Taryn by the river this afternoon had completely vanished with Joely's arrival.

"The beginning is always a good point," he said, turning the bottle of iced tea in his hands round and round, ignoring the shiver zigzagging down his spine.

She nodded. "John Henry was heartbroken when the boys disappeared. You see, he was gone…" She played with the metal clasp on her purse. *Click, click. Click, click. Click, click.*

"He was with you," Taryn said gently, encouraging Joely to go on.

"No." Joely shook her head. "He was…" She leaned forward. "He wasn't a drunk, you have to understand that, but sometimes the pain in his knee from the sawmill accident, well, it got so he couldn't stand it. So he'd binge. He didn't want the boys to see him like that."

She turned her head and her eyes became vacant as if she were viewing ghosts from the past. "He never forgave himself for not being there that day."

"It wouldn't have changed the outcome."

Joely looked at him. A small light of relief shone in her eyes. "I know."

She dug into her purse and extracted a sheaf of folded papers. Smoothing them on her lap, she said, "He took the trust left to the boys by your father and set it up so that the homestead would always be taken care of and the boys would always have a house to come home to. The trust pays for the taxes and the upkeep."

Tears brightened her eyes. "He never gave up on you boys. He kept telling everyone who'd listen that you were still alive. He never gave up looking." The tears fell. "He died looking for his boys."

Taryn handed Joely a tissue. Joely dabbed at her eyes. Holding one of Joely's hands, Taryn asked, "Why couldn't you tell us all this earlier?"

Eyebrows drawn, lips trembling, Joely lowered her gaze. "I was afraid."

"Of what?" None of this was making any sense. How could a trust evoke fear? The slow boil of anger rumbled in his chest. He leaned back more deeply into the sofa, throwing an arm over the back. His fingers dug into the cushion. He had to hold in his temper or he'd never get the answers he needed.

"You have to understand, I never wanted the responsibility of the trust, but John Henry said he couldn't depend on anybody else to look out for his interests."

"Were you…" Taryn blushed. After the way she'd seduced him this afternoon, how could she act so shy?

"Lovers?" Joely held her head high. "Yes. John Henry was a good man."

"Why did he feel he couldn't trust anyone?" Chance asked, trying to get the conversation back on track.

"Because of what happened to Ellen. Sheriff Paxton blamed the boys, and John Henry, as their guardian, became a pariah." She licked her lips, pressed them tight, then said, "He could have left, you know. He could have avoided the daily dose of hatred he got from everybody in town."

"I'm not faulting him. I'm not faulting you. All I want is the truth." Chance took a swig of iced tea, wished for something stronger. "Please go on."

"Your father donated the land for the Woodhaven Preserve. He wanted the old-growth woods preserved for his sons and their sons to enjoy. But the five acres of land this house stands on isn't protected."

She took in a deep breath and handed him the trust papers. Without glancing at them, Chance dropped them onto the coffee table.

"Taxes went up and I didn't want to eat up the capital.

I'd made a promise. I wanted to keep my word to John Henry. Someone made me an offer for the land.'' She shrugged.

"Someone?"

"The Ramsey Lumber Company."

It's a matter of economics, Joely had said when he'd first met her. Did Garth Ramsey's influence color Ashbrook's economy?

"Why didn't you just donate the property to the town as conservation land? Add it to the preserve?" Taryn asked. She was sipping ginger ale again.

"Because of town politics." Joely's gaze shifted from Taryn to him and back. "A change like that has to be approved by the town council and the council's first concern is the economic well-being of the town."

"I'm not sure I understand what you're getting at." Absently, he peeled the label off the empty tea bottle with his thumbnail.

"The main employer of the region is the Ramsey Lumber Company. Two out of three people work at the sawmill off Route 255."

"And Ramsey wanted the Makepeace lumber, so the town council rejected the offer of conservation land." Chance slammed down the empty iced-tea bottle on the table. It rocked before coming to a standstill.

Joely stood and her purse thumped to the floor. Ignoring it, she paced in front of the chair. "Yes. He was pushing me to sell it to him. I knew he'd raze the land, so I said no. The only way I could think to keep the land safe from Garth was to sell one acre to save the rest."

Shaking her head, she silently implored for understanding. "I truly thought you and your brother both had died. And John Henry had expended a lot of money looking for you boys. The trust was running low, eating into the capital. I'd promised John Henry to protect the land.''

"I still don't understand why you couldn't tell me all this earlier."

She stopped, let out a long breath. "Because I thought I'd sold the acre to a man who wanted to build a weekend home, not to Garth Ramsey. When the timber turned up razed not even a month after the sale, I was horrified. I confronted Garth and he told me that the trust clearly stated the trustee wasn't allowed to sell any part of the land for any reason."

She crumpled into the chair. "If the trust money had run out, if it couldn't pay the taxes, then the land would have reverted to the town and Garth could have bought it for next to nothing. I didn't want that to happen. I'd promised."

"Has Garth threatened you?" *A man who threatens a woman is the lowest form of coward,* a voice he didn't recognize echoed in his head. Where had that come from?

Joely's eyebrows rose. The corners of her mouth drooped. "If I was found out, he said I would spend time in jail and have to pay a heavy fine."

Shame colored her face and her gaze fell to her lap. "You have to understand, my salary isn't large and I just couldn't deal with the thought of prison. Not at my age. Garth said he could buy his way out of the penalty for harvesting this old-growth timber, but I was on my own unless he chose to protect me."

"You were acting in good faith," Taryn soothed. "No court would have convicted you of a crime."

"I chose the coward's way out." Joely looked up at him, eyes tense. "When you showed up, I thought you'd come to claim your inheritance. I couldn't bear for you to see it like this. I thought…'' Her fingers knitted themselves into a gnarl.

"I'm not interested in the land. The only thing I want is to know who I am."

A soulful smile graced her lips. "You look just like your grandfather when he was your age."

"But is he Kyle or is he Kent?" Taryn asked. She went to the counter separating the living room from the kitchen and twisted the top off another bottle of ginger ale. Resting her backside against the counter, she rubbed a small circle over her belly.

She'd told him who he was didn't make a difference. Did she regret her declaration? She'd committed to him body and soul, he reminded himself. That couldn't have been a lie. But her actions now spoke of anxiety.

He wanted desperately to see her smile again, to hear her laugh, to make love to her. To regain the peace he'd found this afternoon in her arms, he would do anything.

But if he was Kyle, he realized, he had a debt to pay. Carter Paxton would make sure the price was high, and Taryn would be lost to him. With regret he tore his gaze from Taryn's anxious face and focused his attention on Joely.

Joely stared at him, studied every feature, every line of his face. "I don't know. I saw you boys mostly from a distance. I never came here and John Henry never took you to my place. In his own way, your grandfather was trying to protect you."

Reaching across the coffee table, Joely's hand squeezed his knee. "He loved you very much."

Suddenly choked up, Chance could do nothing more than swallow the hard lump in his throat.

Straightening up, Joely glanced at her watch. "I can't stay. I'm expected at a meeting in half an hour."

She grabbed her purse, hitched the leather strap over her shoulder and walked to the front door. As she opened the door, the sound of the rain battering the porch catapulted inside. The gloomy remains of evening light stained a dark patch on the cabin's wooden floor. With the knob still in her hands, Joely turned. "Do you know where Melody Road is?"

Chance shook his head.

"Take Gum Springs Road to the end, then turn left. I'm the only house on the right side. Come for breakfast. I've got the photo albums John Henry left behind. Maybe we can figure out which twin you are by looking through them."

"I'd like that." Chance rose. Hands stuck in his jeans pockets, he stood next to Joely. He wanted to offer words of comfort for her loss, for the sorrow he and his brother had caused her and John Henry with their disappearance, but could think of nothing that would repair over a decade of pain. "Thank you for the truth."

"I just wish I'd had the courage to tell you sooner." She gave a half shrug. "I wish it could be more."

Chance nodded.

Joely turned to leave. The spew of a pistol rent the silence. With a gasp, she clutched her chest. Another report cracked. Wood splintered from the door frame above their heads. She stumbled backward, fell into his arms. Bright red speckled her white shirt, his fingers.

Taryn screamed. A bottle shattered against the floor. Ginger ale hissed.

"Get down!" Chance ordered.

Taryn dropped to her knees, then flattened against the floor. Eyes rounded with fear, she stared at him.

Like lightning, something struck. In the darkness of his mind, a flash of light. *Bang.* Blood blossoming red on a white blouse. "Get down!" his own voice echoed from somewhere in the past. Taryn, hair cut boy-short, dropped to her knees, flattened against the linoleum of the diner floor. Eyes round with fear, face white with shock, freckles of blood spattering her cheeks, she stared at him. Ten years unfolded before him in a wild spool of fast-forward film. The trial. The courtship. The tests.

The love.

Their marriage.

Oh my God. Taryn.

Another shot cracked, shaking him out of the past. A window splintered.

"Stay low," he ordered Taryn. "Get behind the counter."

Crouching, he slid Joely back into the house and slammed the door shut.

"Where's your cell phone?"

"In my purse."

The purse sat on the kitchen counter. "Can you reach up and drag it down?"

She did.

"Call for help."

He shed his T-shirt, and with it, stanched the flow of blood pulsing from Joely's chest. Her breathing was strained, gurgling. She clutched one of his wrists.

"The truth—" she heaved a breath "—was worth the price."

Her eyes dulled. Her chest rose with a labored gurgle, then fell in the long hiss of an emptying balloon. No other breath followed.

In the eerie stillness, Taryn's voice, brittle and raw, begged for help.

His quest had caused yet another woman harm. Was Taryn next?

Taryn. His Taryn. His wife, his lover, his soul mate. Now that he'd found her again, he couldn't let anything happen to her.

Chapter Twelve

"Kyle Makepeace, you're under arrest."

The sheer pleasure twinkling in Carter Paxton's eyes made Taryn's stomach heave a protest. She threw herself between Chance and the deputies advancing toward him. "No!"

Chance wrapped her in his arms and swung her away from a deputy's grip. "Stay out of this, Taryn. I don't want you hurt."

"This isn't fair. They're not even trying to find who shot Joely."

"I'll handle it."

"Hands up in the air where we can see 'em."

"No!"

"Taryn..."

Heart breaking, she stumbled backward. "You can't let them do this to you."

"I'll get a chance to state my case."

As one deputy held a gun on Chance, another shoved him against the wall like a criminal. While one deputy patted him down, the other Mirandized him. The scene played straight out of a bad movie, and Taryn couldn't believe they were truly arresting Chance.

Officials dressed in black slickers shiny with rain bulldozed their way through the small room. Two of them enclosed Joely in a body bag. The rest seemed to walk in circles smearing muddy boot prints, puddles of water and the pool of blood into a homogeneous mess on the cabin's floor. No one seemed to care that evidence was being destroyed, that no questions had been asked, that rights were being trampled.

"Are you crazy?" Taryn grabbed at the sheriff's sleeve and was swatted away.

"Don't touch her," Chance warned. His voice was low and dangerous as he strained against the deputy's hold.

Sheriff Paxton snorted. "You're not in a position to be making threats, son."

Taryn's fear for Chance overshadowed her anxiety in the face of authority. She advanced on the sheriff once more. "Someone tried to kill him. What are you arresting *him* for?"

"The murder of Joely Brahms."

"You're arresting the wrong man!" She wanted to pummel the sheriff's face with her fists, but sitting in jail for assaulting an officer, would do Chance no good.

"Won't take but a few minutes once he's fingerprinted to prove he's Kyle Makepeace."

"How?"

"Birth records from the hospital in Lufkin."

Why hadn't she thought of that? Chance would have known for sure who he was and they could have been on their way home.

A deputy jerked Chance's arms behind him and snapped cuffs around his wrists. His face was so blank, he looked like a bust in a wax museum. Taryn rubbed at the growing ache bruising her chest. This could not be happening.

"Chance didn't kill Joely. How could he, when he was inside and the shot came from outside?"

"We've got enough evidence to take him in." The sheriff nodded at his deputies and, one holding each of Chance's arms, they led him outside.

Taryn stepped in front of the sheriff, blocking his path. "Evidence? What evidence? He was inside and someone shot from outside."

"We've got the murder weapon." The sheriff reached inside the folds of his slicker and held up Chance's service pistol. Taryn's mouth dropped open. "Recognize this?"

Someone had broken into Lucille's car and stolen Chance's gun. Could this get any worse?

"It was left by whoever really pulled the trigger." The words tumbled out of her mouth. "It was stolen." Why couldn't he see the truth that was so plain in front of his eyes?

"No report of a stolen weapon was made."

"Of course not. We didn't know it *was* stolen. Do the test. Check his hands. You'll see he hasn't fired a gun."

The sheriff said nothing as he supervised the men from the coroner's office.

Her mind spun a tornado of thoughts. She had to make them stop this ridiculous charade. "What's his motive?"

The sheriff snorted. "The oldest one in the book. Greed."

"Greed? What are you talking about?"

He nodded toward the body bag being hefted off the floor. "He asked Ms. Brahms to transfer the Makepeace trust to him."

Taryn frowned and shook her head at the utter absurdity of his accusation. "That's not what happened at all."

"When she refused, he shot her."

Her heart pounded a marathon. "That's crazy. If she's dead, then the trust reverts to the town. What does that gain him?"

"He didn't know."

She was fighting a losing battle. The sheriff wasn't listening to a word she was saying. "I just told you. If I know, then he knows."

"He hasn't read the trust papers yet."

Taryn growled her frustration. "This is pure manure!"

The sheriff slanted her a glance reminiscent of a bull who'd just spotted a red cape. "No, ma'am, it's the facts, and you can't argue with the facts."

"It's just your word against Chance's."

The sheriff's eyes narrowed as he invaded her space. The years of pain had crystallized his hatred to a steely cave of icy stalagmites. Chance didn't stand a ghost of a possibility of getting due process.

"Who is a jury going to believe?" the sheriff said between gritted teeth. His nostrils flared with the heat of his anger. "A servant of the law or a man caught bending over the woman he just killed."

"I'll back him."

"The evidence will back me."

"You can't manipulate evidence like this."

"We've got a witness to corroborate the facts."

A witness who'd more than likely been bought and paid for. The situation was worsening by the second. "Who?"

Ignoring her, the sheriff crammed his hat on his head.

"Why are you doing this?"

"Justice." He tapped the brim of his hat and turned to leave.

Taryn grabbed his shoulder and pulled him around. "If your interest truly were justice, you'd be out there looking for whoever really killed Joely Brahms."

"I got him." He snagged his shoulder free from her grip and strode out into the night.

She followed the sheriff outside. The blue-and-white

lights from three patrol cars swirled the yard into confusion. Radios belched static into the air. Rain splattered against her bare legs. "Where are you taking him?"

"He'll be at the county lockup." The sheriff heaved his body into the patrol car.

"Where's that?"

"Right here in Ashbrook." The sheriff slammed the door of his patrol car, then rolled down the window. "If I were you, I'd head on home."

"You're not me," she whispered, arms rigid, hands fisted at her sides. "What about bail?"

"He'll be arraigned in Angelina County in the morning. But I wouldn't count on bail. He's a flight risk. I'll recommend he be denied."

Flight risk. Bail denied. This could not be happening.

She feared for Chance as she'd never feared for him. Not one of these men saw him as a human being. To them, he was simply a mode of revenge—Carter Paxton's revenge. Would he even reach the holding cell or would they just stop somewhere along the way and shoot him like a rabid fox?

Shoving the rental into gear, Taryn followed the caravan of patrol cars into town, wishing all the way she hadn't listened to Grandy and taken the damn pistol with her, wishing that she hadn't left the thing in Lucille's car, wishing that she had it now to protect the man she loved.

She didn't bother parking the rental behind the courthouse, just stopped it right behind the three sheriffs' cars.

Chance was standing outside a cruiser, a gun trained on him, rain pouring over him while the deputy took his sweet time opening the courthouse's back door.

Taryn ran to him. "Wait!"

"Go home, Taryn."

"No, I'm going to be here for you. I'm not going to le

them railroad you into a conviction that doesn't belong to you.''

"If you stay, I'll worry about your safety.''

"I'll be okay. You're the one in danger. They don't care about the law.''

His eyes grew stone-hard. When he spoke, his voice was cadaver-cold. "I don't want you here.''

"Chance—''

He turned his back to her and glared at the sheriff. "Escort her out of town. I don't want to see her again.''

The sheriff grinned. "Glad to oblige.''

THE IRON DOOR clanged behind Chance.

"Don't get too comfy now,'' the guard said, tossing the ring of keys up and down in his hand. "If things go right, you'll be sitting pretty in Huntsville in no time.''

Comfy wasn't going to be a problem. A solid-steel cot was welded to the wall. A thin, stained mattress covered the metal slab. The gray decor continued in the form of a stainless commode and a sink no bigger than his hand. There were no windows, no carpet, no blankets, just the cold welcome of a solid cage. A spotlight shone into the space and bounced off every shiny surface. Sleep would be impossible. Even the first grade's guinea pig back in Gabenburg had more comfortable accommodations.

He slumped onto the mattress. Elbows on knees, he rested his head on his upturned palms. This afternoon, he'd let himself believe that things could work out right. Taryn's trust had let him think that their love was strong enough to overcome any obstacle.

He'd been a fool to put stock in the illusion. The facts pointed to a different reality. He was Kyle Makepeace. He had harmed Ellen Paxton beyond repair. He would have to pay for his mistake.

The anger that had poisoned him blew out of him. In its place stood resignation.

Sending Taryn home was the right decision. She'd be safe there. Angus and Nola would take care of her. He'd wanted to know his identity. He'd found it. And his past had caught up with him—the good and the bad. She didn't need to witness his final disgrace.

The hurt look in her eyes had cut him down to his soul. Her helpless cry as the sheriff had led her away tore the heart right out of his chest. Refusing to glance back at her had been the hardest thing he'd ever done. But she deserved happiness and she would never find it with him to drag her down.

As he closed his eyes, images of her smile across the years, of her sexy eyes always bright with love for him, of the thousands of nights satisfied with their lovemaking filled his mind. In his blank slate of a mind, the returning memories of Taryn fed him. He hung on to the pictures, savored them, imprinted them deeper. They would have to last him a lifetime.

He loved her. Heart, mind and soul. He loved her. The ten years they'd spent together were a lifetime for him. She'd made a decade feel like a moment, like forever. Even amnesia had not managed to completely sever their deep bond.

Taryn. His soul bayed with loneliness.

Now that he knew her again, she was lost to him.

But she was safe.

That was all that could matter now.

ONCE THE SHERIFF'S LIGHTS faded from her rearview mirror, Taryn stopped the car on the shoulder of the road somewhere south of Ashbrook. Hands tight around the steering wheel, she stared into the black of the night. Rain still poured and her high beams didn't reach far into the gloom.

She didn't want to leave her husband at the mercy of such hatred. If she left, there would be no witness to whatever punishment the sheriff sought to mete out. But what could she do? Who would listen to her? How could she make her voice heard and guarantee Chance a fair shake?

He was her husband. They were bound by more than promises. She couldn't leave him here to face his fate alone. She loved him. She had to stand by him.

Nausea rolled in her stomach. She hadn't eaten any dinner. Good nutrition was important, especially in this early stage of a fetus's development. If she stayed, she risked putting her unborn baby under stress.

If she left, she couldn't live with abandoning her husband in a time of need. If she stayed and her baby was harmed, she couldn't live with the loss. This baby was part of her, part of Chance, part of their future together.

She'd waited too long to give up on either.

There was only one thing to do.

She turned the car around, stopped at a convenience store in a town too small for a welcome sign, and stocked up on food, paper and a couple of disposable cameras. Once again at the cabin, she ignored the crime-scene tape. The sheriff's men had already done their best to muddle the evidence. Back turned to the living room, she forced herself to eat a turkey sandwich and a handful of baby carrots.

With pad of paper and pen in hand, she wrote down everything that had happened since the beginning of their search for Chance's identity. Then she put herself in Chance's skin and walked the crime scene as he might have—as the sheriff and his men should have. Ignoring her disgust at the congealing blood on the floor, she snapped pictures with the disposable cameras. Then she sketched and measured. When she'd noted everything she could think of, she scrubbed the floor using cold water from the mechanical pump outside and a bucket she'd found in the barn. Crying for Joely, for Chance, for herself, she kept going until no stain remained.

By the end of this exercise, she was exhausted. After washing herself as best she could with a cloth, she dressed in fresh clothes.

In the hot and sticky childhood bedroom that had once been Chance's, she sank into one of the twin beds. She tried not to think of Chance caged like an animal, but her thoughts kept straying to him. Would anyone bother to feed him? Was he able to sleep at all? Was he all right or were the nightmares turning his imprisonment into hell?

Staring into the endless womb of darkness, she came to the conclusion that she didn't have the skills or the knowledge to penetrate the depth of deceit found in Ashbrook. If she was to get Chance out of jail, she would have to ask for help.

Cradling her purse to her chest, she picked up her cell phone and punched in a series of numbers. Her throat was dry. Her heart pounded. Her fingers shook as she held the phone to her ear.

She was not going to let Chance go. Not without a fight. Not without exhausting every possibility.

"Angus," she said, eyes closed, tears clinging to her lashes, heart in her throat. "I need help."

Holding back her grief, she explained the situation.

"I'm going to make some calls," Angus said. "I'll be there first thing in the morning. Don't you worry, sweetheart, we'll get him home."

How could she do anything *but* worry?

THE WALLS WERE CLOSING IN around Chance. He couldn't tell how long he'd been here. They'd taken his watch away.

There were no clocks, no windows that would offer him a clue.

He paced the floor, trying to halt the slow narrowing of the cell. All he needed was a squeak and he'd feel just like Peanuts, the first-grade guinea pig when it jogged on its exercise wheel. He was going nowhere fast. And his thinking, endlessly looping from nightmare to nightmare, didn't offer any solutions.

"Stop your pacin'. You're drivin' me crazy," said the guard sitting at the desk outside Chance's cell.

But if he stopped, Chance feared getting mired in the dark soup of his mind. He needed to think, and to think, he needed to move.

"I said, stop your pacin'."

Chance ignored the command. Taryn would be home by now, in her grandmother's care. That was the one positive of this situation. To endure what was to come, he needed to know she was safe.

In the morning, he'd be arraigned. The plea wouldn't matter. His chance of getting an impartial judge and an appointed lawyer who'd fight fairly for him were slim to none. At least in this town. The worst-case scenario would be the death penalty; the best, voluntary manslaughter. Either way, the future looked grim.

"I said stop your friggin' pacin'."

Before Chance could turn around to answer, a bucket of cold water splashed over him.

A powerful claustrophobic feeling seized him. Something tight wrapped around his shoulders. He couldn't move. He couldn't breathe. Panic tore through him, making him shake. *Help me! Help me!* The voice, small and far, echoed inside his head. Pain scraped along his side as if someone were skinning him alive. A piercing scream split his skull. Everything went black.

As GARTH REACHED the sheriff's office, Carter Paxton battered through the front door.

"Come on," Carter said, charging down the stone stairway. "I gotta go down to the courthouse."

"Something wrong?"

"Not sure. Blanchard wasn't making any sense. All I know is Makepeace is down."

"Escape attempt?"

"He's never been one to face the consequences of his actions." Carter snorted. "He ain't gettin' away this time."

"Might save us all the trouble of a trial if he did meet up with an accident."

Carter snorted and wrestled open the door of his cruiser. "Not this time, Garth. I want this one to go through. For Ellen's sake, I want him to be found guilty and sentenced to die. After that, I don't care what happens to him."

Garth settled himself in the passenger's side. Carter snapped on the lights and sirens and streaked his way across town.

Delays in dealing with the situation placed Garth in jeopardy. The trick to success was to take charge. He scowled at the sheriff. "How fast can you move this case along?"

He'd come to Ashbrook to claim Joely's body and do right by her as her next of kin, but he wanted to make his stay as short as possible. Even though half the buildings in town, including the courthouse, bore his name, he couldn't stand spending more time than he had to in this dot on the map. Coming here never failed to bring back memories of being the runt everyone was only too ready to kick.

"I got the ball rolling," Carter said. "Judge Frasier'll be waiting for him when he gets to the courthouse in Lufkin, ready to deny bail. Milton'll act as his court-appointed lawyer. He hasn't got a chance to beat the charges.''

The gleam in Carter's eyes looked maniacal. He leaned forward against the steering wheel as if it would make the car move faster. The way he huffed every couple of breaths made him look like a bull in a rodeo chute. Almost made Garth feel sorry for the short trip Kyle would have through the justice system.

Almost, but not enough to stop the ball once it was rolling, or to pass on arranging a convenient accident once Kyle reached the detention center waiting for his trial. No one would be surprised when he was found beaten or bludgeoned to death after a brawl. Happened all the time to cons with short tempers.

Garth had too much invested in Ellen to risk a return of Kyle's memories at an inopportune time. *Dead men don't talk.* Too bad Kyle hadn't been able to realize how far Garth had come up in the world. But then Garth was never one for sentimentality. Concrete results, that's what counted in the end.

Carter squealed to a stop by the courthouse steps and cleared the stairs by twos.

''Where is he?'' Carter asked the front-desk clerk.

''Out back.''

Carter sprinted down the halls painted puke green. Garth followed at a more sedate pace. Dignity had to be maintained. Impatiently Carter buzzed at the door leading to the holding cells. The heavy door clanked as the guard let them through.

''What happened?'' Carter asked.

The guard raked a hand through his hair. ''I dunno. He was pacin', drivin' me crazy. I told him to stop. When he wouldn't, I pitched a bucket of water at him.'' Blanchard shook his head, scrunched his forehead. "He started gaggin', then he fell. That's when I called you."

Carter nodded toward the cell door. "Open it."

Crouching by Kyle's side, Carter took a pulse. "He's alive. Let's get him out of this wet uniform. Get a blanket and call Doc Macmillan."

Once the guard had left, Garth peered into the cell. An expression of pure terror was etched onto Kyle's face. What had brought it on? The glimpse of a memory? "Might serve us all better if he didn't wake up from his little seizure."

"I told you. I need for him to be convicted and sentenced."

Carter ripped the orange shirt off Kyle's back, exposing a scarred back. Garth's mouth opened and he took a step back.

"Did the prints come in yet?" Garth asked, tabbing through options. Makepeace couldn't see tomorrow. Carter would have to be satisfied with this man's death as his revenge.

"Still waiting for the hospital to fax 'em over. Should be here any minute."

"Where's his wife?"

"On her way home. Escorted her out of town myself last night."

No, Garth thought. Someone as fiercely loyal as this woman wouldn't simply up and quit. She'd stick around, planning, waiting for the opportunity to launch a rescue. A woman like her would be ready to die for what she wanted. On one level, Garth admired that quality—especially in a woman. On another, this could spell trouble. She wouldn't give up.

"I got an errand to run," Garth said. "Buzz me when you're ready to transport."

Time was running short. But he'd faced a stacked deck before and still drawn a pat hand.

Chapter Thirteen

"Is he all right?" Taryn asked Angus, holding on to the cell phone with both hands.

Sunlight eked through the cabin's dirty kitchen window, giving the room a rusty, forgotten look. The nausea wasn't so bad this morning. For the baby's sake, she'd drunk a container of orange juice and forced some cold oatmeal down her throat. Then she'd waited endlessly for the sound of Angus's car down the driveway, for the phone to ring. Yet, when the phone had rung, the sound had caught her daydreaming, making her jump on the stool where she sat next to the counter.

"Chance is fine, sweetheart," Angus said. "They're transporting him to Lufkin for arraignment, so I'm going to follow. I've got a lawyer meeting us there."

"You think the lawyer can get him bail?" She held her breath.

"Even if he can, sweetheart, if the charge is murder, it'll be at least half a million dollars."

"Half a million? Where am I supposed to find that much money?"

Angus huffed a frustrated breath. "Don't give up yet, sweetheart. You said you took pictures of the crime scene."

"Seventy-two exposures of everything from every angle."

"Good. I want you to go out and have two sets made. Mail one to Chance's office in Gabenburg and bring the other to the courthouse in Lufkin. It's off Frank Avenue."

"I'll make a copy of my notes, too, and include them in the packages." She spoke a note into the memo-minder on her key chain. "Okay, I've got a map. I'll meet you there."

"You drive safely, now, you hear. I don't want you or that baby of yours to come to no harm."

Taryn gasped. "How did you know?"

He laughed. "I could say it's my highly intuitive mind, but it's more your grandy's doing. Seems she found a pregnancy kit in your bathroom and she's blabbing the news she's gonna be a great-grandma all over town. Her chest is all puffed with pride every time she mentions that baby."

Taryn groaned. So much for keeping a secret. "What was she doing in my bathroom?"

"Laundry."

"Laundry?"

"She wanted the house all spiffed up for when you got back."

So much for Grandy's threat that she'd never acknowledge her granddaughter again. Not that Taryn had believed her for a second. Well, maybe a second, but not longer. Grandy had lost too much to throw away her last living relative. "Is Grandy driving you and Lucille crazy?"

"Not exactly."

"What do you mean, not exactly?"

His belly laugh shook over the phone. "She's holding court at the Bread and Butter."

Why didn't that surprise Taryn? And Grandy was probably driving half her clientele away with her gossip. How many times would Maud Rankin be willing to gush over

Grandy's baby news before taking her sweet tooth elsewhere? Especially since, much to Maud's chagrin, her own son and daughter were in no hurry to get married, let alone provide her with grandkids.

Angus continued, "Hired the MacKay girl to do some of the baking and she's running the storefront herself. You'll be glad to know, you're now offering a soup of the day to match your bread of the day."

Soup in the middle of June? Was Grandy crazy? "Is it selling?"

"Amazingly enough, there's a line every day at lunchtime. Your grandy was always a great cook."

"Well." Taryn didn't know what to say. Grandy's reaction to her pregnancy and her enthusiasm at running the shop were both unexpected.

"You may have a fight on your hands to take back control of the bakery when you get home."

When she got home. But first she had to free Chance. "Don't tell Chance about the baby. With the accident and everything else—" she blew out a breath "—I haven't had a chance to tell him."

"Then I won't take away your pleasure." There was a commotion in the background, shouts and the clink of chains. "They're leaving now. I gotta go."

"Okay, I'll get the pictures developed and meet you at the courthouse."

Trying not to think of Chance chained and dressed in prisoner-orange garb, Taryn launched into a flurry of activity. She packed the disposable cameras, her notes and a snack into her purse. Grabbing a bottle of ginger ale, she headed for the front door. She was startled to find Garth Ramsey on the other side, fist raised as if he'd been about to knock. She hadn't heard him drive up, yet there was a shiny white Cadillac gleaming in the sunshine.

"I'm sorry," he said, and flashed her a smile so brilliant as to be blinding. The sun glinted off his blond hair, adding to the impression of dazzle. "I didn't mean to startle you."

"I'm on my way out." She hugged her purse closer to her side.

"Kyle—I mean, Chance—is in trouble."

"I know, they're transferring him to Lufkin right now."

She tried to squeeze past Garth, but he put a gentle hand on her shoulder. "Before you head off after him, I'd like to talk to you for a minute."

"I really need to go."

"Won't take but a minute." This close, she could smell his expensive cologne. The scent reminded her of rich leather, fine cognac and aromatic cigars. Any other day, she might have found the aroma pleasant, but today it only managed to stir her stomach into upheaval.

"I've got pull," he said, "and if we can come to an agreement, maybe I can use some of that pull to free your husband."

She eyed him warily. "What kind of agreement?"

He eased on inside. Taking her elbow, he guided her to the living-room cluster in a smooth move. She wanted to tug out of his grip, but the touch was light and nonthreatening, making her wonder at the sharp distaste souring her mouth. Was it just the nausea coming back? Graciously, he held her hand as she sat down on one of the chairs. Straightening the perfect creases of his tan pants, he sat across from her.

"Kyle and Kent and I grew up together. Kyle, Chance—" He shook his head. "I just can't get used to callin' him Chance."

"It's the name I know him by."

"I know, darlin', and I'd like to help you. That's why I came by. Like I said, Kent and Kyle and I grew up together.

Ms. Makepeace used to call us the Three Musketeers. I think I spent more nights under this roof than my own till the twins' accident. They were like brothers to me.''

She opened her mouth to speak, but he held up a hand. ''I know, you're gonna say I was hard on him when he came to see me at my office, but I had to be. Ellen is my wife. She's my first concern. Surely, you can understand my position.''

''Of course.'' Chance was first in her life, too, and she'd do anything to make sure he was safe.

''I'd like to help you,'' Garth said.

''I don't see how you can.''

''Like I said, I've got a bit of pull.''

''What kind of pull?''

''In my line of work, I meet a lot of people, wheel and deal, grant favors. I can place a phone call or two and make sure your husband is offered bail.''

She was reluctant to trust this man, to become dependent on him for any favor. ''My father-in-law brought a lawyer—''

Garth chuffed. ''A lawyer won't do him much good against Carter's determination. You've got to know someone who can put a bug in the right person's ear.''

''And that would be you.''

''That would be me.'' He nodded and leaned forward. ''I don't want to see Kyle behind bars. I'm willin' to pay the bail myself.''

''What's the catch?''

He chuckled. ''Kyle got himself one smart lady. He always did have an eye for quality.'' He straightened and slung an arm casually over the back of the sofa. ''As I'm sure you understand, with Carter bein' my father-in-law, it wouldn't look good for me to go against him on his stand against Kyle. If I give you the bail money, no one can know where it came from.''

"Not even Chance?"

"Sorry, darlin'. This has to be our little secret."

She hadn't kept anything from Chance since the day they'd met—except for her pregnancy, and he'd know about that if it weren't for the accident. She didn't like adding an extra barrier of caution between them.

"And once he's freed, I want you to make sure he goes back to Gabenburg."

That was too easy, too close to her own desire. She had to be missing something, but what? "Why?"

"Because if he's back where he belongs, he'll be out of Carter's reach. I don't want him hurt any more than you do."

"After what you say he did to Ellen, how can you be so forgiving?"

He reached forward and squeezed her knee. His fingers lingered too long on her skin. Although the touch was light, the fingers felt like talons. She eased her knees sideways. He took the hint and sat back, elbows at his side, fingers interlaced and tented above his lap.

"I haven't forgotten," he said. "But I also remember all the times he and Kent got me out of hot water. I owe him this one." He shrugged. "If he stays, I won't be able to guarantee his safety."

Another convenient accident arranged by Sheriff Paxton? Another shot ringing out unexpectedly in the night? Another nightmare yet to be imagined? Would Chance be safer in jail or out here where they could at least see danger coming and try to get out of its way? The questions tossed and turned like the bad dream they were, miring her in indecision, until she didn't think she could handle any more stress. She wanted to grab Chance and head home and forget any of this had ever taken place. "I want him home even more than you do."

He flashed her another of his bright smile. "So we're agreed."

The brown eyes were clear and frank. The face appeared affable enough. Honesty seemed to pour off him like sweet milk. Why was she so ready to believe he was all hat and no cattle when he was going out of his way to help a child-hood friend?

Because, until Chance, she'd never known that type of enduring friendship. Because she'd been raised never to trust strangers. Because life's lessons had taught her not to rely on others for her well-being. But what choice did she have? Chance couldn't survive behind bars—not alone, not without his memories, not with all the guilt he wore like a horsehair shirt. With too much time to think, he would drown in his own despair. And caged, he'd make too easy a target for Sheriff Paxton's unrequited revenge.

She'd do anything—even bargain with the devil—to save Chance from that miserable fate. With him out of jail, they could try to prove he hadn't murdered Joely Brahms.

And if she set everything right, she could fill the missing scene behind Chance's nightmare. Maybe then, the memories would tumble back and she could show him he was a good man, not the monster he thought he was. Nature didn't change. She was sure, despite all evidence, that he wasn't Kyle.

And if he wasn't Kyle, then they would never have to set foot in Ashbrook or Lufkin again. She could have her life back. Their future as husband and wife, as parents, was worth the price of a breath of silence.

"We're agreed." She hitched her purse onto her shoulder. He offered her his hand. Reluctantly she shook it. "As soon as he's released, we'll head on home."

"Good." Garth nodded. "I'll get the ball rollin'."

AFTER THE COURTHOUSE'S artificial light, the evening sunlight outside blinded Chance.

His arraignment ordeal in Lufkin was followed by transportation back to Ashbrook to process the release paperwork. The sheriff had taken his sweet time, double crossing every *t*, triple dotting every *i* before setting him free.

Chance blinked several times. When his vision came into focus, the first thing he saw was Taryn waiting for him at the bottom of the stone steps. Something in him shifted, warmed, settled.

Taryn. His wife, his lover, his friend.

He loved her so much his heart was heavy with the feeling. He wanted to race down those steps, take her into his arms and hold her forever.

But he couldn't.

If she thought he'd regained any part of his memory, she'd insist on finding the rest. He couldn't stay here. He couldn't risk any harm coming to her. Every minute they spent in Sheriff Paxton's arena of influence spelled danger. Paxton's raging reaction to the bail sentencing had echoed in the courtroom like laments of the damned. The roar of outrage had continued when bail was posted for him. The sheriff's warning as Chance was handed back his belongings still echoed in his ears.

Sheriff Paxton would not give up on revenge. Not by a long shot.

Chance found himself scanning every rooftop, every corner for a sniper with a rifle. He couldn't ease his vigilance—not until they were home in Gabenburg, where his own circle of influence would help protect Taryn.

Coming up behind him, Angus gently slapped an open palm on his back. "I'm gonna go get the car and meet you at the rental drop-off, then we can go to the campground to pick up Lucille's car and get on home.''

Chance nodded. ''The sooner, the better.''

Angus leaned in close and whispered, ''Go on, son. Go kiss that wife of yours.'' After another encouraging thump to the shoulder, Angus was gone.

Stepping down to Taryn, an odd nervousness danced inside Chance. His fingers itched to touch her. His mouth watered at the thought of a kiss. A helpless groan of desire formed low in his throat. Swallowing it back was like eating glass. But if he touched her, if he kissed her, if he held her, she would know. He'd never been able to keep anything from her. That had been the hallmark of their relationship from the start. Cards on the table—the good, the bad, the ugly. Keeping this secret from her felt like betrayal.

''Where did you park?'' That wasn't what he wanted to say at all. *I remember, Taryn. Our love. Our marriage. Our plans. The past fifteen years are mine again. I love you.* That's what he'd tell her if he could.

She stuffed her hands in the pockets of her shorts. Rocking one foot from side to side, she eyed him with a wariness that made him curse the heat, the humidity, the memories hiding and resurfacing in the folds of his brain.

''Down the road a bit,'' she said. ''Want me to go get the car?''

''No, let's walk.'' There was no way he was letting her out of his sight until they reached Gabenburg.

Stiffly, they walked side by side. The sheen of sweat dewed her face in the nearly unbreathable air. She looked exhausted and pale. When they got home, he'd make her soak in a tub. He'd cook her a meal. He'd rub her back. He'd let her sleep for a day. And when she was all nice and rested, he'd make love to her until she fell asleep in his arms, sated and relaxed.

She unlocked the door, slipped into the passenger's side and handed him the keys. Her gaze, wide and open, scanned him like an X ray. Could she sense the change in him?

"We're going to meet Angus at the rental drop-off," he said, "then head-on home after we pick up Lucille's car."

"I know." She fiddled with the strap of her purse, her frowning gaze riveted to her lap. "We've got to stop by the cabin for my things."

"Okay."

"I think we ought to make a detour by the river while we're there."

"No." He overcranked the starter, making it whine.

"This might be your last chance to remember. The sun, the heat—"

"No."

"Be reasonable."

The engine started with a roar. Chance switched the air-conditioning to maximum. A hot draft blasted his face. Sweat dripped down his back. The seat belt stuck to his T-shirt. "Reasonable is leaving this hellhole as soon as possible."

"I've got to get my things."

Her voice was close to a whine, and that only made Chance worry more. Taryn never whined. The closest she'd come was two winters ago when she had the stuffy-head-itchy-eyes-drippy-nose-sneezing kind of flu and the stomach flu at the same time.

"Are you all right?" He maneuvered his way out of town, checking every shadow for a phantom enemy.

"I'm fine. I just need some ginger ale."

"We'll get you some once we're on the road."

"I've got a bottle left at the cabin. I need to get my stuff. Why don't you just drop me off, meet Angus and come back to get me."

"No."

"It'll save time. I want to get back home as soon as possible, too."

"Where did you get the bail money?" he asked to derail her from that hard-and-narrow track he didn't want to visit.

"Does it matter?"

"Yes."

She wouldn't look at him. Gaze narrowed, she stared out at the passing scenery of pines. "I borrowed it."

"From who?"

She rounded on him. Her face was flushed too red. Her eyes were too close to tears. "I got you out, that's all that matters."

His jaw stiffened. He stared at the road. Taryn had a secret, too. He didn't like that. Not one bit. After enduring ten years of openness envied by all who knew them, the doors between them were slamming shut faster than a farmer closing his barn before a tornado.

"Stop the car!" She leaned forward, one hand over her mouth, the other cradling her stomach.

Before the car was stopped all the way, she shouldered open the door and emptied the contents of her stomach on the side of the road. He stood by her helplessly, wishing he could take her place. When she was done, he handed her the bottle of water that had been sitting in the car all day. She took a swig of the hot water and rinsed out her mouth.

"Take me to the cabin, please." She heaved herself to her feet, then collapsed into the car. "I need to sit for a bit."

As much as he wanted to, as much as every instinct in

him screamed, he couldn't refuse her. Not when she was sick. "Okay."

Once at the cabin, he made her lie down on the couch, wet a cloth and laid it on her forehead, then held her up as she sipped a few swallows of warm ginger ale.

She looked too pale and drawn. "You ought to see a doctor as soon as we get back."

Eyes closed, she nodded. "Go drop off the rental and meet Angus."

"What if you get worse?"

She shook her head. "I'll be okay. I just need to sit for a few minutes while the nausea passes."

He couldn't get Sheriff Paxton's warning out of his head. *I'll get you or I'll get yours. Either way, Makepeace, Ellen will be avenged.* But he couldn't ask Taryn to get into a hot car and ride on bumpy roads in her condition. "Are you sure?"

She nodded. "I'm perfectly healthy."

"Not from where I'm looking."

Her half smile eased a slice off his worry. "Geez, Chance, with lines like that you'll never get very far."

If she could crack a joke, she'd be okay. He fingered a lock of her hair. "I'm only interested in the lines that'll make you melt in my arms."

She slit one eye open. "You are?"

He kissed her temple. "Of course."

With both thumbs he caressed her cheeks. She'd be okay here. No one had followed them. If anything, Sheriff Paxton would have Lucille's car under surveillance. What better place for an old-fashioned ambush than in the thick of the woods where it was easy enough to make a body disappear? Taryn would be better off here where no one expected her to be. "I want you to wait for me. I'm going to lock the door. Don't answer to anyone but me. Got that?"

She nodded.

Gently, he shook her shoulders. "Taryn, it's important."

She opened her eyes and the deep blue took his breath away. "I'll wait for you."

He could almost hear the echo of forever in her voice. Swallowing hard, he rose. "I'll be back in no time."

"I'll wait for you."

With that, he left, heart in his throat.

TARYN COULD NOT BELIEVE she'd puked her guts out on the side of the road. Embarrassing, to say the least. And when Chance had looked at her so worried, she'd been afraid he'd guess about the baby. She didn't want to blurt out this kind of news with her mouth tasting sour, on her hands and knees on the side of a road in the middle of nowhere. She wanted to be home where their love had created that child. She wanted the moment to be special.

Dragging herself from sofa to chair to stool, she made her way to the kitchen and nibbled on saltines. In all the commotion at the courthouse in Lufkin, then with the long wait at the courthouse in Ashbrook, she'd forgotten to eat lunch. Now it was dinnertime. She was paying the price for her neglect. When she most needed her strength, it was deserting her.

She sipped ginger ale. Something about the way Chance had looked at her before he left had given her a surge of renewed hope. She'd seen the old Chance again. That crooked smile, the teasing voice, the gentle touch. He was in there somewhere.

Swiping her wet hair from her forehead, she realized she had one last opportunity to set the scene and make him remember the facts as well as the feelings of that day fifteen years ago. She couldn't pass it up.

She riffled through her purse and found paper and a pen.

Quickly, she scribbled a note, then hiked her purse over her shoulder.

With the bottle of ginger ale in hand, she unlocked the door and strode through it. Looking at the sun setting over the trees, she said, "I'll be waiting for you, Chance."

Chance—
The heat was too much. I decided to cool down by the river. I'll be waiting for you.

Love,
Taryn

Garth carefully placed the note back on the kitchen counter and strode out to his car, leaving the cabin's front door open.

He'd sent a boy to do a man's job. Not once, but three times. That was two more mistakes than he usually allowed. Carter was too volatile to be trusted. His hired gun couldn't seem to hit more than one target. He'd take care of the problem himself.

Makepeace was going to go in the river, and this time, he wasn't going to come out.

Chapter Fourteen

Taryn walked along the river until she found an open spot where the sun hit the water. She applied her last ribbon of paper to a low-hanging hickory branch. With the trail she'd marked, Chance could easily find her.

She wiped away a strand of damp hair from her forehead, plucked at the T-shirt sticking to her chest and took a look around.

A cocoon of trees surrounded the clearing, creating an enchanting oasis. The sound of a squirrel chewing on a nut carried over the still air above the din of running water. Sun touched the treetops, shone golden-red through the leaves then shimmered crimson on the ripples of the Red Thunder River. The chirr of cicadas added a jingly counterpoint to the early-evening concert. The whine of mosquitoes provided the only sour note.

Using the cardboard backing from her pad of paper, she fanned herself and sat on the riverbank. She took off her canvas shoes and cooled her feet in the rushing water.

She'd barely caught her breath, when the crack of a branch made her whirl her head around. "Chance?"

A head of hair gleaming reddish-gold in the setting sun appeared from between two pines. "Sorry, darlin'. It's me."

"Garth, what are you doing here?"

Garth brushed pine needles from the sleeves of his light-weight jacket. "Well, you see, I've got myself a little problem that needs takin' care of."

"What kind of problem?"

"Chance."

Not until this moment had Taryn realized how isolated this spot was. Suddenly, she felt as vulnerable as a turtle without its shell. The leer in Garth's eyes didn't help dispel her uneasiness, not when he seemed to undress her and taste her with just a crooked look. Barefoot, she couldn't outrun him. She had no weapon but her purse, and unless she got close enough to clobber him with it, that would do her no good.

Keep 'em moving, keep 'em talking. That had been Grandy's advice to her on dating. They can't get you in trouble if they're moving and talking. She drew her feet out of the water and spun around on her bottom to face Garth. He was leaning against a tree, looking relaxed and nonthreatening.

Maybe she was overreacting. Maybe the reason he was here was sentimental and not sinister. Maybe he just wanted to know why she hadn't kept up her part of their agreement.

"We're leaving," she said, scrambling to her feet. "Chance just went to pick up the car at the campground. As soon as he's back, we'll be on our way to Gabenburg and you won't have to worry about Carter or about Ellen." God, she was babbling. This wasn't going to do her any good.

"I know. And we'll wait right here until he comes to fetch you."

Okay, so he just wanted to be sure they really left. Nothing wrong with that. But she couldn't seem to stop shaking inside. Her anxiety spilled outward in a spew of words.

"You won't lose your bail money. Chance'll show up for the trial. He's in law enforcement. He knows how these things work."

"I'm not worried." He waved a hand at her. "Why don't you have a seat. Might take a while."

"Oh, no. He should be back any minute now. He was dropping off the rental, then he and Angus were going to pick up the car, and Angus was going to go home and Chance was going to come pick me up." *Shut up, Taryn. Just shut up.* She hugged her purse in front of her like a shield.

"Sit."

Like a docile child, she obeyed. The keys in her pocket dug into her thigh when she sat down. "He won't be long. We'll be on our way. You don't have to worry about him being around."

"I need to have a private conversation with your Chance." He looked around. "You found it."

"Found what?"

"This is where Kyle and Kent fought and ended up in the river."

"I'LL MAKE SURE you're both on your way," Angus said from the rolled-down window of his car, "then I'll follow you out."

Chance nodded and trotted over to the cabin. He came to a sudden halt. The door was wide open. "Something's wrong."

Cautiously, Chance made his way to the cabin. There was no activity, no sound. His pulse jumped. His heart sped. "Taryn?"

A quick glance at the living room showed him the sofa was empty.

Angus joined him. "You're worrying too much. Last we saw the sheriff, he was still trying to untangle the red tape."

"No. The sheriff's car followed us from the rental place. Taryn? Where are you?"

No answer. The stillness inside the house raced goose bumps down Chance's back. The rusty red light of evening filtered through the dirty windows, making the interior look bathed in blood.

"She's not here," Chance said.

"Let's check to make sure. Maybe she fell asleep."

"Then why was the front door wide open?"

"She's fine, son." Angus disappeared into one of the bedrooms.

Chance circled the open space and ended in the kitchen. On the kitchen counter, he found Taryn's note.

Angus came up behind him. "See, I told you. She's all right. She just went by the river. I'll go with you."

Swearing, Chance crumpled the note. "I told her to wait for me."

Somehow, he must have given himself away. He'd known this would happen, that she would try to force his memory to return.

"She *is* waiting for you, son," Angus said.

Chance turned and faced Angus. "You don't seem worried at all."

"There's no reason. The sheriff can't afford to hurt you before he gets you into court."

But the drooping of the corner of his eyes, his mouth, said otherwise. As Angus tried to walk away, Chance detained him. "Angus?"

"She just wanted to give you this one last gift. Won't take but a few more minutes to go check it out. If it doesn't jog your memory, we'll be on our way."

"You knew." The ticking inside Chance's chest was like a flock of birds pecking at his flesh. "You knew."

Angus seemed to wither before his eyes. He slumped onto a stool like an old man. He gave a sad shake of his head. "There seemed no reason to say anything when you were so happy."

"Taryn—"

"Is waiting for you by the river. I would never do anything to put her in danger."

"Tell me why you're so sure she's not in any danger."

"I tried to make her stay home and wait for you." Angus looked away. Eyes unfocused, he talked. "When I found you, Lucille was with me. We were on our way to the farmer's market when the call came in. You know how she likes to go every Saturday morning."

Chance nodded, wondering if the pain of betrayal would ease with time.

"You also know we had a son, Tyler. We lost him when he was twelve. Drowned in that same damn river." He shook his head. "Part of Lucille died the day we lost him." He turned to look at Chance. "That part came back to life the day we found you."

"She thought I was Tyler?"

"No, she didn't delude herself that badly." He shrugged. "I just couldn't take another son away from her, even—maybe especially—after I found the truth."

"Which was?"

"That there was nothing for you here. Your parents were dead. Your grandfather was a drunk. Lucille, she needed a son to love...." He held his hands up helplessly. "I thought everything here would settle itself, that's why I wasn't worried when you set off. I thought you'd find what you needed and come back home where you belong."

Anger burned in Chance's chest, deadening him. "You were wrong."

Angus nodded. "Taryn's waiting for you."

The longer they stayed here, the greater their danger. Despite Angus's belief that Carter wanted a legal outcome for his loss, Chance couldn't forget the sheriff's threat. A man who'd waited fifteen years for revenge would take it any way he could. Chance couldn't relax until Ashbrook was nothing but a dot in his rearview mirror.

He'd spotted a sheriff's car following him. Leading them to an isolated area wasn't the smartest move to make. But what choice did he have? He couldn't leave Taryn behind. He needed her home where she was safe.

Regaining his memory would mean nothing to him if he lost Taryn in the process. "Let's get this over with."

He parked Lucille's car where the sheriff couldn't miss it, then, driving Angus's Jeep, they cut across the razed forest to the abandoned mill. They backtracked to the trail-head. After hiding the vehicle behind some bushes, they jogged onto the trail.

HER MOUTH DROPPED OPEN and her eyes widened, just as Garth knew they would. She was as easy to read as fiction.

"Tell me about that day," Taryn said, her voice squeaking like a mouse. And what a pretty mouse she was. Even with sweat plastering a strand of her brown hair against her forehead, there was something sensual about her. It was those incredible eyes, he decided. That smoky blue against the soft pink of her skin and her gentle features promised a hidden excitement.

But he wasn't going to taste it. Not today. He had other plans for her, for her husband.

"We were sittin' here." He pointed to a group of three trees hugged close together. "John Henry was away on one of his binges, so we'd picked up some burgers and fries at the Burger Station. Place closed about five years back.''

''I thought Ellen was here, too.''

''No, she didn't come till later.''

How much should he say? There was no danger in the truth. Not today. Besides, he liked seeing her eyes widen with shock, that pretty mouth of hers open like an invitation. Maybe he would take a sample after all. Who would know? Who would care? By day's end, she'd be just another victim of Kyle's rage.

''Why did you marry Ellen?'' Taryn sat cross-legged, body rounded. Her gaze darted here and there as if looking for an escape. But he knew her type. She'd stay as long as he told her to. She wouldn't give him any problems. Not until Chance got here. And he was prepared for that event.

Garth shrugged. ''I married Ellen because it was convenient.''

''Convenient?''

''I'd gotten in a spot of trouble and the sheriff needed some monetary assistance for Ellen's care. He didn't like her bein' in the state facility. He wanted the best and the best meant private care. Of course, on a sheriff's salary, he couldn't afford it.'' He slanted her a sheepish grin. ''And I'd done quite well for myself buyin' and sellin' real estate. You could say I had a nose for investment.''

She nervously licked her lips. ''So you came to an agreement.''

Garth chuckled. ''That we did.''

''I still don't get why you married her.''

A dutiful wife like her probably wouldn't understand the logic of such an arrangement. The marriage was a technicality that any court could overturn, should anyone care to look at the paperwork. But who would? ''Havin' an invalid wife allows me the freedom of relationships without the danger of permanent entanglements, if you know what I mean.''

"The pity angle?"

"The best of both worlds. A wife who can't object and a ring to ward off the messy expectations of matrimony."

He could see his image tarnishing for her. Too bad.

"Why was Ellen here?" she asked.

Garth was disappointed at her obvious disgust. "She was trying to win back her man. She didn't want Kyle to take the job he'd been offered out on a ranch in West Texas. They broke up over the fact."

Her eyebrows scrunched in confusion. "So it was Ellen and Kyle who were arguing?"

"No. She was tryin' to get to Kyle by cozyin' up to Kent."

"Kyle didn't like it." She fanned herself lazily, pretending she was relaxed, but there was a jerky quality to her ease that didn't fool him.

"Not by half."

She glanced at her watch.

"Don't worry, darlin', I made sure your Chance would be able to find you." He'd left the note where he'd found it and hadn't touched a single one of Taryn's paper-trail markers. He'd hiked the woods with Kent often enough to know how to leave no trail of his own.

"I still don't understand how they ended up in the river."

"Kyle was in what we called one of his moods. He was lookin' to pick a fight. Kent didn't want to get involved so he was leavin'." And Garth had been bored enough to want to see a good fight culminate from this mood.

"Kyle pushed him in the water for stepping back from a fight?"

Garth shook his head. "He was mad at Ellen, so he took

it out on his brother. He shoved him, Kent fell backward and into the river." He could still see the fear on Kent's face, the shock on Kyle's. "The river was runnin' fast because of all the rain we'd had. Kent got swept away."

He strode toward her, stopped when she had to look up at him. "You want to know a secret nobody else knows?"

She shivered as if she'd read his intention. "No."

He crouched beside her, rested the side of his hands on her shoulders and cupped her nape with his fingers. "Kyle jumped in the water to save his brother."

"But you said—"

He shrugged. "I had a lot to protect."

"I don't understand."

"There was nothin' to be done for them. Kent didn't know how to swim and was petrified of water. Kyle was a good swimmer, but with that current, there was no way he could rescue his twin."

She swallowed hard, shifting backward, hiking her hands and purse up higher on her chest.

"Ellen, she wanted me to jump in, too," Garth continued. "But you see, I've always been good at sizin' up a situation, calculatin' the odds and makin' decisions. This one wasn't in my favor and I wasn't goin' to ruin a good future over losin' odds."

"So Ellen jumped in instead?" Her voice cracked.

He shook his head. "She tried blackmailin' me."

Her breathing quickened, shallowed. "With what?"

"I got myself a scholarship." He stroked the back of her neck, felt her shiver for him. "It was my ticket out of this one-stoplight town. She said she'd tell her father and the editor of the *Ashbrook Herald* and the committee that I got the inside track by gettin' Alice Addison to write the winnin' essay for me. Alice was on the committee, you see. She knew just what they were lookin' for."

"How did you get her to write your essay?"

He laughed. "She wanted sex. I gave it to her."

She gulped and swallowed. His pulse quickened. His taste for her sharpened. He leaned forward and whispered in her ear.

"Without that ticket, I couldn't have afforded an education. Now, in real life, a degree doesn't mean much, but it's an introduction. It tells people you're somebody even before you get a chance to prove it. I had plans, big plans. I needed that piece of paper and I needed the scholarship to get it. I wasn't about to let someone ruin it all for me just because I wasn't fool enough to jump in a ragin' river and die before I got to live."

"How did Ellen know about Alice Addison?"

He had to admire someone who could keep pushing even when she was scared halfway to death. In spite of the sweat pouring down the side of her face, the fresh scent of flowers after a rain wafted up to him.

"She saw me with my fly open." He exaggerated his drawl, knowing it sounded almost like a purr. "My hand was up horse-face Alice's skirt, my tongue halfway down her throat. Ellen'd come by to drop off a kitten Alice had wanted."

"What happened when you refused to help the twins?"

"Ellen pushed me. I pushed her." He rocked back on his heels and pointed at an outcropping of rocks. "She fell over there. Hit her head. I knew she'd talk, so I did the only thing I could."

"Which was?"

He stood, forcing Taryn to look up at him again. "I rolled her into the river and watched her drift away."

"But she made it out."

"Yes, she did." His gaze drifted to the stampeding water. He saw the scene again with crystal clarity. His jaw tightened. "Thanks to Kyle."

Taryn gasped. He looked down at her again, amused. "That's right, darlin', he shoved her on the shore and went back into the water after his brother."

She started fidgeting as if she were sitting on top of a fire-ant hill. "Kyle didn't try to kill Ellen?"

Garth sneered. "Fool tried to save both her and his brother. The river wasn't about to give all of them up. Not as hungry as it was."

"And Ellen hit her head because you pushed her."

Garth frowned. Taryn seemed eager now. Why? He bent down and pierced her gaze with his sharpest stare.

"When the search party got here, I conveniently found Ellen. She was still alive. I was plannin' on rollin' her back into the river, only the park ranger chose that time to appear, and I had to make it look as if I was attemptin' to save her."

He wrapped his hand around her ponytail and yanked it until her neck was extended and exposed. "I got in one good hit. Thankfully it scrambled her mind." There was no one left to deny whatever story he made up. There would be no one this time, either.

"The blow was enough to keep her in a coma for a couple of years. Then the care at the private facility was workin' too well."

Her eyes were so lovely when they were wide with fear. Her pale skin was temptation itself. Her swallows were making him hard.

"What do you mean?"

"The trick to influence," he said, "is findin' out what's in it for the other guy, givin' him what he wants in exchange for what you want. Ellen got a little help to keep her brain scrambled."

Taryn gasped. "You drugged her."

He raised his eyebrows. "I gave her peace."

He dropped his hold on the ponytail and rose. "I thought they'd both drowned. I was real surprised to see Kent again after all this time."

"Kent, but—"

He grinned and cocked his head. "I thought he was Kyle, too. All that anger. It had to be Kyle. Then I saw the scars on his shoulders."

Kyle was easy to manipulate. His anger was his downfall. As long as Carter believed Chance Conover was Kyle Makepeace, any accident that happened to "Kyle" wouldn't be investigated too closely. Kent was another matter. So he'd swiped the fingerprint report from the fax machine. "Kyle" would be dead before Carter could order a second set, and the point would become moot. His secrets would stay safe.

"I don't understand," Taryn said. The least he could do is let her die knowing the man she loved was as honorable as she thought he was.

"When he was five, Kent crawled into a drainage ditch to retrieve a ball. He got stuck. Kyle and I poured water over him, thinkin' that would make him slip out. It didn't. So we pulled him out by his feet. Tore his shoulders up bad."

"I thought the scars had come from being tossed in the river."

"We learn something new every day, don't we?"

"Well," Taryn said, getting up, "I've enjoyed our conversation, but I'd better get going. After all, I did promise you I'd get Chance out of town, and it's getting late."

"Stay." From under his jacket, he pulled out a gun. The movement caught the sun, making the barrel flash. He'd always enjoyed a bit of drama.

She froze. Her eyes grew impossibly wide. He imagined that's what she looked like in the throes of an orgasm. But work always came before pleasure. He had to preserve what he'd built.

She clutched her purse with both hands until her fingertips were red from the effort. "Is that really necessary?"

"I'm afraid so." He chuckled, waving the gun around. "It has no emotions."

Then he pressed the muzzle of the pistol against her temple. Marring this beautiful face was a shame, but there was no getting around the problem.

The scenario was all planned out. Guns were easy enough to come by. It was human nature to follow patterns. Angry because his wife had accepted bail money from his ex-girlfriend's husband, Kyle had flown into a rage and executed Taryn. Then realizing what he'd done, he'd pushed her into the river and turned the gun on himself, following her to her watery grave like some Romeo after his Juliet.

Why wouldn't everyone believe it? History was repeating itself.

"You'll be dead before you can feel the pain, darlin'. I promise."

Chapter Fifteen

With Garth's gun pressed against her temple, Taryn's mind scrambled to the past. She was twenty-one watching her mother die. Blood and brain sprayed all over her. Her own scream echoed in her mind, paralyzing her with fear.

She didn't want to die. Not then. Not now.

Chance's insistence she learn to handle a weapon was worthless in the face of this lethal power ready to blow a hole through her head. This time there was no dodging the bullet. Not this close.

Chance, where are you?

You've got to face the thing you fear. When you're facing that gun, you've got to be willing to get shot. Chance's words floated in the chaos swirling in her mind.

Be willing to get shot. How she'd balked at that concept. It went against every survival instinct. In the face of danger, you ran, you fought, you screamed, you did *something*. You didn't calmly face the weapon and accept to be shot. To do so meant accepting death. Hers and her baby's. And Chance's. Because the hard edge to Garth's gaze told her there would be no survivors here today.

To give her unborn child life, to give Chance the truth of his past, she had to be willing to take that bullet.

Once she made the choice, the chaos in her mind van-shed. In its place fell a calm so serene, the whole world seemed to slow. Every detail of the woods surrounding her came into sharp focus. The green of the leaves, the roughness of the bark, the rusty litter at her feet. The scent of Garth's cologne became a locator beacon.

Her breath puffed evenly. The drum of her pulse beat unhurried. Options opened before her. She remembered all the self-defense moves Chance had insisted she learn. They flowed from her instinctively.

She had all the time she needed.

She dropped her purse. With an open palm, she slapped Garth's forearm. The gun dislodged from her temple. Before Garth could straighten, she cuffed him on the ear with the opposite hand, knocking his sense of balance for a loop. Then she swept his feet from under him. He pitched onto his back. The wind was knocked out of him. Stepping on the wrist of his right gun hand, she released the weapon from his grip, then pointed it at him.

"You wouldn't use it," he said, looking up at her. For the first time since she'd met him, his hair wasn't perfectly coiffed and his air of smooth confidence looked rumpled.

Taryn took the balanced stance Chance had shown her. Braced as she was, this close, there was no way she could miss, and Garth had to know it.

He tried to scuttle on his back.

"Don't move."

"You can't pull the trigger," he said. "It's not in your nature."

"Go ahead, Garth," she said, teeth gritted, "just give me a reason."

He was wrong. Pulling that trigger was in her nature. She never would have believed Chance if he'd told her that faced with protecting the ones she loved, she would be willing to kill a man.

A feeling of fierceness growled in her. She had a child
to defend and she wasn't about to give Garth an inch.
Crouching carefully, she reached for her purse and her cell
phone. Never wavering from her aim, she dialed Angus's
number and got no answer. She pondered for a moment
and dialed 911. She had proof. The sheriff would have to
listen.

As she stood there, gun aimed at Garth's chest, waiting
for help, a terrible sense of sadness swamped her. She
thought back to ten years ago, to the night she'd lost her
mother. Instead of worrying over a few lost dollars, her
mother should have emptied the till, shoved the money at
the thief, told her daughter to run—anything to save the
life of the child she'd brought into the world. But she'd
grown so hard and bitter that her values had warped. Taryn
swiped at the tears running down her cheeks.

Garth took advantage of her momentary lapse in vigilance, jumped up and advanced toward her. He extended a
hand forward, smiled his most brilliant smile. "Give me
the gun, Taryn. I know you don't want to use it. Just give
it to me."

She squeezed the trigger, deliberately grazing his biceps.
He fell to one knee, gaped at the red stain coloring his
jacket. "You could have killed me!"

"Believe me, if I'd wanted you dead, you'd *be* dead."

THE SOUND OF A GUN ripping through the air momentarily
paralyzed Chance.

Taryn.

The single word propelled him forward. He fought off
the wave of terror sweeping over him and sprinted as fast
as he could. Taryn. He had to help her.

"Chance, wait," Angus called after him, but Chance ignored him, pounding into the dense foliage of fully leafed trees.

He should slow down. He should call for backup. He should do a million things, but he could focus only on one thought—getting to Taryn.

Weapon. What could he use for a weapon? His gun was held in evidence. His diving knife was at home. "Angus, hand me your weapon."

"Not when you're running this hot."

Chance cursed and snagged a branch on the fly. *Taryn, wait for me. Hang on.* Leg muscles straining over the uneven path, breath burning in his lungs, he shot into the clearing and came to a grinding halt.

There before him stood Taryn like some Valkyrie, holding a quivering Garth Ramsey at gunpoint.

Chance didn't know what he'd expected, but this wasn't it. Relief was so great, he deflated like a nicked balloon.

She turned her head and smiled at him. "Well, it's about time."

Out of the corner of his eye, Chance saw Garth move. Before he could react, Garth snapped an arm around Taryn's neck. One good yank and he could break her neck. The gun was in his left hand and aimed at Angus, who'd just walked onto the clearing.

"Looks like we've got ourselves a bit of a situation," Garth said.

Chance couldn't move. Any movement would cause the death of one of the people he cared for the most. Whatever Angus had failed to tell him, one thing couldn't be denied—he'd been a good father to him, and his and Lucille's love had given him an anchor from which he'd built his life with Taryn.

Staring at Angus, Garth said, "Drop the gun, old man."

"Taryn, sweetheart, are you all right?" Angus asked as he placed his weapon on the ground.

"Shut up, old man. Kick the gun toward me."

Angus did as instructed.

"I'm fine," Taryn said, but her voice was strained over the arm crushing her vocal chords.

Chance gripped the oak branch in his hand tighter and wished he could whip it against Ramsey's head. But he couldn't make a mistake. Not with Taryn's life in the balance.

"Maybe we can reach an agreement," Taryn croaked. "What do you want?"

"It's too late for agreements," Garth said.

Garth was in too deep, Chance realized. He couldn't let any of them get away.

Red Thunder rumbled. Sweat slicked Chance's skin. He didn't like being cornered like this. He wanted to rush forward and pluck Taryn from the arms of danger. But rushing at this stage would set the stage for a scuffle. Someone would get hurt. Red-hot rage burned in his chest.

Something flashed across his brain. A picture, fully formed. *Can you stop the river?*

Swallowing back the bitter taste in his mouth, Chance spoke calmly. "It takes a lot to stop a river."

"What did you say?" Garth's eyes widened with shock.

Chance would have only one opportunity to save Taryn and Angus. He would have to count on both of them reacting without thinking.

Priming himself for action, he yelled, "Get down!"

Everything happened at once. Angus flattened to the ground. Taryn sank, her weight taking Garth with her. He hauled her back up. But with his grasp loosened, she could butt her head into his forehead. Garth brought his gun around to Chance, opening his stance. With the advantage of momentum, Taryn rolled sideways, wrenching Garth's arm and freeing herself from his grip. Chance rammed Garth with all his might. Angus rushed forward, protecting Taryn with his body.

The sandy bank crumbled beneath the weight of Chance's and Garth's bodies. The river roared around them as they smacked into the turbulent water. Surrounding them, it whirled and spun them downriver.

Taryn screamed.

At that sound of pure despair, something cracked. From the deep recesses of his mind, memories spilled like a stack of dropped photographs. The fight. The fall. The hands pushing down on him. The body bumping up against him. Hanging on to a tree for his life. Water streaming over him. He couldn't breathe.

Then all the pieces fell together in one flowing picture, and he knew. He relived the fear that had paralyzed him, that had warped and stolen his memory, that had nearly killed him. Midgasp, he remembered how to breathe, how to use the water, how to make it his friend.

Red Thunder had no more power over him.

Someone latched onto him, dragging him down. Chance didn't fight the downward momentum. His lung capacity was great. He could hold his breath for a full two and a half minutes.

Garth quit struggling, and with powerful strokes Chance swam for shore. He dragged Garth onto the bank.

"Chance, Chance, where are you?" Taryn's voice floated to him from beyond the trees. Never had anything sounded so beautiful.

As his mind scrambled to order all the information resurfacing, one thing became clear—Taryn's love. Through all this nightmare, it was the one constant. She'd given him his past. She was his future. He was the luckiest man on earth.

"Over here."

Taryn and Angus crashed through a cluster of bushes. Garth squirmed like a beached fish, gasping for breath. Chance raised his fist. With both hands around his, Taryn stopped the downward blow.

"This nightmare is over, Chance, don't start a new one."

He looked up at her, at those blue eyes filled with love for him, and knew she was right.

The nightmare was over. All of it.

A CUFFED GARTH SAT crumpled on the ground, moaning about his injuries. Taryn had taken a quick look at his wound and his wrenched arm. He'd survive. The sheriff, along with two deputies, had walked onto the scene a moment earlier. He studied the faces before him, uncharacteristically silent.

"He's not Kyle," Taryn said to the sheriff as she hung on to Chance's arm. "He's Kent."

"I know," the sheriff said. "The prints didn't match." He nodded toward Garth. "He swiped them. I got the hospital to refax them."

Holding Taryn by the waist, Chance faced the sheriff. "I don't know what happened to Ellen, but Kyle didn't hurt her. She was already hurt when she floated down to the cove where I was stuck. Kyle put her back onshore, then came back to get me."

"I do." Taryn raced to her purse, rummaged through the contents and brought out her key chain. She pressed the Play button and Garth's mocking voice warbled onto the clearing.

"*Fool tried to save both her and his brother. The rive.*

wasn't about to give all of them up. Not as hungry as it was.''

''And Ellen hit her head because you pushed her.''

''When the search party got here, I conveniently found Ellen. She was still alive. I was plannin' on rollin' her back into the river, only the park ranger chose that time to appear, and I had to make it look as if I was attemptin' to save her.

''I got in one good hit. Thankfully it scrambled her mind.

''The blow was enough to keep her in a coma for a couple of years. Then the care at the private facility was workin' too well.''

''What do you mean?''

''The trick to influence is findin' out what's in it for the other guy, givin' him what he wants in exchange for what you want. Ellen got a little help to keep her brain scrambled.''

''You drugged her.''

''I gave her peace.''

The sheriff's face turned red. His fists were clenched. His body was so stiff, his muscles shook from the force. ''I trusted you.''

''I did what you wanted. I took care of Ellen.''

''If it weren't for you, she wouldn't have needed care in the first place.'' The sheriff rammed his foot into Garth's ribs. He was about to hit him again, but Chance and Angus held him back. ''You drugged her, you bastard. You kept her from me all these years.'' He spit in Garth's face. ''You are going to pay for this. You will rot in jail.''

''I've got records of everything you did for me.''

''I don't give a damn. I'd rather die behind bars than give you one more minute of freedom.''

The sheriff motioned to his deputy. ''Garth Ramsey,'' he said as they hefted Garth to his feet. ''You're charged with the attempted murder of Taryn Conover, Chance Conover and Angus Conover."

As he was marched back to the cruiser waiting on the old lumber road, Garth was read his rights.

"I'll need y'all to stop by the office and give a statement," the sheriff said. His defeated look reminded her of Billy Ray's aged bull, plodding in the pasture.

"If you'll excuse me," he said, tipping his hat at them, "I've got some phone calls to make."

As Angus started to follow the sheriff out, Chance said, "You were right, Angus, there was nothing here for me."

Angus's eyes watered and a small smile shook on his face. He gave a nod. "I'll wait for you at the station."

As THE LAST OF THE SUN bled into the river, Taryn stood next to Chance. She wrapped her arms around his waist and laid her head against his chest. The slow, even drumming of his heart soothed her.

She glanced at the water, still rippling golden red in the dying sunlight. "Do you think he survived?"

"Kyle?" Chance bent to place a kiss on top of her head. "I don't know."

She found herself hoping he had, that he'd found a good family like the Conovers to take him in, that he'd grown into an honorable man like his brother. She hoped that his memories weren't haunting him the way they were haunting Chance.

"I don't care," she said.

"About what?"

"If you never remember the life we had together."

"Taryn—"

She shook her head and placed a finger against his lips. "We'll just make new memories." She leaned back in his embrace so she could look into his eyes. "I'm pregnant. Come January, we're going to have a baby."

The shock of her announcement widened his eyes. A slow smile spread over his lips, tipped up slightly higher on the left side, lending his sharp features a boyish charm. "A baby? Really?" He cocked his head, and the look in his eyes was positively beaming with pride. "Had to have been the weekend we spent in Beaumont a couple of months ago."

It was her turn to gape. "You remember!"

He raked his fingers through her loosened hair, held her face in his hands and peered deeply into her eyes. There were no shadows left in his eyes, just a crystal clarity that reflected the goodness of his soul. "I remember everything. Our marriage, the accident—both of them. Everything."

A sudden pang of fear whittled at her newfound joy. "Being Kent?"

"Being Kent." He pressed her hard against his heart. "The dead eyes, the hair. They were Ellen's. She floated against the same tree I was hanging on to. Things are still a bit fuzzy, but I know Kyle wasn't trying to drown me. He was trying to save me. My foot got caught in an uprooted tree. He was pushing me down so he could release me. I panicked. That's what I saw. The face like mine above the water—it was my twin trying to save me."

He remembered all of his past. Not quite knowing how to phrase the question weighing heavy on her heart, she licked her lips. She fiddled with the mud encrusted on Chance's T-shirt.

"What's wrong?" Chance hiked her chin up until their gazes met once again.

"Who are you now?"

A heartwarming laugh boomed from him. "Who do you want me to be?"

"Whoever your heart tells you you are." She held her breath, not knowing what to expect.

He kissed her once, twice, three times. "Then I'm Chance Conover, husband, friend, sheriff."

"Oh, Chance." Arms snaking around his neck, she kissed him back.

When the kiss ended, Chance said, "You'll do to run the river with."

Heart glowing warm, she said, "You're not half-bad yourself."

He took her hand in his, and together they started up the path in the woods.

Epilogue

"It's time."

Chance tripped out of bed and stood rooted, helpless in the dark. "Now? Are you sure?"

"My water just broke."

Water had brought him to a new life fifteen years ago. New life was coming to him now with the discharge of water from Taryn's body.

I'm not ready, he wanted to say. He didn't think he'd ever be ready. He didn't know anything about kids, let alone about babies. Would he make a good father? What if he didn't do it right? He fumbled for the light switch and found it.

Blinking at the sudden brightness, he went from drawer to closet throwing on clothes. "Where's your bag?"

"By the door."

"Should I call your doctor?"

"I'll do it."

For the life of him, he couldn't remember where he'd put the keys to his truck.

"On the dresser," she said.

He grabbed the keys and the bag and darted through the door. Taryn, he forgot Taryn. She was shuffling behind him, one hand on her lower back, the other skimming the hallway wall. Then she doubled over.

Racing back to her, he dropped the keys and the bag. "Are you okay?"

She patted his cheek and puffed hard for a couple of breaths. "Contraction. I'm fine. Are you going to be okay to drive?"

"I'm fine. I'm fine." He took a couple of deep breaths. "I'm fine."

Somehow, they made it to the hospital, and five agonizing hours later, their daughter was born. Pink and wrinkled, she howled her way into the world. Taryn had done well. He was wrung out. While Taryn rested, he called Angus, Lucille and Nola. Another call to the station ensured RoAnn would let the whole town know about the birth.

He couldn't stop looking at his new little girl. Every few minutes, he found himself reaching into her bassinet and fingering the shock of dark hair on top of her head. His baby. His daughter.

There was a soft knock on the door and a blond head poked inside. "Hi."

"Ellen, come on in."

"Taryn's sleeping. I don't want to disturb her."

"I'm awake," Taryn said, waving their guest in. "I was just enjoying watching Chance cuddle his daughter."

Ellen squealed softly as she peered at the baby. "She's beautiful. What's her name?"

"Shauna Tyne," Chance said.

"It means 'present from the river.'"

"And what a present she is," Ellen agreed.

"Do you want to hold her?"

A shadow passed over Ellen's gray-green eyes. She shook her head. "I don't want to drop her." Her fine motor skills still needed work.

"You'll be fine." Taryn patted the bed next to her, inviting Ellen to sit. "Chance…"

Chance picked up his daughter. She weighed nothing and he could understand Ellen's reluctance. He was glad enough to place her into Taryn's arms.

"What are you doing at the hospital?" Taryn asked Ellen.

"A pain and torture session. I'm due at physical therapy in a few minutes, but I heard you were here and I had to visit."

Ellen's recovery was nothing short of miraculous. She'd regained most of her strength, bought a piece of land outside of town and was starting a new life. She didn't take kindly to any meddling, even the well-meaning kind.

"I'm picking up my own baby in a few days," Ellen said. Her smile reminded him of a pixie with a trick up her sleeve.

"You're adopting?" Taryn asked, gawking at the child in her arms.

Ellen nodded. "A beautiful dappled gray mare. She was in an accident at the racetrack and she needs slow recovery—just like me."

"Are you sure you're strong enough?" Chance asked. He worried about her all on her own, but she insisted that after living in a cage for fifteen years, she was ready for some freedom.

She laughed. "If I can handle all the stretching and mauling they put me through downstairs, I can handle anything."

And the look in her eye said she just might.

Shauna Tyne, realizing she was no longer the center of attention, made her presence known with a bawling cry. Taryn fussed over her and soon the child contentedly suckled at her mother's breast.

He barely registered Ellen tiptoeing out of the room. The look of contentment on Taryn's and Shauna's faces was one he wanted to memorize.

Right here, right now, he couldn't think of anywhere else he wanted to be. He wrapped an arm around Taryn's shoulder. She tipped her head up to smile at him, then leaned her head against his chest. Heart overflowing with love, with his wife and his child by his side, he was home where he belonged.

*   *   *   *   *

What happened to Kyle Makepeace?
Find out next month in
the final installment of

FLESH AND BLOOD:
RED THUNDER RECKONING

By Sylvie Kurtz

Chapter One

"What is this?" Nina Rainwater asked in disgust, flipping through channels and landing on the only one showing news. "A million channels and this is what I get? I'm in Colorado, how come I've got to listen to weather from Beaumont, Texas?"

"Satellite dish, Grandmother," Kevin Ransom said as he entered the hospice room. Nina looked out of place in the pink frill of the room. He'd always associated her with blue skies and green pastures, with the scent of sweet hay and the smoke of a wood fire—with undying energy.

She didn't look well this evening. Strands of hair, dull as a rainy November sky, poked out of her usually neat braid. Her brown eyes were listless and her breathing seemed more labored in spite of the tubes feeding her oxygen through the nose.

The mock disgust was for his benefit. She didn't want him to worry about her. But he couldn't help himself. She'd given him his life back after he'd thrown it away. He owed her more than gratitude, and now, when she needed him most, he was helpless again. "Sometimes you can't get local news with a satellite dish."

"Pah!" She pitched the remote and looked longingly at the sun starting to set outside her window. The bearberry flowers, pussytoes and columbines in the rock garden bordering the property swayed in the breeze.

"Want me to turn off the TV?" Kevin asked.

She shrugged.

Kevin reached for the remote—a mere five inches from where she'd launched it—and aimed the gadget at the television set on the roll cart at the foot of Nina's bed. He was about to press the Power button, when the image on the screen jumped straight out of his nightmare. It rose like a ghost from his past and laughed at him with satanic glee.

You can run as fast and as far as you want from trouble, but it will never let you forget.

He dreaded evenings when his mind had time to catch up with his body, prompting the assault of all he longed to forget. For sixteen years he'd lived a lie, trying to erase the mental picture of his brother's lifeless body ripped from his grasp on the Red Thunder's flood-swollen waters.

Like some punishment cursed upon him by a Greek god, Kent, Ellen and the accident on that awful evening visited him nightly, torturing him with all he'd lost.

The television screen showed a transport van filled with racehorses toppled on a rain-slicked highway outside a small East Texas town. As much as his life revolved around horses, it wasn't his equine brothers that held him entranced, but the man swaddled in a black slicker trying to save them. Watching the sheriff on the screen was as if he were viewing his own face, had the rocks in the Red Thunder River not altered it all those years ago.

He couldn't breathe. He couldn't move. Blood roared in his ears. Thoughts tumbled through his mind like debris on a storm-tossed sea. It's the rain, he tried to convince himself. It made him think of the river, of that night.

It's not him. It can't be. Look, the name's different. Con-

over, not Makepeace. And Beaumont is at least a hundred miles from Ashbrook.

Downriver, he reminded himself. The sharp cheekbones. The hard eyes. The mantle of responsibility square on his shoulders. Familiar. Could Kent have survived such a long trek down the raging Red Thunder?

The face on the screen joined the haunted memories preying on his mind, overlapping, morphing one into the other, mocking him. Kent, Ellen, anger, so much anger.

"Pajackok? What's wrong?"

When Nina had found him, his broken jaw had made him unable to talk. She'd renamed him Pajackok, the Algonquian word for thunder. She'd told him he was all thunder and no lightning. Told him she'd help him find his spark. He'd done his best to discourage her care, but she'd ignored him.

She still didn't know about Ellen, about his brother, about the damage he'd done with one raw burst of anger.

Pajackok...Kevin Ransom. Both lies.

If he'd changed his name, maybe Kent had, too, and given himself a second chance. Kent hadn't been happy in Ashbrook, but he'd been the responsible one, and those self-imposed responsibilities had weighed him down and cemented him into place. Would he have welcomed the chance at freedom?

Could it be? Could Kevin have avoided all this torture if he'd just had the courage to face the consequences of his actions? Was Kent alive?

"Pajackok?"

His brother was alive. He had to find him. He had to humble himself and ask for forgiveness. Only then could he stop working so hard at trying to forget the brother he thought he'd killed and the woman he'd loved too much.

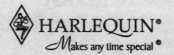

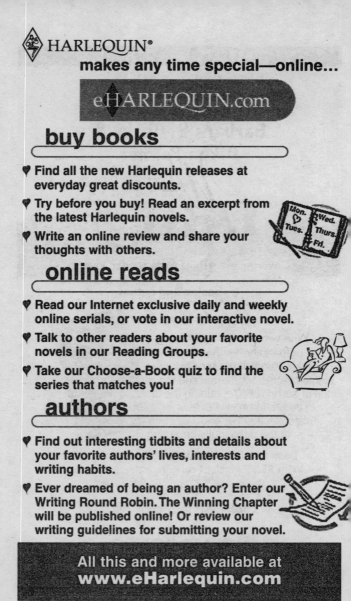

Meet the Randall brothers...four sexy bachelor brothers who are about to find four beautiful brides!

WYOMING WINTER

by bestselling author

Judy Christenberry

In preparation for the long, cold Wyoming winter, the eldest Randall brother seeks to find wives for his four single rancher brothers...and the resulting matchmaking is full of surprises! Containing the first two full-length novels in Judy's famous *4 Brides for 4 Brothers* miniseries, this collection will bring you into the lives, and loves, of the delightfully engaging Randall family.

Look for WYOMING WINTER in March 2002.

And in May 2002 look for SUMMER SKIES, containing the last two Randall stories.

HARLEQUIN®
Makes any time special ®